DATE DUE

Joyce and the G-Men

J. Edgar Hoover's Manipulation of Modernism

Joyce and the G-Men

J. Edgar Hoover's Manipulation of Modernism

By Claire A. Culleton

First published 2004 by
PALGRAVE MACMILLAN™
175 Fifth Avenue, New York, N.Y. 10010 and
Houndmills, Basingstoke, Hampshire, England RG21 6XS.
Companies and representatives throughout the world.

PALGRAVE MACMILLAN IS THE GLOBAL ACADEMIC IMPRINT OF THE PAL-
GRAVE MACMILLAN division of St. Martin's Press, LLC and of Palgrave Macmillan
Ltd. Macmillan®is a registered trademark in the United States, United Kingdom and
other countries. Palgrave is a registered trademark in the European Union and other
countries.

ISBN 0-312-23553-4 hardback

Library of Congress Cataloging-in-Publication Data

Culleton, Claire A.
    Joyce and the G-men : J. Edgar Hoover's manipulation of modernism / Claire A.
Culleton.
      p. cm.
    Includes bibliographical references and index.
      ISBN 0-312-23553-4 (alk. Paper)
  American literature--20th century--History and criticism. 2. Modernism (Literature)-
-United States. 3. United States. Federal Bureau of Investigation--History--20th
century. 4. Politics and literature--United States--History--20th century. 5. Literature
and state--United States--History--20th century. 6. Authors, American--20th century-
-Political and social views. 7. Joyce, James, 1882-1941--Appreciation--United States. 8.
Hoover, J. Edgar (John Edgar), 1895-1972--Influence. 9. Censorship--United States--
History--20th century. 10. American literature--Foreign influences. 11. Joyce, James,
1882-1941--Censorship. I. Title.

PS228.M63C85 2004
                                                                        810.9"112--dc22
2003068919

A catalogue record for this book is available from the British Library.

Design by planettheo.com

First edition: July 2004
    9 8 7 6 5 4 3 2 1

Printed in the United States of America

Also by Claire A. Culleton:

Working-Class Culture, Women, and Britain, 1914-1921
(St. Martin's Press, 2000)

Names and Naming in Joyce
(1994)

Permission Acknowledgments

A portion of chapter 1 was first published in the *James Joyce Quarterly,* 32.3-4 (Spring/Summer 1995): 748-54, as "Joyce and the G-men."

A portion of chapter 4 was first published in *Eire-Ireland: A Journal of the Irish American Cultural Institute* 35.3-4 (Fall/Winter 2001): 238-259, as "James Larkin and J. Edgar Hoover: Irish Politics and an American Conspiracy."

Three letters, written by Morris L. Ernst to J. Edgar Hoover, have been reproduced with permission by the Harry Ransom Humanities Research Center, The University of Texas at Austin.

Photographs reproduced from the Collections of the Library of Congress.

Contents

For Chris
my best bro
who could always make the alphabet sound great

Joyce and the G-Men

Several years ago, following a hunch that seemed ridiculous even to me, I wrote to the Federal Bureau of Investigation and asked whether they had kept a classified dossier on the Irish writer James Joyce (1882-1941). After three years of back-and-forth correspondence, a slim, 20-page dossier marked "James Joyce" arrived from bureau headquarters in Washington, D.C. It was almost entirely blacked out. Since then, I have turned my attention to researching and investigating the mysterious and complex relationship between James Joyce and the FBI, trying to imagine what it was that Joyce might have represented to J. Edgar Hoover and the bureau. In this book, I trace Hoover's career and reveal his doggedly persistent intervention in one of the most important critical constructs of his time: literary modernism, a movement rife with diverse, inconsistent, even over-determined approaches, practices, and responses to early twentieth-century cultural, aesthetic, and political events and attitudes. That his reach extended to American, British, German, Irish and other writers participating in the literary movement is particularly important today at a time when the cultural foundations of modernism are undergoing sharp academic and critical reevaluation.[1]

Nobody ever believes me when I tell them how this all got started, but my friend Beav was there, and Rocco, too, and I know they can back me up. People always say, "be careful what you wish for." In 1992, I thought I was on to something when I requested James Joyce's FBI file from bureau headquarters under provisions of the Freedom of Information-Privacy Acts (FOIPA; also referred to as FOIA). I hoped to find something to write about in those papers, if they existed. I got what I wished for all right, and since then, my research into the topic has not let up.

This all began in a small club in Cleveland when Beav and I went to see a show up in The Flats district. At the door we were given cards to fill out for one of the singers' fan lists and were promised we'd get something in return by mail if we sent the cards in. I figured there'd be a free cd in it, so why not? We each filled out cards, and in about a year's time received what amounted to little more than a press packet featuring the singer David Baerwald. The packet contained lots of copied newspaper clippings on the artist, some copied photographs and lyrics, a few reviews, and Baerwald's tirade against political corruption and subterfuge. Included in the tirade was his warning about the FBI: "They're watching you," he said. You need to know how much, when, and why, he added, and said that everyone should write to the bureau to request a copy of his or her FBI file under the Freedom of Information Act. Conveniently, two FOIA forms were included in the packet.

I remember stopping for a while and thinking about this. Hadn't I gone through the trouble of getting Secret Service clearance back in college when the president met in a press conference with college newspaper editors in New York City? And didn't I march every Saturday morning, it seemed, in the 1980s outside the British Consulate on Manhattan's East Side to protest Margaret Thatcher's monstrous treatment of Irish political prisoners, her unyielding response to the H-Block situation, to hungerstriking men and women, and prisoners who refused to wear British prison uniforms and went "on the blanket" instead? I recalled those days and remembered that off to the sides, at each end of the demonstration circles, there were always two men—Feds, we assumed—taking photographs of all the demonstrators as they marched by. It occurred to me then that yes, I just might have an FBI file, so I proceeded to fill out the form.

When making a FOIA request, you are asked to supply a wealth of personal information about the subject whose file you're requesting on these forms: the subject's date and place of birth, the jobs the subject has held, the cities the subject has worked in, his or her old and present addresses, her maiden name (if applicable), and anything else that may help FOIA to locate materials and records on the subject if any exist. I filled the form out as fully as I could and when I got to the bottom of the sheet, I remember that there was space to describe your relationship to the subject whose file you were requesting. It was then that I realized, almost as if it were a "V-8 moment," or an epiphany, that I could get an FBI file on just about anyone. Since I had an extra FOIA request form, I thought it would be fun to ask for someone else's file, too. I toyed with the idea of requesting JFK's file but since Oliver Stone's movie had recently come out, I thought that my request would wind up buried in a pile with hundreds of others like it. Who else did I know such intimate information about? I wondered. The answer came quicker than I expected: James Joyce.

I have been a James Joyce scholar for decades, and have been fascinated with him since my first introduction to *Ulysses* in John Nagle's classes at Manhattan College in the Bronx. I went on to write my master's thesis as well as my doctoral dissertation on Joyce, and at the time I made the FOIA request, I was in the throes of finishing my first book on the Irish writer. If I knew anyone's life backwards and forwards, it was his. So with considerable aplomb I filled out the sheet from memory, knowing exactly where Joyce was born, several of his addresses, a variety of jobs he held to make ends meet, his wife's first name, maiden name, shoe size, etc. I remember that at the time I didn't think for one minute that there would actually *be* a file on Joyce. If nothing else, I thought it would cost me 29 cents (the price of a stamp back then) to get a letter back from the bureau saying "there's no file on James Joyce." I'd get a good laugh at my own expense, hang the letter on my office wall, and amuse myself now and again with my fearlessness and tireless penchant for mild self-humiliation.

But that was before the file actually arrived in December 1994, some three years after I initially requested it.

After I sent in the two FOIA forms, I instantly got a letter back saying that bureau records contained no information on Claire Culleton. Fair enough, I thought; but what about Joyce? More than three years later, I got a letter saying that FOIPA requests are handled on a first-come, first-serve basis and that my request for Joyce's materials is assigned a number reaching beyond 11,300. By the time any one of the more than 200 FBI employees assigned to handle FOIPA requests gets around to handling mine, the letter continued, assessors will have reviewed an estimated 4.8 million pages. They'd get back to me, the letter assured me, but it may take more than a year, it warned (May 5, 1994).[2] I could hardly believe it. Earlier that year, on March 17th (it was Saint Patrick's Day, I'll never forget) I had been in the English office of Kent State University and one of the secretaries said, "Professor Culleton, it's for you. It's the FBI." I froze. The voice on the other end said she was calling from the FOIA headquarters about my James Joyce request and wanted to ask me would I please send proof that James Joyce was dead. I remember being so flabbergasted that I could only respond something like, "For God's sake, turn on your television. It's Saint Patrick's Day. He's probably all over the news being quoted by *somebody!*" Nonetheless, I dug up his obituary (surprised to learn that his death didn't make front-page news) and sent it in. By the end of the year, but not before another letter from the FBI informed me that they had lost the file with my request in it (Aug. 18, 1994), a slim dossier arrived at my Kent, Ohio apartment wrapped in a brown envelope, just a week before Christmas and hours before I was ready to leave for home. The timing was perfect. I would take the file with me to New York City and try to get in to speak with someone in the bureau at 26 Federal Plaza to help me go over the papers. Little did I know that I was living a pipe dream if I thought I could ever get into the FBI.

What I received from the FBI numbered only 20 pages and was a collection of cross-referenced pages taken from the files of others: his daughter-in-law Helen Joyce's brother Robert Kastor, Ezra Pound, Whittaker Chambers, and others. Most of the 20 pages I received were almost entirely blacked out with the exception of words like "Irish" or "Finnegan's [*sic*] Wake" or some other set of words that were little help to my project. I remember thinking that Yossarian Yossarian of *Catch-22* must be the bureau censor, since only inconsequential words were left for review. (Bureau censorship was taken to the extreme, I think, in Lincoln Steffens's file, which I received a few years ago. One page is entirely blacked out line by line except for the phrase "further advised Agent, that." Another page is fully blacked out with nothing readable on it except for the FOIA exemption notations scribbled in the margins.) I remember wondering at the time just how "free" is the "freedom" of information when it takes so long to arrive, and when it arrives so heavily redacted?

Looking over Joyce's file, however, I laughed to read the lone uncensored bit from a page out of the file of "Dr. Ezra Pound": "he has also done a similar thing with notes he has made on 'Finnegan's [*sic*] Wake.' It is my understanding that 'Finnegan's [*sic*] Wake' is a book written by J. Joyce, the author of 'Ulysses.' This book has created quite a controversy, inasmuch as, many books have been written by other individuals trying to explain what it means."

Once I got to New York City, I called my friend Rocco, told him about the bare-bones Joyce file I had received, and asked if he wanted to accompany me to Federal Plaza to try to meet with some FBI people to get more information. He was up for it, and the trip downtown that followed was nothing short of hilarious.

For reasons I couldn't actually put my finger on, I had become paranoid that the bureau would want to take the papers away from me, even though I had waited three years to get them. So I wanted to Xerox them before "going in," but the only copy machine Rocco and I could find around Chambers Street was in a small news-and-cigarette shop that wanted 25 cents per page and, well, I was just too cheap to pay that. Rocco laughed anyhow at my paranoia and convinced me that the FBI wasn't going to want to take back the papers. He was right, I thought, and felt foolish for being so possessed. Two native New Yorkers, we then set our attention to finding 26 Federal Plaza. We had both been down in that section of New York dozens of times for jury duty, to do something at the DMV, to eat in Chinatown, or what have you. But I'll be damned if either of us could find 26 Federal Plaza. We found Federal Plaza itself, and other addresses on Federal Plaza, but we couldn't find 26 Federal Plaza without circling the area several times. I remember us laughing to each other saying that it was part of the big conspiracy that no one can even FIND the FBI. We even were approached by a young Russian couple who asked us whether *we* knew where 26 Federal Plaza was. We said we didn't, and from that point on, Rocco and I adopted fake Russian accents and started talking to each other as if we were Boris and Natasha from the Bullwinkle cartoons.

Long story short, we finally found the building, made it through the metal detectors, and headed toward the clearly marked FBI Offices elevator bank. A security guard stopped us and pointed us in the direction of a very old man, old like the character in Beckett's *Krapp's Last Tape,* doddering around in a huge booth made of plexiglass in the lobby. No, I didn't have an appointment, I explained as best I could through the small talk hole. I was hoping to get upstairs to talk with an agent about a file I'd received on James Joyce. I had questions about the file, I explained. I wasn't sure how to read or interpret it. Couldn't I just go up and speak with someone who could help me read and interpret the file? I asked. The old man in the plexiglass booth looked at me funny, asked Rocco what *he* was there for, and then made a series of muffled telephone calls upstairs, turning frequently to look at Rocco and me in order to describe us to voices on the other end. After the phone calls were over, the man stooped over to the talk box and said to me, "They said they want you to leave all of the papers you have and they'll get back to you." He pushed out a noisy, deep drawer into which he expected me to put the papers. This fed right into my paranoia, and though I don't want to put too dramatic a spin on things, Rocco and I hightailed it out of that building like nobody's business, looking back only to see if any suits were following us.

By the time I had gotten back uptown to my mother's apartment, she'd already gone to her night job but left a phone message for me that was one of those "while-you-were-outs" that you never think you're going to get. "Claire," it read. "The FBI called. They want you to call them back."

I called them back, eventually, but got nowhere, which is why I started writing this book. What *was* it, I wondered, that could be so provocative about James Joyce's FBI file? I mean, I knew even when I filled out the original FOIA request that Joyce had never stepped foot in the United States; that he had refused to sign his name to political manifestoes or petitions; that he successfully stayed apart from the politics of his day so much so that his friend André Gide responded to the question "Maître, when we have communism in France, whatever will we do with Joyce?" by saying, "We'll leave him be" (Ellman, 695). Why all this bizarre behavior over such a small file, then, especially one so cryptically censored by FOIA workers? It was a little too bizarre, I thought. When I got back to Ohio, I met with Beav's dad, a retired FBI agent, and he helped me to understand the codes, the notations, and the shorthand in Joyce's file.

So, was Joyce a political threat? Did the bureau see in him any risk to national security? What I have figured out since my experiences in the early 1990s is that all of this craziness and insanity has very little to do with James Joyce but everything to do with the FBI—most pointedly, with its director, who for more than 50 years manipulated the relationship between state power and modern literature during his tenure in the bureau. While the file pages disclose information that relates to Joyce and his family's life, they betray, as well, a history of the FBI and its special watchdog division that targeted twentieth-century writers, artists, and intellectuals.

Though I received only what are called cross-referenced pages, I do not know whether there exists a separate or main file on Joyce. Such information is impossible to obtain in the wake of Ronald Reagan's 1986 order giving agencies the authority to refuse to supply information about the existence or nonexistence of main files.[3] In fact, I have come to distrust the words "file" and "main file" altogether, having received letters from the FBI that state while "no main file records responsive to your request were located," we have identified some material that "might possibly be responsive. . . . [S]hould it be responsive . . . it will be processed pursuant to the FOIA and you will be advised of the results." I got a letter to this effect after requesting a file on Samuel Roth, the man who pirated Joyce's *Ulysses*. I was surprised to learn in the letter that "no main file records" existed on Roth. However, a few months later, I received more than 300 pages of Roth's main file, replete with memoranda from Hoover that discussed the bureau's continuing investigation of Roth and his wife Pauline. I would call that a file, wouldn't you?

Does it matter that it winds up that Joyce in fact *was* quite political but that his critics failed to look into his political past, if for no other reason than they assumed he didn't have one? Joyce certainly made his allegiance to the nineteenth-century Irish political hero

Charles Stewart Parnell public knowledge. Trevor Williams and John McCourt raise such points in their recent work on the writer, focusing especially on Joyce's political activity during his years in Trieste and his involvement with socialists there and with Italian irredentists who hoped to recover the city for Italy from Austria. Joyce referred to himself as a "socialistic artist" in a May 1905 letter to his brother Stanislaus, who wrote in *My Brother's Keeper* that during the years Joyce was writing *Dubliners*, "At Trieste, [Joyce] still called himself a socialist" (170). Joyce expressed his political views in columns that he wrote for the Italian newspaper *Il Piccolo della Sera*, and was stirred by the irredentist movement that was gaining ground in Italy. John McCourt reports that Joyce found the Triestine situation so compellingly similar to the Irish push for nationalism that he attended socialist meetings and lectures there, and regularly read Trieste's socialist newspaper, *Il Lavoratore*. It seems then that Joyce was not so apolitical as his early biographer Richard Ellmann, for whatever reasons, painted him. Uncovering Joyce's political past has been one of the remarkable and exciting additions to new biographies and critical works about the writer over the past decade. In new work on Joyce and censorship, for example, Katherine Mullin argues that a "still entrenched view of Joyce the apolitical writer [working] in splendid isolation, preoccupied with style rather than the substance of ideology and history is . . . insidious, since it deflects attention from the 'manifestly political content'" of Joyce's works, directing attention, instead, to his unarguably important stylistic innovations (210). In Joyce, the "threat or expectation of censorship is not incidental but integral to [his] aesthetic," she adds.

Just because critics failed to look at Joyce as a political figure doesn't mean the bureau had to follow suit. In fact, pages in Joyce's file are marked "Internal Security-C" ("C" meaning Communist) and, like the files of other writers, it contains information (often incorrect) about his works and his life, though most is blacked out and thereby unintelligible as a cultural document and artifact.

Because of these unrecoverable redactions, and because of the ultimate unavailability of the true scope of the FBI's interest in James Joyce, I learned early on that if I were going to turn this into something bigger than an article about Joyce's cryptic file, then I would need to widen the scope of the project. I began to request the files of some of Joyce's friends and acquaintances, and then the files of his publishers and editors, and then the files of his contemporaries, and so forth, until I had amassed piles and piles and bookshelves and closets full of FOIA documents. From these, an alarming pattern began to emerge, which led me to reconceive the project and to organize it around a different critical argument, that J. Edgar Hoover and the FBI grew to contain and thereby structure expressions of literary modernists. What follows is the result of more than a decade of investigative research and critical inquiry inspired by that single and startling assumption.

"It is no easy task to narrate the story of a cultural movement engaging hundreds of writers and influencing thousands more, over several decades," Alan Wald is correct to point out in *Exiles from a Future Time* (4). His work signals a continuing scholarly effort to discover, examine, and theorize elements of a hardly coherent yet identifiable tradition. *Joyce and the G-Men: J. Edgar Hoover's Manipulation of Modernism* extends such remarkable efforts.

I have organized this book into chapters that contextualize and examine specific episodes of J. Edgar Hoover's interaction with literary modernism. Chapter 1 is a discussion of Hoover's rise to fame, his ideology for the bureau, and his effort to pursue and harangue modern writers in an attempt to challenge and limit the dissemination of their art. Chapter 2 focuses on modern literature and Hoover's anxiety, his fears that the nation was being corrupted right before his eyes, that its moral fabric had thinned, and that "loyalty" had become its most pressing issue, anxieties fueled by his antiradical hysteria and by his intense paranoia that Bolsheviks and

"Reds" had infiltrated America and that their numbers were growing.

American playwright Clifford Odets, whose literary attention to class and labor issues earned him a 30-page FBI file, bemoaned that, in the course of his reign as director of the bureau, Hoover had cultivated a generation of Americans "processed by democracy" (Odets FBI file). Drawing from that comment, I use Chapter 3 to discuss Hoover's processing of Americans, especially his use of technological apparatuses as he tried to manipulate and control the masses through regular radio broadcasts, pop culture novels, comic books, special appearances, pamphlets, articles, and so forth. An early media manipulator as savvy as FDR would grow to become when he tried to hide the physical manifestations of his polio through his radio talks, Hoover made sure that Americans not only tuned in regularly to his shows but that they believed America needed his protection more than ever. America's most famous "top cop," Hoover had the public and the media eating out of the palm of his proverbial hand.

Chapter 4 focuses on the American labor movement in the early part of the twentieth century, and identifies Hoover's assaults against "insurgent" and "radical" writers and other key figures involved in the movement. Since many had come over to America from Europe or elsewhere to galvanize sentiment for a proletarian work force, Hoover deemed their work anti-American, and worked to capture and deport them, often literally by the boatload. Many modern writers were engaged with labor issues and supported striking workers who were involved in labor disputes across America. They traveled to and reported on their experiences at contested work sites such as Harlan County, Kentucky, where Theodore Dreiser, John Dos Passos, and others traveled to show their support of striking miners. Other writers went to Lawrence, Massachusetts, or to Paterson, New Jersey to galvanize the spirit of abused and striking textile and silk workers, as John Reed, Mary Heaton Vorse, and others did. Max Eastman reported from Colorado on the Ludlow strike and massacre, where striking workers' tent-colonies had been burned and subsequently ravaged by gunmen representing and sustaining the mine owners' interests. Eastman's reports to the *Masses* quoted verbatim what he overheard: "Twenty-eight of the dirty brutes we've roasted alive down there," the wife of the company's physician boasted to the wife of the mine superintendent (*Echoes of Revolt,* 154). Muriel Rukeyser in *The Book of the Dead* catalogued what she saw and learned at Gauley Bridge, West Virginia, during the aftermath of Union Carbide's 1930s industrial atrocity, incorporating into her epic poem testimony, personal letters, and interviews of sick workers, bereaved family members, and guileful corporate spokesmen involved in the Hawk's Nest Tunnel project, a disaster that remains one of America's worst industrial tragedies. Martin Cherniack's book on the subject reports that "more people died during the drilling of the Hawk's Nest Tunnel than in the Triangle Shirt Waist fire, the Sunshine Mine disaster, and the Farmington Mine disaster combined" (vii). Rukeyser's poem gave voice not only to the Gauley Bridge dead and to the silicosis-infected workers who remained there biding what time they had left, but to a new generation of writers who marked themselves as modernists by engaging in the lyrical documentation of cultural wrongdoings and moral transgressions. Outraged at the plight of labor in the early twentieth century, and sickened by dangerous working conditions and below-subsistence wages for workers, modern writers labored to summarize historical events as they were happening. To this end, Sherwood Anderson, Mary Heaton Vorse, and several other novelists, for example, captured in their novels the violent drama at the Loray Mill strike in Gastonia, North Carolina in 1929; others bore witness to the violent attacks against striking workers in Passaic in 1926, or spoke loudly and long against the impending execution of workers Sacco and Vanzetti, or traveled to many other troubled work sites in the uneasy American landscape during the first decade of Hoover's involvement in the bureau in efforts to capture the spirit of the age as they saw it unfold. Moreover, they engaged with class struggle issues as they affected white as well as black workers. Through their involvement with the burgeoning labor movement as newspaper correspondents capturing the aura and the brutality of the episodes, groups of modern writers worked together to restore a civic function to art. Their writings, so politically charged, would also capture the attention of and invite censure from J. Edgar Hoover's FBI.

Chapter 5 examines the role of little magazines popular at the time, such as *The Egoist, Blast, Fire!!, Vortex, The Little Review* and other small press magazines, as well as newspapers such as the *Masses,* the *Liberator,* and the *New Masses,* which worked collectively to disseminate this new kind of literature (modernism) and regularly inculcated readers with radical and highly determined politicism that sought to develop and articulate, among other things, a concept of cultural freedom. Many of these publications were forced out of print by bankruptcy—but not before their editors, writers, or publishers had been dragged into court on obscenity or sedition charges, and as a result of court mandates, were forced to close or lost their mailing privileges. This chapter tells the story of how Hoover's antiradicalism joined forces with a growing censorship campaign to break young publications just as they were getting their legs. Correlatively, Chapter 6 looks at social purity discourses during the time and discusses how bastions of social purity affected the lives of modern writers, printers, publishers, and editors, and how they affected the narratives of characters in modern literature.

The short epilogue charts, as so many books dealing with J. Edgar Hoover do, what has been called "Hoover's Legacy." Some 80 years after his appointment as FBI director, I consider what impacts his efforts to monitor and manipulate aesthetic expression have had on the course of modern literature, on the evolution of the bureau, on forensic criminology, on obscenity laws, on radical discourse, and on nationalist discourse.

Herbert Mitgang closes the introduction to his fine work, *Dangerous Dossiers,* by noting that not one of the Nobel laureates whose FBI files he obtained and scrutinized under FOIA "ever threatened the President, the United States government or its institutions. As their dossiers sadly show, it is the government that found them suspect. Despite thousands of pages in their files, none was ever convicted, let alone accused, of violating federal or state laws" (3). For all of Hoover's mad pursuit of these writers, it is tempting to argue after looking at evidence gathered in files from card indexes, phone taps, personnel files, mail interception, interviews, press clippings, and an ingenious organization of spies and informers, that his work, so full of sound and fury, ultimately yielded nothing. But it did yield something. Hoover's pursuit, and his watchful eye trained, as it were, on writers and others in the book industry, allowed him to manipulate modern literature at its roots, at its origins. His bureau would come to influence the decisions of other agencies, steer political developments, and affect legal proceedings against writers, editors and publishers; the reports that he and his agents issued would cost many modern writers national and international recognition and prominence, prestigious and handsome awards or medals, publication contracts, book club selections, speaking engagements, and in some cases, would even jeopardize a writer's entitlement to a burial spot in America's National Cemetery at Arlington. Equally criminal, the chilly climate he would create for writers engaged with modern literature would dissuade some from writing altogether; would lead others to seek out alternative publication strategies (which would thereby remove them from a historically constructed "mainstream" modernism); and would compromise their constitutional right to privacy, affect their health, and distress their daily lives. As "America's 'top cop' propagated his ideology of the American Way, as vague as it was influential" (Stephan, 2), his efforts to oppress the literary counterculture still follow us today. At a time when the cultural foundations of modernism are undergoing reevaluation, garnering academic and critical reanalysis, we need to question in what directions the movement might have traveled without Hoover's persistent interventions.

CHAPTER ONE

Joyce and the G-Men: J. Edgar Hoover's Manipulation of Modernism

"J. Edgar Hoover was like a sewer that collected dirt. I now believe he was the worst public servant in our history" (Summers, 193). These words, obviously holding nothing back, were spoken by Attorney General Laurence Silberman, the first person to go through Hoover's secret files after his sudden death in 1972. Considering that things had started out so well for J. Edgar Hoover—born on January 1st, he was 1895's "Baby New Year" and was later voted 1930's "Bachelor of the Year," two quite notable if strikingly incongruent honors—how did it all go so wrong? How did he wind up being compared to a "sewer that collected dirt," and what circumstances led to his being called "a martinet, a preposterous figure" (Robins, 353) by poet Theodore Roethke in a 1963 issue of *Harper's Bazaar?*

J. Edgar Hoover, nicknamed "Speed" as a boy, was raised in a family of mapmakers, something William Beverley proposes had a "suggestive influence upon the man and administrator he would become" (Beverley, 30).[1] After working from 1913 to mid-1917 in the Library of Congress, Hoover began his career with the Justice Department working in the Aliens Registration office, where he developed knowledge of and cultivated information about political radicalism that would prove useful to him in the future (Jeffreys, 55). "Hoover's first months in the Justice Department put him in the middle of . . . hysteria over traitors, spies, and saboteurs," Richard Gid Powers notes (47). Later that year, Hoover would be responsible for organizing the haphazard files of the Justice Department, and would organize them obsessively, "out of a great personal and political need to control the flow of information in America" (Robins, 33). Though a functionary in the Aliens Registrations office, Hoover's reputation as a Red-baiter matured when at the height of the Red Scare in 1919, he successfully deported hundreds of alien radicals and foreign-born agitators following November and December raids. The hysterical search for anarchists and radicals that would eventually be called the Red Scare began in mid-1919, when, as Christopher Finan explains,

> eight bombs exploded outside the homes of prominent men, including the mayor of Cleveland and judges in New York City, Boston, and Pittsburgh. . . . The June bombings convinced many that the United States must be ruthless if it was going to meet the threat of Communist revolution. A Montana senator introduced a bill making it a crime to advocate violent revolution. [Attorney General A. Mitchell] Palmer appointed a new chief of the Justice Department's Bureau of Investigation to take charge of the search for the bombers and created a new assistant attorney general to help. Congress gave the federal Red hunters $500 million to speed their work. (Finan, 127)

Manifestations of postwar antiradical hysteria, the 1919 raids resulted in one thousand arrests and netted some 25 tons of seized documents.

Hoover's reputation further developed in 1920 after he coordinated with the attorney general the "Palmer Raids," dragnets organized to arrest without warrants some 10,000 "subversives" nationwide in one simultaneous action. It was an operation that surpassed even the fierceness of some of the Lusk Committee (an anti-red investigative body) raids the year before; it climaxed with the deportation of those radicals who were arrested, brutalized, and compelled to sign false confessions about their radical activities in the United States. Paul Buhle notes that the Palmer Raids were "a government show of force" organized in response to "real and/or orchestrated bomb threats" in 1920. "Palmer and the vastly expanded Bureau of Investigation . . . ran roughshod over legal niceties. . . . A procedure historically famous in legal circles for the virtual absence of due process, the indiscriminate grounds for arrest, brutality, threats, and extorted confessions, the manner of the raids drew wide complaints from Congress and the Press" (647-48). The Palmer Raids, like the many other Red raids that preceded them, were designed to flush out and test burgeoning immigrant and alien populations, and targeted 33 of America's largest cities. The *Liberator* humorist Howard Brubaker lampooned the police's lack of evidence to hold any of the suspects when he wrote pithily in May 1919, "New York Police recently rounded up 164 Bolshevik suspects. All were held for further examination, except 160" (May 1919: 25). It was a crusade that flung a wide net, and culminated in deportation mania, with many of its victims charged with sedition or criminalized as anarchists. Brubaker would later write "The backbone of radicalism was officially pronounced BROKEN at 12:30 on the morning of January 3rd" (Feb. 1920: 20). To point out the magnitude of the raids, editors of the *Liberator* reproduced headlines taken from only a single issue of the *New York Times:*

ONE HUNDRED TAKEN IN AND NEAR BUFFALO; RAIDS IN 17
CONNECTICUT TOWNS; FIFTEEN TAKEN IN BRIDGEPORT;
SEIZE 150 RADICALS IN NASHUA; 65 ARRESTED IN MANCHES-
TER; SEIZE 30 RUSSIANS IN BOSTON; SEIZE EIGHT AT
LAWRENCE; NINE ARRESTS MADE AT HOLYOKE; WORCESTER'S
TOTAL EXCEEDS 50; TAKE THIRTY AT LOWELL; TWENTY ONE
ARRESTED IN HAVERHILL; SPRINGFIELD ROUNDS UP 65; SEV-
ERAL ARRESTS IN RHODE ISLAND; ROUND UP EIGHTEEN AT
BALTIMORE; OAKLAND RAID NETS 15; LOUISVILLE BAG IS
TWENTY. (Feb. 1920: 14)

It is no coincidence that these roundups came during a time of
growing unrest on American job sites. Palmer assumed that the labor
agitation came from "Reds," a wrongheaded assumption that led
Robert Minor to argue in the *Liberator* that because "[he] thinks that
'Red' agitators are the cause behind the 'outlaw strikes' which have
been chewing up the railroads and many other industries. . . . Mr.
Palmer is like a doctor practising obstetrics on the theory that storks
bring babies" (June 1920: 3). J. Edgar Hoover, Palmer's right-hand
man, oversaw the delivery of hundreds of insurgents. The Palmer
Raids, like New York City Police Commissioner Grover Whelan's
Red raids a few years later, abrogated the First Amendment in the
name of anticommunism, and lumped together, according to Herbert Mitgang, "college-cafeteria radicals, Socialists, anarchists, members of the International [*sic*] Workers of the World, and activists on
union picket lines" (*Once Upon a Time in New York,* 27). Such mad
pursuit would test or crack the backbone of any movement, and
Hoover knew it.

This degree of brutality worked for and against the radical
movement, in that it worked to curb membership temporarily but to
increase it subsequently as the violence escalated. This is precisely the
case for Philip Schutz, who wrote in 1930 about his experiences
during and after the First World War:

Those were stirring days. Several times in the midst of meetings, strange men with gutting jaws, thick necks and bulging hip pockets entered the hall and ordered everyone to remain seated while they inspected draft registration cards.

It was often my duty under these circumstances to slip past the Department of Justice agents surrounding the building to warn approaching comrades that there was another raid in progress.

I saw these unfriendly, overbearing radical-hunters abuse men whom I respected. I saw the rudeness and hatred with which they handled the girls and women whom I knew. . . .

These men were part of America's holy crusade. (*New Masses*, Dec. 1930: 10)

Schutz continues describing a pivotal event in his childhood. His father took him on Labor Day 1917 to the mass meeting of the Cleveland Federation of Labor. C. E. Ruthenberg, then secretary of the Socialist Party in Cleveland and also a candidate for mayor, stepped forward and spoke to some 5,000 persons. Schutz writes: "At the climax of his speech, half a dozen [Ohio] national guardsmen leaped to the platform and seized Ruthenberg. . . . Other guardsmen poured into the auditorium. . . . That settled it for me. It seemed incredible that Socialists must be hunted and beaten to make the world safe for democracy" (11). As Schutz describes, the climate after the Palmer Raids encouraged brute vigilantism on the part of American citizens. Christine Stansell notes, for example, "soldiers and sailors based in New York led roving mobs looking for radicals to intimidate" (*American Moderns,* 314). Schools, too, were subjected to raids in the wake of post–World War I antiradical hysteria. The Rand School, for example, a workers' school founded in 1906 with some 90 students, was investigated for subversive activities, raided for confiscable material, and subjected to a series of police interferences and mob attacks. It was an all-out war waged against radical writers, thinkers, workers, teachers, students, and activists.

Labor organizer Elizabeth Gurley Flynn describes the postwar climate in her autobiography *The Rebel Girl:*

> after the war ended, lawless force and violence continued, now led by ex-soldiers, fomented by stay-at-home patriots, employers and their hirelings. Many violent scenes had occurred in 1918 and 1919. The Rand School in New York City was attacked by a mob of soldiers and sailors who tore down the American flag flying from the building. The Socialist daily paper, the New York *Call,* was raided and wrecked. Employees were driven out and beaten as they were forced to run the gauntlet of armed men. (261-62)

In 1919, a newsstand operated by a blind man in Centralia, Washington was broken into, ransacked, and burned. Tom Lassiter, its operator, sold issues of Seattle's *Union Record* and the IWW's *Industrial Worker.* A note left behind signed "U.S. Soldiers, Sailors and Marines" warned Lassiter to leave town. When he refused, Flynn notes, Lassiter was "seized, beaten and dropped in a ditch over the county line. When he returned to Centralia, he was arrested under the criminal syndicalist law" (Flynn, 262). Though his lawyer Elmer Smith tried to bring the actors to justice, his attempts failed, which emboldened and animated unruly mobs in Centralia. Antiradical hysteria quickly escalated and leaflets and bulletins produced and distributed by the Employers Association urged its members to "deport the radicals or use the rope in Centralia." Use the rope they would in Centralia, to carry out a notorious crime of postwar vigilante brutality. It would mark the climax of a veritable reign of terror sanctioned by employers in business and industry against workers associated with the IWW and with other labor organizations, as we shall see.

Three years earlier, in July 1916, Dante Barong had reported on the Pittsburgh strike for the *Masses* and illustrated with a simple anecdote the fierce animosity of employers towards workers involved in the labor movement. He wrote: "With a beginning of 60,000 workers on strike for the 8-hour-day in the Pittsburgh district, Isaac Frank, multi-millionaire, president of several great machine works and head of the Employers' Association of Pittsburgh, told the writer of this article that Frank F. Walsh, Chairman of the Committee on Industrial Relations, 'ought to be assassinated'" (July 1916: 17). Five months later, another writer provided another anecdote detailing the commentary of another "captain" of industry who advocated the same kind of force to put down the labor movement. In "The San Francisco Frame Up," the writer explained:

> Last spring during the strike of the Longshoremen, the San Francisco Chamber of Commerce held a huge meeting of manufacturers, bankers and big merchants, and openly pledged one million dollars to "stamp out Union Labor in the city." The keynote of the occasion was struck by Captain Robert Dollar, of the Ship-Owner's Association, one of the bitterest foes of organized labor in the country, who said: "The only way to settle the strike is to send several ambulance loads of strikers to the hospital." (Dec. 1916: 15)

The reign of terror against labor and activists and writers associated with the labor movement would last some ten years, but its half-life would be perpetual, since involvement with labor or with other activist organizations earned writers their own FBI files, and in some cases won them criminal charges and police records that would haunt them or their families even after their deaths. In fact, we now know that Joseph McCarthy used information gathered by the bureau on writers during the 1910s, 1920s, and 1930s to torment and badger them in the 1950s. More on that later. For now, let us return to Centralia, Washington, where in 1919 the unthinkable occurred.

Centralia was the site in November 1919 of the fierce raid of an IWW hall by uniformed American Legionnaires, who voted earlier in the week to march their Armistice Day parade past the IWW hall, halt in front of the building, raid the hall, and then proceed with their march along the publicized parade route. Because the American Legion plans were leaked, IWW lawyer Elmer Smith learned of the campaign and advised his clients to defend themselves if necessary. They did, and one of the hall's defenders—Wesley Everest, who shot and killed an invading legionnaire—was attacked by the mob, kicked and beaten, dragged by a rope around his neck to the local jail, taken from his cell that night, castrated, and lynched. Everest's dangling body was then used for target practice. The next day, the mutilated body was cut down, returned to the jail, and thrown in among the other arrested and tortured IWW prisoners. One of the arrested men, Lorens Robert, went insane as a result of the experience. When ten IWW men were brought to trial, two were acquitted, one was declared insane (Robert), and seven were sentenced to the state penitentiary for 25 to 40 years on charges of criminal syndicalism. After 17 years, five of the men were paroled, and the others, who refused parole, were released shortly thereafter. Whereas the IWW men bore the brunt of the criminal charges, no legionnaire was ever arrested or brought to trial, though a legionnaire writing to the governor ten years later urged him to release the IWW men, admitting it was now clear to him that the "Centralia Legionnaires were used by local business interests to eject the IWW. On Armistice Day, 1919," he continued, "the workers' hall was raided before a shot was fired in self-defense. A gigantic frame-up followed, and the trial at Montesano bears all the earmarks of being an attempt at 'lynching'" (Flynn, 265). In *The Rebel Girl*, Elizabeth Gurley Flynn says it is nearly impossible to "recreate a picture of the long years of intense brutal reaction that lasted from 1917-1927" (265), but she accurately attributes the hostility to a capitalist class gone mad with fear, eager to dismantle the strengthening American labor movement.

Modernist writers who aligned themselves with issues affecting workers, or whose writings championed the cause of labor, sentimentalized the working class, highlighted their invisibility and growing powerlessness, or issued calls for solidarity and/or action were yoked together with other radicals who advocated, just as dangerously, for social change in other aspects of American life. Since literary modernists were beginning to investigate the voices of the underclass, the underrepresented heroes of society, it is these writers who naturally were drawn to the revolutionary movement, and thus suffered attention and harassment from Hoover's FBI. By 1920, J. Edgar Hoover "would add the names of many writers to his index," Natalie Robins notes (55), and after changing the name of his Antiradical Division to the General Intelligence Division (a name that reveals his broadening interests in gathering "general," noncriminal information), Hoover began to demonstrate a marked interest in writers, and nurtured a culture in the bureau where agents ardently gathered "general" information about them.

Hoover's marked interest in writers extended to their circles of friends, as well. In the bureau file of writer Mary Heaton Vorse, a writer best known for her proletarian novel *Strike!,* Hoover's special agents note her animated reveries with fellow writers. Surprising, to me, Mary Heaton Vorse's file also contains transcripts of telephone conversations, incoming and outgoing. It also contains handwriting and signature samples of the subject, and Office Memoranda stating that the records of the New York City Boards of Health for the boroughs of Manhattan and Brooklyn had been checked under the subject's maiden and marital names. Clearly, the marriage of Vorse's activism with her literary output marked her as one of the insurgents so terrifying to Hoover and so threatening to his concept of "Americanism." Even the writers with whom she associated (though their names remain blacked out in her FBI file, despite my appeals) are noted in Vorse's file. One such report, made in New York City on May 29, 1944, notes that Mary Heaton Vorse entertains and receives writers into her home:

[CENSORED] further advised that the subject occasionally enter-
tained guests at the hotel, writers and editors of her own generation,
including [CENSORED] novelist, and two persons whom he
understood to be editors connected with the *New York Times* and
Harper's Magazine.
        . . . He stated that the subject occasionally received as visitors well
known writers who were old friends of the subject. He identified these
persons as [CENSORED], poet; [CENSORED], author;
[CENSORED], and [CENSORED], writer, [CEN-
SORED]. (Vorse FBI file)

Further complicating the question of the importance of the noncriminal information being gathered by Hoover's men is this 1946
notation assessing the Vorse household: "Confidential Informant
[CENSORED], stated he believes the occupants of 2949 Mills
Avenue, N.E. are "nutz, they have a house full of cats and the house
stinks and they are odd actors."[2]

To combat the growing antiradical aggression that had begun to
feel so oppressive to modern writers and activists, networks of writers
developed over time to support one another in crusades against
harassment, violence, censorship, and interdictions. To this end,
writers were bent on using their art as a vehicle for historical change.
Christine Stansel notes in *American Moderns:*

Across the country, when radicals went to jail for fulminating against
capitalist injustice, they gained support from local doctors, editors,
and progressive thinkers. Writers, theater people, and sex radicals
became involved, because an 1873 federal law—one of the famed
"Comstock laws," after vice-crusader Anthony Comstock—inter-
dicted "obscene" material from being published, mailed or per-
formed. The Comstock law was used to suppress birth control
literature, and sex information, but from 1910 on, agents also went

after novels, reproductions of nudes, and eventually avant-garde literature. (Stansell, 76)

Engaged as they were in the same effort to protect free expression, writers, artists, editors, and publishers linked arms to struggle against federally imposed censorship. Their free-speech politicking, however, would mark them indelibly as insurgents in bureau files created by the very sources of the aggression they fought.

To be sure, A. Mitchell Palmer's "Leave it to Me" attitude, coupled with J. Edgar Hoover's "I Never Fed a Red" arrogance (as Art Young, political cartoonist for the *Liberator,* pictured the two in March 1920),[3] characterized what soon would become a force to be reckoned with. Feared and scorned, Palmer had earned himself the nickname "Simon Legree Palmer" and frequently was caricatured as such by Boardman Robinson, another political cartoonist for the *Liberator* (though he preferred to be called the "Fighting Quaker").[4] One cartoon showed Palmer and another Department of Justice agent surrounded by headlines and front pages that read

No Riots at Radical Meeting; Bomb Discovered in U.S. Mail, a Baseball; Torture Fails; Palmer Suspects 10-Year-Old Boy of Criminal Anarchy; Plot Fails; May Day Revolt a Fizzle; Imbecile Given a Bomb Throws it at a Cow, Intended for Millionaire; Judge Anderson of Boston Discovers (What Everybody Suspected) that Palmer Agents Try to Incite Workingmen to Riot and Illegal Acts.

In the cartoon, a panicky Palmer says to the other agent, "Say, look here—if something doesn't happen pretty soon, I'm a ruined man!" (11). Throughout the publicity, J. Edgar Hoover was at Palmer's side. His allegiance would pay off and his accumulation of power would grow exponentially as his own paranoia developed. Fred Jerome notes in his work with Albert Einstein's bureau files that

[w]hen the Palmer raids brought an unexpected public backlash, and Congress launched an investigation into possible violations of human rights, Hoover publicly minimized his role in the raids and kept a low profile as he maneuvered his way to appointment as the director of the new FBI. At the same time, he quietly began to develop his extensive files on suspected 'Reds' and others he didn't like. (*The Einstein File*, 20).

As a result of Hoover's role in orchestrating the raids, he was named special assistant to the Attorney General, then served from 1921-1924 as assistant director of the Bureau of Investigation under William J. Burns, a former New York City detective, until being appointed by Harlan Fiske Stone to be the acting director of the FBI at the astonishingly young age of 29. From that appointment in 1924 until his death 48 years later in 1972, J. Edgar Hoover's preoccupation with political radicalism, especially communism, would become a feature of the Hoover bureau, and the strength of its force would affect writers, intellectuals, activists, and artists not only in America but in several nations across several continents. Its standards, for example, would be upheld and preserved by the deportation from America of alien radicals, intellectuals, and provocateurs, by the criminal trials of "anarchists," "spies," and "subversives," and by the legal battles forced upon writers, booksellers, editors, and publishers of radical books, journals, and magazines. This climate, in fact, would lead anthropologist Franz Boas to write in the *New Masses* six years after Hoover's appointment, "I regret with you exceedingly what appears to me as entirely unwarranted hysterical fear of radical opinion and I consider it a most regrettable assault upon the principle of freedom to discriminate against those who hold radical opinions and who have the courage to express them" (June 1930: 9). Michael Gold also complained about the culture of the day: "These investigations! These committees!" he wrote with exasperation. "They are shyster tricks" (*New Masses,* July 1930). This book is a story, in part, about J. Edgar Hoover's dossier on James Joyce and on other suspected "Reds," "subversives," and "anarchists"; but it is also a story about literary modernism, and how Hoover managed to control the movement when it was spreading quickly and was in the hands of a young, vibrant collection of international writers, editors, and publishers. To accomplish this, Hoover had access to virtually unlimited funds and uncompromising strategies,[5] and equally important, he had a cartel of prosecutors standing at the ready to aid him in his work.

In the early half of the twentieth century, modern writers had come together to form an international and overt movement. Progress in the postal service and the mails allowed the free exchange of literature to take place across oceans that had separated continentals, Americans, and Eastern Europeans for centuries. Travel exigencies allowed more people to move about the world to meet other writers, artists, and thinkers. Newspapers and magazines enjoyed an international readership, and the success of John Reed clubs in the United States brought together like-minded artists and workers. The purpose of the Reed Clubs was to unite creative workers with members of the American revolutionary labor movement, according to one of the club's New York City secretaries. The clubs aimed to join

> radical artists and writers. . . . all creative workers in art, literature, sculpture, music, theatre and the movies. . . . The purpose of the club [was] to bring closer all creative workers [and] to maintain contact with the American revolutionary labor movement. . . . For the first time, a group of socially conscious creative workers has been organized in America to compare with existing groups in Europe. (*New Masses,* Nov. 1929: 21).

These conditions nurtured the prospects for an international movement of modernist literature, and many, many writers and activists participated in it.

William Everdell describes this exciting moment in his book *The First Moderns:*

> The great cities of 1900 where the first Modernists found themselves were already very populous, and usually multicultural. The nineteenth century had accomplished that. Communication was extremely swift, whether by postal correspondence (five deliveries a day in Munich), by publication (one month plus one week from contract to presentation copy for Kafka's first book of fiction), or by telephone and telegraph. It was possible for the poet Jules Laforgue to be born in Uruguay, educated at one of the best provincial secondary schools in France, employed as a reader by the Dowager Empress of Germany, and commissioned to translate the American works of Walt Whitman. James Joyce could write a novel meticulously set in the Dublin of 1904 while he was teaching English to Italians in the main seaport of the Austro-Hungarian Empire. In this sort of world an aristocratic Russian like Igor Stravinsky could change the course of Western music with a ballet score written in Switzerland and performed in Paris. Niels Bohr could write his classic paper on the atom in English while teaching in his native Denmark, publishing it in the journal of the British Royal Society under the guidance of a New Zealander who had made his scientific reputation in Ontario, Canada, by extending the work of a Polish woman living in Paris. This kind of "hopscotching the world," as early film newsreels called it, suggests an absence of system, certainly to those who prized 19th Century distinctions based on ethnicity and language. But the system was there, and it was itself transnational. In fact, the insistence on a supra-ethnic community of thought and of art is one of the positions now often defined as Modernism. (2-3)

Everdell is correct in pointing out the importance of "supra-ethnicity" to modernism. It was the newly discovered freedom to move around the world, the freedom to exchange ideas, and to participate in international demonstrations and nationalist causes, to communicate in several languages and to write in or to translate into even more languages that gave this moment in cultural and literary history a distinctly new advantage. It reinforced for twentieth-century writers the notion that there could be no more genuinely isolated historical episodes; that with developments in travel technology, eye witnesses could be anywhere history was breaking, and could have their reports published and disseminated instantly, as John Reed was able to do from Petrograd with his serialized accounts in 1917 of the Russian Revolution as it unfolded. By 1919, he had published the first major account of the event, *Ten Days that Shook the World.*

Literature, like art, was fast becoming not only a site for communication and reportage but potentially a weapon, though this was nothing new for American literature. In fact, the Irish labor leader James Larkin testified during his New York trial for sedition that it was through American literature that he learned rebellion. When questioned about the origin of his socialist ideas and ideologies, and when asked by the federal prosecutor where he picked up his seditious ways, the Irish radical addressed the court and said:

> How did I get the love of comrades, only by reading Whitman? How did I get this love of humanity, except by understanding men like Thoreau and Emerson and the greatest man of all next to Emerson—Mark Twain? Those are the men I have lived with—the real Americans, not the Americans of the mart and the exchange who would sell their souls for money and sell their country too. (O'Riordan, 71)

Larkin even quoted Walt Whitman as he boarded the S.S. *Majestic* in 1923 after being deported following his controversial unconditional pardon from Governor Al Smith. "I'm like the man in Whitman's poem: 'Free and light-hearted I take to the open road'" (Nevin, 279).[6] J. Edgar Hoover spent a great deal of energy assisting Larkin's prosecutor Rorke, and I do not think the linkage of literature and revolution that he heard that day was lost on the bureau director. Hearing Larkin, one of Hoover's most detested agitators, testify to the political power of literature alerted Hoover to its perils, and he would spend decades in rabid pursuit of the world's most powerful writers. He likely began tracking James Joyce because the British were—the Queen's MI6 files on writers are as extensive as the FBI's are—but his interest in modern writers, especially his desire to limit the dissemination of their work through censorship, bullying, and courtroom dramas, would come to define the bureau's attitude towards modern literature, and, in turn, would affect the nation's taste.

What was it about Joyce and his literary, artistic, and intellectual contemporaries that so threatened the bureau director? Joyce certainly associated with "known" communists—Harriet Shaw Weaver, for example—but Joyce himself? It seemed outrageous that Hoover would even want to keep tabs on Joyce, since the writer refused to become even minimally involved in the great European issues of his day. What possible interest could the FBI have had in him, I wondered.

One of Joyce's more recent biographers, John McCourt, notes that while early biographies of the writer tended to ignore or conceal Joyce's political allegiances, James Joyce was quite political; he notes that there is scholarly consensus that biographer Richard Ellmann's downplaying of Joyce's interest in socialism and Irish nationalism is one of the many weaknesses now recognized in a work that had been touted as one of the best literary biographies ever written. Published in 1959 and revised in 1982, Ellmann's biography is often held up as a magnificent achievement, though it is sadly wanting in its descriptions of Joyce's political beliefs. My research with the FBI under the Freedom of Information Act has turned up files dealing not only with Joyce and some of his more politically active associates and acquaintances, but with others involved in the production and dissemination of modernist literature. Possessed by J. Edgar Hoover's paranoid suspicion of anything that could not be fitted into his narrow conception of "Americanism," the FBI targeted well-known intellec-

tual and artistic figures precisely because their originality, prominence, and emphasis on the free exchange of ideas made them seem
threatening. Hoover, in fact, thrived on collecting noncriminal
information about his subjects. The revelation three or four years ago
that the bureau carried out surveillance against Groucho Marx is one
of the many absurdly comic highlights in this history. But there is a
serious side as well, and my study of the FBI's surveillance of people
associated with one of the twentieth century's most important prose
writers has interesting implications.

A founder of literary modernism, Joyce likely epitomized for J.
Edgar Hoover everything about the modernist literary movement (still
in transition and flux) that Hoover deemed loathsome, obscene, and
corrupt: its experimentation with forms, styles, and voices; its efforts to
articulate crises of authority and anxiety; its seemingly impenetrable
intellectualism; its exploration of sexuality, eroticism, and the libidinal
currents that give shape to the subjects and styles of the movement; its
examination of sexual energies and errant sexualities; its investigations
into identity, psychology; and its apparent willingness to confront and
challenge capitalism and enter into political debate about its failures and
its degeneracy. At a time when members of John Reed Clubs all over the
United States were brandishing the slogan "Art Is a Class Weapon" and
likening the potency of journalism and literature to "paper bullets,"
Hoover was growing uneasy about the changing relationship between
art and politics in the early twentieth century and worked to beleaguer
writers, artists, and intellectual leaders during his tenure as director of
the bureau, frustrating, as best he could, their insurgent cultural
practices with a special watchdog division. While Hoover and his
henchmen knew little, if anything, about art or literature per se, because
so much of it (it seemed) had begun to transgress the boundaries
between art and obscenity, or art and political insurgency, it was
identified as a legitimate area of exploration for the bureau.

To this end, Hoover ordered an FBI study to look for "subversive
factors" in the backgrounds of prominent writers, editors, book club

judges, and others associated with book clubs. For example, when a book subscribing service called The Reader's Club was starting up, the FBI procured a copy of the invitational circular sent out on Club stationary with Clifton Fadiman, Sinclair Lewis, Carl Van Doren, and Alexander Woollcott's names on the letterhead. The circular promised that these "famous men of books will help you discover some of the best already-published books for only one dollar a copy" (Mitgang, 38). Mitgang reports "the FBI used false names as subscribers to the club in order to find out what was being published and by whom" (38). A notation in Nobel laureate Sinclair Lewis's file, for example, reads "From a review of these pamphlets, it appeared that 'The Reader's Club' would be similar in operation to the well-known Book of the Month Club. The committee designated to select the books that were to be made available to the members of the club included Sinclair Lewis" (39). Lewis had been a suspect writer certainly since the late 1920s when Army Intelligence had begun to keep tabs on him: he endorsed the Viking Press's publication of the *Letters of Sacco and Vanzetti*.

Some of the other stories are already well-known: Hoover's "red-hot" pursuit over decades of writers like Pearl Buck, Theodore Dreiser, James Baldwin, Langston Hughes, Thomas Mann, Richard Wright, Bertolt Brecht, Carl Sandburg, Frank O'Connor, George Bernard Shaw, Susan Glaspell, Eugene O'Neill, John Steinbeck, Claude McKay, Elmer Rice, Edna St. Vincent Millay, and more—writers who endured surveillance, full-scale assaults, and privacy violations. What ties these people, these subjects, together is that they were writers participating in modernism, one of the first overtly acknowledged literary movements in history. Shari Benstock notes in *Women of the Left Bank,* a study of modernism, that modernism's "aesthetic principles and literary claims were codified in a series of manifestoes whose texts were printed in journals specifically dedicated to the propagation of Modernist literature" (32). Under

Hoover's direction, the FBI was acting out a self-appointed role as a police force against writers aligned with modernism.

Modern literature was a particular lightning rod for Hoover's paranoia and anti-intellectualism; it excited his anxiety more than other twentieth-century art forms, though he certainly kept files on modern artists such as Picasso, Chagall, Steiglitz and O'Keeffe.[7] Hoover even grew to suspect there was collusion among American publishers who agreed not to publish anticommunist works, and among book reviewers, who gave negative reviews or worse, ignored, such books (Theoharis, *Secret Files,* 311). What Hoover seemed to fear most was the ultimate effect art might have on the masses, and he did not know or understand what modern art could lead to. Modern art, so deliberately nonrepresentational, confused early twentieth century viewers and readers. One apocryphal story that made the rounds at this time poked fun of Picasso's abstractions: "Picasso replied to a lady who wanted her portrait done and asked him for an appointment for a sitting [that] 'You need only send me a lock of hair and your necklace'" (Hall and Wykes, 118). What many Americans feared was what Jonas Atwater would aptly explain in the *Masses,* "Art is long—it is too long for any man to see where it ends and the end is a long, long way from the beginning" (Oct. 1911: 16). Modern art and literature seemed to provoke thought more than earlier art movements. Such thinking could spawn a revolution, Horatio Winslow warned in "Eight Hours and a Revolution": "Two ways there are to make a Revolution. The first way is to put a gun into a man's hands and tell him to kill. The second is to put an idea into a man's head and tell him to think" (5). The culture of modernism was spreading rapidly, especially among intellectuals and young writers. Not only were young writers making indelible impressions on culture; their work was also gaining recognition and notoriety with liberal teachers and college professors who were teaching modern literature at some of the schools and college campuses that Hoover already had under surveillance (New York University, Columbia University, Harvard University, and the Rand School, to name a few). Ultimately, Hoover's mistrust of professors would lead to the 1953 House Committee on Un-American Activities (a.k.a. House Un-American Activities Committee or HUAC) hearings on Communist Methods of Infiltration in Education, in which Professor Granville Hicks and others would become star witnesses.[8] Interestingly, one of the items in Joyce's FBI file is a course description of an undergraduate *Ulysses* seminar; another item is a memorandum sent to Hoover from New York with the notation: "the following books and plays are the subject's choice for student reading during the fall semester." The list attached to the file includes Joyce's *A Portrait of the Artist as a Young Man* and two plays by his compatriot George Bernard Shaw. Such scrupulous watchfulness, Michael North suggests, may be why F. Scott Fitzgerald exploits the trope of Dr. T. J. Eckleburg's eyeglasses in his novel *The Great Gatsby,* set in New York during the *annus mirabilis* of literary modernism, 1922, when America was under the vigilant eye of federal agents and local citizens, whose courage to snitch on their neighbors was buttressed by a police force eager to eradicate radicalism. F. Scott Fitzgerald had been a member of the Communist Party, USA (CPUSA) and his FBI file grew once J. Edgar Hoover found out that his story "A Diamond as Big as the Ritz" was going to be made into a Broadway musical.

Hoover enjoyed being "seen" at Broadway premieres and at long-running shows, and often took these as good photo opportunities, as was the case with Jack Kirkland's Broadway adaptation of Erskine Caldwell's *Tobacco Road,* produced in 1933 at the Masque Theater by Sam Grisman.[9] Caldwell's book had seen much controversy, as would his later work, *God's Little Acre,* which would be attacked for its obscenity by John Sumner and the New York Society for the Suppression of Vice in April 1933 two months after its publication. When the dramatic version of *Tobacco Road* reached the heights of unprecedented success (it eventually would break records on Broadway), J. Edgar Hoover himself made an appearance at the theatre and "raved about the play," according to Caldwell's biographer Dan B. Miller (197). Cartoonist Abe Hirschfeld immortalized the Broadway cast by caricaturing them into celebrity and "gossip columnists followed their every move" (197). Meanwhile, Caldwell and his publishers were engaged in a New York City courtroom battle over the propriety of *God's Little Acre*. Sumner, so often a champion and protector of social purity, charged Viking Press with disseminating pornography through the sale of the book. In a planned effort to "initiate a national test case" (Miller, 175), Sumner purchased his copy of Caldwell's novel through the publisher's office at Viking. This allowed him to name the press directly in the suit without having to focus legal attention on mere booksellers or other retailers. This suit, predicated on section 1141 of the New York Penal Code, which forbade the sale of literature that was "obscene, lewd, lascivious, filthy, indecent or disgusting," went right for the jugular and hit Viking Press, Caldwell's new publisher after he split with Scribner's, hard.

By the early 1930s, as Caldwell found himself and his work knotted with legal and social complications in New York City courtrooms, the American Communist Party was enjoying its greatest popularity and influence in literary circles. Dan Miller describes the city as being "alive with Communist rallies, bookshop debates, political dance groups and theater, films, and mass meetings—the city was, a bewildered John Orrick Jones wrote, 'as full of dates as festas in Italy'" (157). All over America, active chapters of John Reed clubs were springing up, in small towns as well as in large cities; their purpose was "to win writers and artists to the revolution," Alexander Trachtenberg declared in 1934. Months later, in 1935, the *New Masses* published Granville Hicks's "Call for an American Writers' Congress," which sought to engage poets, novelists, dramatists, critics, short story writers, and journalists in the struggle to speed up the obliteration of capitalism and to launch a workers' government. Shortly thereafter, the League of American Writers was formed, and in a two-day inaugural conference remembered by Waldo Frank for its energy, intellectual solidarity, and most important, its *youth,* 216 delegates met to discuss and forge alliances between literature, intellectualism, and politics, a consolidation that coupled some of the twentieth century's most creative minds with its most commanding activists. It would be a movement that was at the same time young and alarmingly mature; and it would be a movement fueled by politics and poetry, animated by brawn, and compelled by bravado.

That so many modern writers were politically aligned with the Popular Front (a loose conglomeration of organizations steered by the American Communist Party), or were aligned with the League of American Writers, the American Committee for the Defense of Leon Trotsky, John Reed Clubs, the Committee for Cultural Freedom, the Nonpartisan Labor Defense, or the American Civil Liberties Union, or worked in the editorial offices of literary and political magazines such as the *Masses, Liberator, New Masses, Nation, Anvil, Transatlantic Review,* the *JRC Bulletin,* the *New Republic, Little Review, Modern Monthly,* the *Partisan Review,* the *New Age,* or *Marxist Quarterly,* seems indicative of the way modern writers and intellectuals came to express the period in its transition. Their words not only reached and affected intellectuals working within other social movements— galvanizing collective political action, as discussed later in this book—but they attracted the attention and censure of Hoover's antiradical FBI. Hoover continually redefined the role of the bureau during this period of cultural history, decades that teemed with political chaos, economic depression, and emergency. As a result of what Kenneth O'Reilly calls "the FBI's red-hot surveillance and counterintelligence pursuit of 'communists'—a category less ideological than convenient and elastic" (9-10), Hoover's hand touched, and often revoked, even modest civil rights and privileges, and intro- duced into the daily lives of the writers and intellectuals he shadowed elements of compulsion and paranoia. His assaults were persistent and serious, and ranged from routine reports to scandal-filled dossiers, from detailed analyses to random fragments of information (Summers, 53). Hounded for years by Hoover and his government men, many writers, editors, publishers, critics, lawyers, civil rights and antiwar activists, labor leaders, academics, and other intellectuals saw their careers disfigured and their lives come undone because of bureau records that linked them to anarchy, treason, sedition, or criminal activity.

John Steinbeck, for example, wrote to Attorney General Francis Biddle in 1942 and asked, "Do you suppose you could ask Edgar's boys to stop stepping on my heels? They think I'm an enemy alien. It's getting tiresome" (Steinbeck FBI file). Biddle contacted Hoover about this, who immediately responded to the Attorney General:

> Reference is made to your memorandum dated May 11, 1942, transmitting a letter addressed to you by John Steinbeck, in which Steinbeck complained that he was being investigated as an enemy alien by representatives of this Bureau.
>
> I wish to advise that Steinbeck is not being and has never been investigated by this Bureau. His letter to you is returned herewith. (Steinbeck FBI file)

The Steinbeck situation escalated. In October, Miss Collins of the Attorney General's office advised via telephone "the Attorney General want[s] to see the Bureau's file on John Steinbeck tomorrow morning (Oct. 28th)." A notation at the bottom of the message reads: "5:45 P.M. Miss Collins was advised that the Bureau had conducted no investigation concerning John Steinbeck and her attention was called to the Bureau's memorandum of May 21, 1942, in which the Attorney General was so advised" (Steinbeck FBI file). Despite these claims, a file on John Steinbeck does exist; I received a copy of it under FOIA. The file was opened as early as 1936, after the writer attended a writer's conference.

The file provides evidence that bureau Special Agents in Charge (SACs) had conducted interviews with Steinbeck's neighbors; checked his credit records at the Retail Credit Association in San Francisco; located two of his several commercial and savings accounts at the First National Bank in Los Gatos, California; interviewed a Mr. Roberts, bank cashier, a Frederick Bechbolt, postmaster in Carmel, California, Carol Steinbeck, the writer's ex-wife; and probed into the holdings of his personal library. In fact, the "non-investigation" continued for decades. In 1961, M. A. Jones sent a memo to Mr. DeLoach abstracting Steinbeck's recent publication, *The Winter of Our Discontent*, and pointed to two instances in which the writer mentioned the bureau in his book (Steinbeck FBI file). When one SAC found a Mr. Hugh Porter residing at an old Steinbeck address, he interviewed him:

> **MR. PORTER** did not know Subject personally but had Subject's belongings moved from the house. He stated that the Subject's second-class mail was tremendous, much of it apparently communistic. Subject's library, left in the former residence, contained many radical books. Informant's opinion of Subject based upon observation of conditions under which Subject lived is that Subject is very impulsive, eccentric, and unreliable socially. (Steinbeck FBI file)

Steinbeck's file also contains memos from Special Agents (SAs) who captured in minute detail their activity in the non-investigation. Among the many records bureau agents gleaned for Steinbeck information were these, checked by SA Nicholas Zavinsky: "the Office of Naval Intelligence, 12th Naval District; the American Legion Radical Research Bureau, the San Francisco Field Office of the Federal Bureau of Investigation, the San Francisco Police Department, all of San Francisco, California, regarding the Subject" (Steinbeck FBI file).

Another agent, Charles Shields, indicates that he "checked the records of the Sheriff's office, Santa Clara, California, and the Police Department, Los Gatos, California, regarding the Subject" (Steinbeck FBI file). SA Martin Frankel indicates that he had checked the records of the police departments in "Salinas, Carmel, and Monterey" (Steinbeck FBI file). By 1954, the bureau had enough information on Steinbeck to author an eight-page report on the writer, including a full page of material gathered under the category:

"INSTANCES WHEREIN AMERICA'S ENEMIES HAVE USED OR ATTEMPTED TO USE STEINBECK'S WRITINGS AND REPUTATION TO FURTHER THEIR CAUSES" (Steinbeck FBI file).

The report also notes that "During 1942, 1943, and 1944, Steinbeck was listed as one of the individuals in the United States who received Russian literature. Office of Censorship; 65-1674-809, p. 8; 65-49085-81" (Steinbeck FBI file). A second report on Steinbeck, written several years later and placed in the writer's file, numbers 12 pages. How was it then that Hoover could insist to the Attorney General that no investigation was or had been taking place on John Steinbeck?

No doubt such semantics can be exasperating. Time and time again in FBI files I have come across copies of the following form letter sent out by the bureau in response to requests for dossier information: "No investigation pertinent to your inquiry has been conducted by the FBI concerning the captioned individual. However, a review of FBI files reflects that . . ." and the letter outlines a variety of information gathered from various sources. So while the bureau is able to claim that "no investigation has ever been conducted" on a subject regarding enemy alien status, communist affiliations, or suspicion of radical activity, that does not mean the same thing as saying "we are not actively collecting and gathering information on this person."

When Max Eastman was handed a torn-off piece of drawing paper with the words "You are elected editor of *The Masses*. No pay" inscribed on it by a paintbrush, he was understandably shaken. There wasn't much he could do for the bankrupt cooperative magazine (Fishbein, 35), abandoned by its original editor, Piet Vlag. Eastman would stay with the *Masses* as its editor until the paper ceased publication in 1917. Eastman's FBI file contains among other things a report that begins with the seemingly exculpatory statement "The FBI has conducted no investigation concerning the captioned individual." He is incriminated in the next sentence, though. "This Bureau's records reflect, however, that Eastman, a well-known author, editor and lecturer, was admittedly an advocate of the Communist system, who for many years lectured in support thereof in the United States and also wrote several books on the subject" (Eastman FBI file). The report continues for seven pages and outlines all of the information gathered on Eastman during the bureau's "non-investigation" of him. Though Earl Browder proclaimed in 1937 "Communism Is Twentieth Century Americanism," Hoover found such Americanism contemptible, and he made its prosecution a bureau priority. As Herbert Mitgang reminds us,

> The FBI's hidden power had not yet developed when Upton Sinclair wrote *The Jungle*, a novel that led to federal regulation of the meat-packing industry. However, by the time John Steinbeck wrote *The Grapes of Wrath*, which helped bring awareness of the plight of migratory workers and some improvement in their conditions, the FBI recordkeepers were inscribing his name as an author to be watched. (*Dangerous Dossiers*, 303)

Timing, as the man said, is everything.

Using a sophisticated coalition of agents and informants, as well as information supplied by international intelligence agencies, international police forces, legal and civil attachés in foreign embassies, confidential informants, and confidential files, the bureau spent hundreds of man-hours painstakingly cross-referencing dossier material on modern writers. The James Joyce file proves no exception, containing information about his early friendship with American writer Ezra Pound, his introduction to Samuel Roth (the man who published pirated episodes of Joyce's novel *Ulysses* in 1927), his association with the not-yet notorious Whittaker Chambers (who would write a cover story on Joyce and *Finnegans Wake* in 1939 for *Time* magazine), and information about his family. The bureau continued to track information on Joyce well into the late 1960s, as it kept tabs on Joyce's son Giorgio, Giorgio's wife Helen, and her brother Robert Kastor, a member of the Young Communist League (and also the person responsible for talking Bennett Cerf into offering Joyce a Random House contract in December of 1931 for *Ulysses*. The following February, Kastor sailed to Europe to present Joyce with the contract and a check from partners Cerf and Klopfer if he signed it. Joyce signed the contract with Random House in early March). Because of the bureau's pursuit of "communists," Joyce was targeted early as a likely communist, not merely because of his association with politically charged figures Ezra Pound and Whittaker Chambers, but I believe because of his Irish citizenship as well.

Hoover had sent so many Irish labor agitators back to Ireland after the Palmer Raids that I think he began to think of them all as anarchists—probably as dangerous as Russians, in his mind. The Irish Transport and General Workers Union (ITGWU) strike and the ensuing Dublin "Lockout" in 1913, for example, was followed in 1916 by the remarkable Easter Rising, which took place in Dublin and in other parts of Ireland. These episodes prefigured what Russian workers would stage a year later in 1917 during what John Reed would call the "Ten Days that Shook the World." Moreover, Ireland had been caught conspiring with Germany during the First World War for arms sales. These circumstances, I would argue, led to a bureaucratic red-flagging of important Irish and Irish American figures. Joyce likely fell into this pile.

Hoover's distaste for modern writers, especially his desire to limit the dissemination of their work through censorship, bullying, and courtroom dramas, would come to define the bureau's attitude toward modern literature. Because modernists were writing literature that deliberately turned away from the tyranny of the family reading audience and were orienting readers towards forbidden and illicit subject matter, it was seen as contemptible and dangerous. Just as Hoover believed that Russian Communists and Jews were subsidizing pornography in an effort to destabilize American culture— Walter Winchell would declare in radio broadcasts, "Communists have circulated pornographic pamphlets and books in the 48 states"—or as a Confidential FBI Memorandum records, that the Japanese were "sending obscene photographs of American girls through India and other such countries in an effort to create the impression of lax morals on the part of Americans" (*Secret Files,* 301), he saw in this revolutionary new style in the arts (backed certainly, he thought, by Communism) the unraveling of the very fabric of American democracy and capitalism.

Hoover argued that Communist doctrine was supported by "intellectual perverts" and was "atheistic" (Stephan, 11); he even dared to blame deteriorating race relations in America on Communist activities: "a good proportion of unrest as regards race relationships results from Communist activities" (quoted in Messick, 99). Here, actually, Hoover may have been right.[10]

Evidence gathered by bureau agents and deposited into the files of modern writers would clearly suggest that such a link existed between writers and pornographers. In Samuel Roth's FBI file, for example, there are subscription cards announcing that each new subscriber to Roth's publication *Good Times: A Review of the World of Pleasure* would receive a free copy of the collected poems of Ernest Hemingway. The subscription flyers were customized to attract local subscribers. "Special to Chicagoans," for example, "Free copy of Hemingway's poems" (Roth FBI file). This sort of collected evidence would suggest that Ernest Hemingway, one of the more notorious literary modernists of the time, was publishing his poetry in cahoots with pornographer Roth. It would even call into question the contents of such poetry. Most likely, Hemingway knew little of Roth's distribution tactics; Roth was a nefarious pirate.

Much of the information gathered in Joyce's bureau file is marked with the assessment "Internal Security-C," the "C" being bureau shorthand for communism; but were the bureau's suspicions warranted? From what the FBI could tell, Joyce's 1939 *Finnegans Wake,* like his *Ulysses* of 1922, was a bizarre novel written by a man who, suspiciously, had dozens upon dozens of addresses during his lifetime, many of these under false names—but only to avoid debt collectors, a trick he learned from his father. Even as early as 1920, Joyce had been plagued by rumors about him and his work, and was (laughably) reputed to be a spy for the Austrians, the British, and the Italians. He even complained to his brother Stanislaus that *Ulysses* was believed to be a prearranged German code; Ezra Pound had heard that "British censorship suspected *Ulysses* of being a code" (Ellmann, 510). Frustrated by the wildness of the rumors, Joyce wrote to his friend and publisher Harriet Shaw Weaver in 1921 to complain:

A nice collection could be made of legends about me. Here are some. My family in Dublin believe that I enriched myself in Switzerland during the war by espionage work for one or both combatants. . . . that I am a cocaine victim. . . . In America there appear to be or have been two versions: one that I was almost blind, emaciated and consumptive, the other that I am an austere mixture of the Dalai Lama and sir Rabindranath Tagore. Mr [Wyndham] Lewis told me he was told I was a crazy fellow who always carried four watches and rarely spoke except to ask my neighbour what o'clock it was. Mr Yeats seemed to have described me to Mr Pound as a kind of Dick Swiveller. . . .

I mention all these views not to speak about myself but to show you how conflicting they all are. The truth probably is that I am a quite commonplace person undeserving of so much imaginative painting. (Ellmann, 510)

Ellmann notes, "the stories about Joyce grew more extraordinary as his life became outwardly more domestic. Journalists indulged their fancy freely, and mentioned his daily swim in the Seine, the mirrors with which he surrounded himself while he worked, the black gloves he wore when he went to bed" (512). Ellmann adds that Joyce both resented and enjoyed the proliferating rumors; he perhaps unwittingly aligned his situation with compatriot Oscar Wilde's, recalling his oft-quoted remark on being, and not being, talked about.

Joyce didn't have to worry about a lack of attention, though. By 1920, the FBI had an extensive newspaper clipping service—some 625 papers were read and clipped daily by bureau assistants. Moreover, Herbert Mitgang reports that several newspapers, including the New York *Journal American* and the *New York Times,* opened their "morgues" to bureau SACs—these morgues contain "usually guarded, private staff material" (*Dangerous Dossiers,* 142). In this amalgam of sources, Joyce's name kept coming up, not only in newspapers, magazines, and photo spreads, but equally important, in the files of other subjects—Ezra Pound, Whittaker Chambers, Samuel Roth, Michael Gold, and in the files of Hoover's detested Provincetown Players, to name a few. More importantly, Joyce's work had been tried two times in major United States obscenity cases, and because sections of his novel *Ulysses* were pirated by Samuel Roth and published (unauthorized) in *Two Worlds Monthly,* Joyce's novel was once again the subject of a courtroom drama and getting media attention. Another reason why Joyce's name was all over the place was because Joyce's son Giorgio was visiting the United States in 1934, the year of the landmark Woolsey decision, which ruled that *Ulysses* was not obscene and could be printed and sold in the United States. Georgio was interviewed by the *New Yorker* magazine about his father and about the family's reaction to the Woolsey decision. There had also been a spread on Joyce in *Vanity Fair* magazine. Hoover couldn't have missed the attention being showered on Joyce. He might have cared nothing for modern literature but he knew a cultural icon when he saw one.

Moreover, as I will show in chapter 4, the Joyce-Roth connection likely troubled Hoover, who loathed, pursued, and prosecuted Roth several times for trafficking in pornography. Reputed to be "the largest dealer in obscene material in the United States" (Roth FBI file), Roth would wind up in the U.S. penitentiary in Lewisburg, Pennsylvania for his obscene dealings. Interesting to our purposes, in late December 1957, he would contact Hoover by letter to offer information about a communist spy ring in Mexico and to seek exoneration in the form of a "comprehensive Presidential pardon." In his five-page handwritten letter to Hoover (which no longer exists, apparently; only a transcription of it remains in Roth's FBI file), Roth promoted himself as having paved the way for Joyce's apotheosis. He wrote:

> The matter I was found guilty on was so far from being obscene that in its answering brief before the High Court, the Department of Justice described it (and all other publications that have involved me with the law) as "borderline entertainment!" . . . In pronouncing sentence, Judge Cashin spoke indignantly of my "record" on nine previous violations. These included arrests in cases I won, cases on books later exonerated in other court actions and in the highest court of Public Acceptance—one, *Ulysses* by James Joyce—being now required reading in our colleges. (Roth FBI file)

The unwitting connection, then, between Joyce and Roth (though Joyce despised it) would have made him "guilty by association" with the world's foremost peddler of obscene material. Roth's point about Joyce's public acceptance is an important one, since we know that Hoover's G-men certainly kept tabs on what was "required reading" in colleges. In 1928 Michael Gold acknowledged "college professors and fat magazines have at last 'recognized' the American Literature of 1914-1928. Daring young instructors in English courses can now safely recognize Edna Millay, Sherwood Anderson and Carl Sandburg" (*New Masses,* Sept. 1928: 13). The bureau would have noticed the sea shift, as well, and its attention to college campuses and on the reading lists of certain professors would lead eventually to HUAC investigations of college instructors who were scrutinized for what they taught and what they required their students to read.

Hoover looked suspiciously at all "molders of public opinion," domestic or international, and he focused inordinate energy on the writers. In a declassified internal memoranda, for example, he lists as dangerous and subversive "prominent columnists, editors, commentators, authors, et cetera, which could be influencing such slanted views" (Mitgang, 17; Robins, 183). While this project, then, started out as a project that would investigate the relationship between Joyce and the G-men, it rapidly has grown into an examination of Hoover's institutional intervention into the private lives and careers of modernist writers. The argument not only demonstrates that J. Edgar Hoover and his G-men monitored the literary output of the world's hottest and most influential writers in the 1920s and 1930s; because the bureau exhibited such conspicuous control over those writers, the FBI as an institution grew to shape and thereby limit what we recognize as literary modernism. In other words, not only did Hoover structure American experience during his reign in the bureau from 1924 until his death in 1972, but I am convinced he structured the course of modern literature as well, by doggedly shadowing writers who were too politically radical, too stylistically experimental, too critical of twentieth century culture, too sexually frank and explicit, and too likely to influence public opinion. Proving the depth of his paranoia, Hoover called such writers "Communist thought-control relay stations" (Robins, 50), and established within the bureau's Domestic Intelligence Division the Publications Section (later called the Book Review Section) to monitor, manage, and manipulate literary production.

He accomplished this by developing a network of journalists and reporters who gobbled up his daily FBI handouts, begged for what have been called "grace-and-favor" interviews, and hoped to be kept on his list of "Friendlies." In terms of public relations, Hoover kept two running lists: the Friendlies, also known as his "Special Correspondents," and the Unfriendlies, those on his "Not to Be Contacted" list. You didn't want to get on the Unfriendlies list. It was Hoover's way of blacklisting reporters and journalists who weren't eating out of his hand, as Louella Parsons, Walter Winchell, Hedda Hopper, and George Sokolsky were. As Robins points out, "From the time he took over the Bureau in 1924, Hoover used the power of the FBI to make and break relationships" (110). Athan Theoharis notes that the reporters who were deemed reliable "were carefully recruited and stroked. They benefited from well-orchestrated leaks on the condition that they did not disclose the FBI as their source. In return, these journalists provided information of interest . . . and were contacted to write needed 'corrections' to unfavorable stories" (*Secret Files,* 303). Even Hoover's second-ranked man, Cartha "Deke" DeLoach, grasped at euphemisms to describe Hoover's network. He said, "Mr. Hoover didn't have such a thing as a list of sources. He had a list of friends" (quoted in Robins, 109). Often, the technicalities of who was, and who wasn't, a "friend" stirred up jealousy in the press business. The file of Leonard Lyons, a writer for the *New York Post,* contains a letter from a disgruntled fellow journalist, jealous of not getting the "leads" from Hoover, who always gave them, the letter charged, to Winchell and Lyons. Natalie Robins notes that Lyons's wife, Sylvia, understood the antagonism. "Any columnist would have been jealous—if that's the right word—to have a pipeline, so to speak. . . . Winchell," she added, "was Hoover's number one outlet" (139).

If he wasn't setting reporters like Walter Winchell on his literary targets and supplying the reporters with scandalous tidbits from bureau files that they could run in their newspaper columns or glossies to tantalize the public, Hoover was having his SACs from FBI field offices cozy up to lunch with their favorite book club or Book-of-the-Month Club (BOMC) judges, making sure that none of them would help to mass-produce the literature.[11] In her fascinating study of the Book-of-the-Month Club Janice Radway writes that "it is clear to anyone who examines those lists [of main selections] with care that one literary category did not make its way automatically to the club's subscribers. Literary modernism is conspicuously absent from the list of books the judges recommended as appropriate to a large general audience" (*A Feeling for Books,* 279). Radway writes at length of Henry Seidel Canby's dislike of literary modernism, and notes his contempt for modernists Joyce and Faulkner (291-93). "It was the distance and the dispassion Canby instinctively disliked. He believed that an art that produced only contempt, disgust, and shame in the reader could never do positive work in the world" (293). As Radway describes him, Canby sounds like the social puritarian John S. Sumner, secretary of the New York Society for the Suppression of Vice. Sumner's crusades for social purity are outlined in the next and in later chapters.

An earlier account of the Book-of-the-Month Club, *The Hidden Public: The Story of the Book-of-the-Month Club,* written by Charles Lee in 1958, notes that William Allen White and Heywood Broun vehemently objected to the club's signing on Steinbeck's *The Grapes of Wrath* in 1939 as a Club selection, for example, and that their opposition vexed fellow judge Henry Seidel Canby, who was surprised by their positions (113). In a letter the following year inviting J. Edgar Hoover to speak at the Peace Officers gathering in Emporia, Kansas, William Allen White assured Hoover that they were cut from the same cloth. He wrote,

The kind of Americanism that you and I stand for is in the blood here and also I think it would be well if you could come out this way and talk for what you say here would be read widely in the Western Missouri Valley, Oklahoma, Kansas, Nebraska, Iowa and Missouri, Minnesota and the Dakotas. We will see that you have every implement of publicity and give your remarks the widest circulation. (White FBI file).

Hoover usually enjoyed making such appearances, especially when the invitations came with the promise of "every implement of publicity," since he was obsessed with making appearances that helped to shape the public's sentiment about crime and law enforcement; but Hoover declined White's request saying the date was not open. White responded by changing the date to accommodate Hoover but he continued to decline the invitation. More than 15 letters back and forth catalog in White's FBI file their exchange on this invitation. No doubt exasperated, White sent Hoover a telegram on September 14, 1940 urging him to reconsider:

I KNOW OF NO OTHER PLACE IN COUNTRY WHERE YOU CAN SAY VITAL NECESSARY T[*sic*] THINGS BETTER THAN THIS. PERSONALLY I SHOULD BE GLAD IF YOU CAN COME.　W A WHITE. (White FBI file)

Hoover continued to say no.

Dorothy Canfield Fisher, another of the Book-of-the-Month Club judges, notes that one of the questions bandied about at monthly judges meetings was "will the distribution . . . be socially desirable, that is, influence readers toward a more civilized attitude toward human life?" (123). John Marquand, who was appointed a BOMC judge in 1956, recalled that the judges turned down Faulkner's *Intruder in the Dust* simply because it made one person nervous. Before my time,"

Marquand continues, "*The Grapes of Wrath* was turned down for some similar captious reason" (124). Along the same lines, Malcolm Cowley criticized the Book-of-the-Month Club in 1953 for its lack of attention in particular to modernist writers among the club's main selections. He complained, "Among the names that are missing, note Faulkner, Proust, Joyce, Kafka, Gide, Pirandello, Rilke, Lorca, D. H. Lawrence, Sherwood Anderson, Dos Passos, Yeats, Eliot, Mauriac, Conrad Aiken, Valéry, Claudel, Colette" (Lee, 203). As Hoover tried to reconfigure the geography of modern literature, how did his bureau's association with club judges and other literati influence the course of modern literature?

Christopher Morley, one of the founding judges for the Book-of-the-Month Club, selected a lesbian coming-of-age novel for his first recommendation in the club's newsletter, which attracted the attention of the bureau. Later, in January of 1936, Morley's regular column in the *Saturday Review of Literature* was specially titled "*Questio Quid Juris,*" and was written in defense of André Gide's *Si le grain ne meurt* (trans. *If It Die*), a book Frances Steloff of New York's Gotham Book Mart had been arrested for selling. One of Morley's biographers, Helen Oakley, recalls in *Three Hours For Lunch* that

> One Fall day in 1935, Frances Steloff put in a frantic phone call to Bennett Cerf at Random House. She told him she had been arrested! What for? For a curious crime which in those days was called (in hushed tones) buggery. . . . [W]hen Miss Steloff decided to promote André Gide's autobiography, . . . Sumner promptly sent a seedy-looking customer off to the shop to buy a copy—and request a sales slip. All unsuspecting, Frances Steloff complied. Next thing she knew, she was summoned into court. (250)

Cerf contacted Random House's legal counsel, Horace Manges, to handle the defense and then telephoned Morley with the details.

Three weeks after the publication of Morley's column, Judge Nathan D. Perlman dismissed the case. In his ruling, Perlman quoted from Morley's *Saturday Review of Literature* essay. Steloff said years later "that her case, and Morley's article, were responsible for changing the law in regard to 'obscene matter'" (Oakley, 251). Not much later, Christopher Morley would turn his attention to the *Ulysses* obscenity trial, involving yet again Bennett Cerf and Random House. He would cast Judge Woolsey's pronouncement of the theme of sex in the novel into one of his Old Mandarin witticisms (Woolsey ascribed the sexual presence in Joyce's book to the fact that the book was situated in Ireland in the spring):

> He heard the clock its knell tick
> He heard the blackbird sing:
> Reaction peristaltic
> And psychic too, they bring.
> For his locale was Celtic
> And his season, spring. (*The Middle Kingdom*, 108)

Hoover's manipulation of modernism also included having inside men at some of the country's most important downtown New York publishing houses such as Doubleday, Holt, Scribners, and William Sloane Associates.[12] His functionaries there and in the bureau would read books and provide Hoover with "convenient and timely access to what Americans were writing, [allowing] him the opportunity to monitor the written word and discover writers who should be deemed suspicious" (Robins, 50). By 1920, publishing and printing comprised one of the largest industries in New York, second only to the women's garment industry, according to Ann Douglas in *Terrible Honesty: Mongrel Manhattan in the 1920s* (14). New York's largely "imported" group of publishers needed to be monitored (Douglas 14). The bureau kept close watch over the new generation of young publishers, "a group of independent publishers . . . emerged to take on work that the older firms left up for grabs. Small operations at first, presses run by the young Alfred Knopf, Mitchell Kennerley, Horace Liveright, B. W. Huebsch, and bookseller Albert Boni published young writers from downtown and reprinted contemporary work from Europe" (Stansell, 156-57). In his book on Joyce titled *Our Joyce: From Outcast to Icon,* Joseph Kelly identifies small publishers such as Thomas Seltzer, Benjamin W. Huebsch, Albert Boni, Horace Liveright, Pascal Covici, and Donald Friede as "modernist publishers, for their goals (besides, of course, the goal of making money) were sympathetic to the goals voiced in the manifestos of the modernist writers and editors of little reviews" (137).

Not inconsequentially, many of the new publishers were Jewish and had to battle longstanding anti-Semitism in the industry and in the nation. Horace Liveright was the first of these up-and-comers, and he had the field just about to himself, Jason Epstein notes in *Book Business: Publishing Past Present and Future.* Liveright had an "uncanny eye for talent and the promotional instincts of Barnum at a time when writers of genius were turning up on both sides of the Atlantic but were generally shunned by the genteel publishers of the day. . . . Liveright was the first of the so-called Jewish publishers, who as a group would soon energize the somnolent book trade long dominated by houses rooted in the prejudices of the previous century" (Epstein, 45). Looking back on the book industry and praising the kind of publisher typified by this new breed, Malcolm Cowley wrote in January 1929 that the men working the industry back in 1916 were of a different kind, and he eulogized them in an essay for the *New Masses:*

> In 1916, publishers were comfortably uncertain of their position in the world. They hovered on the vague borders between business and art, between the trades and the professions, meanwhile deriving advantages from each of these fields—from business their profits, from the trades their pride in workmanship, from art a faint halo of romance and sin which did not interfere, however, with their professional dignity. . . .

[T]hey regarded themselves as public servants, whose duty was
to care for the minds of the nation in much the same way that
dentists cared for its teeth. To this end they provided aseptic novels,
mildly bracing essays, therapeutic biographies, all of them bound in
cloth as sober as hospital linen. Their profits—their "emoluments"
for these services—were never very great. ("Portrait of a Publisher,"
Jan. 1929: 5)

Though he goes on to bemoan the state of publishing in 1929,
Cowley's portrait of the sincere and benevolent publisher of 1916
contributes to our understanding of the industry at a time when it
changed dramatically due to an influx of fresh, young talent.

Biographer Tom Dardis similarly describes the cultural context
that these young publishers entered when they entered the American
industry. Dardis explains in *Firebrand: The Life of Horace Liveright*:

The presence of Jews in American book publishing was an anomaly in
the pre-World War I years. When Horace and Albert Boni created their
firm in the late spring of 1917, they were entering a Christian industry—
owned by Christians and staffed by them. Anti-Semitism was the main
factor but there were other causes working to keep book publishing a
WASP business from top to bottom, especially the top. The vast
majority of the prominent New York firms had their roots in the mid
and late nineteenth centuries: Harper and Brothers, Charles Scribner's
Sons, G. P. Putnam's Sons, and Doubleday. In Boston, the past ruled
supreme: Houghton Mifflin and Little, Brown. All these old firms were
controlled by the heirs of the original founders, a fact that left its mark
on the books they published. Max Schuster, the Jewish cofounder of
Simon and Schuster, observed that before the war "publishing had the
position of being a closed universe for the elite and the Brahmins in
Boston, and for the high and mighty publishers in New York." Nearly
all the editors of these firms had been educated at Yale, Harvard or
Princeton. In short, American book publishing was something of a

gentlemen's club, which rigorously rejected outsiders. But by 1917 the
outsiders included several young Jews who had decided to be included
by creating their own houses. (Dardis, 50)

Hoover was particularly interested in the Jewish brothers Albert and
Charles Boni, for example, committed socialists whose shop "became
a center for Villagers in the movement who made the store a port of
call where they met their friends" (Dardis, 46). In fact, when Albert
Boni had the idea to publish his "little books," many friends in the
Village were happy to assist: "Among them was Horace's erstwhile
rival for Lucille [his future wife], Walter Lippmann, as well as Harry
Scherman (later to create the Book-of-the-Month-Club), and
Lawrence Langner, a founder with Boni of the Washington Square
Players, a precursor of the Theatre Guild" (47). Keeping track of the
associates of men in the industry was important, too.[13]

G-men shadowed Horace Liveright. Dardis explains in his
biography of the man Ezra Pound called a "pearl among publishers"
that Liveright was making significant changes in the industry by
publishing writers whose works were radical in several ways: "From
the outset, Liveright defied convention by publishing writers whose
books were considered obscure, revolutionary or obscene. Dubbed
'The Firebrand,' Liveright spent many days in courtrooms defending his right to publish writers like Sigmund Freud and Bertrand
Russell. He was loathed by the self-righteous, as much for his books
as for the flamboyant lifestyle he pursued" (Dardis, xiv). Throughout his career, Liveright published the work of some of the most
celebrated modern writers: Djuna Barnes, Hart Crane, e. e. cummings, Theodore Dreiser, T. S. Eliot, William Faulkner, Mike
Gold, Ernest Hemingway, Lewis Mumford, Eugene O'Neill, Dorothy Parker, Ezra Pound, and Nathanael West, to name a few; but
he paid a price for such literary midwifery, and was often in U.S.
courtrooms opposing censorship. The censorship contest, Stansell
argues,

was a battle over who was to determine the content of literature: fusty unlettered zealots who rarely read themselves—"ignorant postal clerks, clergymen of archaic convictions, and lower court judges of the tobacco-chewing, common saloon type," as a *Little Review* writer described the censors—or an "advanced" public of serious readers and eager intellectual consumers. (159)

It is precisely this fight over the content of literature that most effectively paved the way for the kind of writing known as "high modernist" that came to define literary modernism, as I will show.

Censored or not, who could resist a Liveright party? A number of modern writers frequented Liveright's wild brownstone parties, where one also could find and rub elbows with the Gershwin brothers, Paul Robeson, and a magnificent array of Golden Age creative thinkers, artists, and operators. Liveright also was friend to the famously corrupt mayor Jimmy Walker, "a notorious nonreader" (Mitgang, *Once Upon A Time,* 27) who once boasted of his city "I'd rather be a lamppost in New York City than Mayor of Chicago."

The bureau also investigated Benjamin Huebsch, whose B. W. Huebsch publishing firm had done so well that it was able to merge with Viking Press in 1925. Huebsch, the American publisher of Joyce's *Dubliners* and *A Portrait of the Artist as a Young Man* had hoped to publish Joyce's *Ulysses;* but after the 1920s obscenity trial, he wrote to lawyer John Quinn on April 5, 1921, to express his unwillingness to pursue the American rights without manuscript changes. He wrote:

A New York court having held that the publication of a part of [*Ulysses*] in *The Little Review* was a violation of the law, I am unwilling to publish the book unless some changes are made in the manuscript as submitted to me by Miss H.[S.] Weaver who represents Joyce in London. In view of your statement that Joyce declines absolutely to make any alterations, I must decline to publish it. (Gorman, 280)

It was not until 1931 that Benjamin Huebsch formally withdrew from negotiations with Sylvia Beach (who by that time controlled the U.S. rights to Joyce's novel), which cleared the way for Bennett Cerf's Random House to pick it up, and for the infamously orchestrated defense of *Ulysses* to begin to get under way.[14]

Huebsch had attracted the attention of the bureau in 1912 after publishing the anonymously authored *Philip Dru: Administrator: A Story of Tomorrow, 1920-1935*. The novel went into several subsequent printings. An Office Memorandum to J. Edgar Hoover from a New York SAC dated 1954 in Huebsch's file quotes from a *New York Journal American* article by Westbrook Pegler that recalls the 1912 *Philip Dru* publication. Pegler calls the book "[a] cabal against the Constitution," and says of Huebsch

> He is now treasurer of the Civil Liberties Union and a member of the American Commission for UNESCO, the "educational" and "cultural" arm of the U.N. . . . Mr. HUEBSCH over a stretch of 20 years has been connected with 13 organizations which were described by the House Committee on Un-American Activities as subversive. Five of them were so described by Attorneys General. Usually, persons in this position insist that such descriptions are unjustified and HUEBSCH may want to make this reservation, too. (Huebsch FBI file)

What we see in this 1954 memo is obviously HUAC-baiting on the part of one of Hoover's grace-and-favor reporters. A charge is made and then a statement is issued saying that the person ought to dispute those charges if they are inaccurate. It's a foolproof plan and it works every time. This is the way Hoover and his men operated. It was a culture of severe oppression, one driven by fear, fueled by subterfuge, and bent on deceit. Cat-and-mouse games such as this one seemed a bureau standard. Huebsch's file also notes that he was a member of the advisory council of Book Union, described in a file notation as "A Communist 'Book-of-the-month' club."

In Huebsch's file, as in so many others, there are lists and lists of petitions and letters that have been signed by the publisher (to name a few, Huebsch joined an appeal to President Roosevelt on behalf of Earl Browder, signed a letter to President Roosevelt "protesting the attacks upon the Veterans of the Abraham Lincoln Brigade and condemning the war hysteria now being whipped up by the Roosevelt Administration," and was "signer of Golden Book of American Friendship with Soviet Union, date unknown" [FBI file]). The richness of information in these bureau files points to serious misdeeds and privacy violations.

Apart from keeping a watchful eye on the men holding the reins in the book publishing industry and noting their involvement, if any, in radical activities (Henry Hart, editor in chief of G. P. Putnam's Sons, was on the preplanning committee of the First American Writers Congress, for example), the bureau also had in-house sources who would supply Hoover's special agents with notes from editorial board meetings at magazines such as *Time, Life, Collier's, Fortune, Newsweek, Look,* and *Reader's Digest* (Gentry, 388), or with copies of minutes taken during Advisory Council meetings at newspapers such as the *Daily Worker.* Louis Budenz, for example, managing editor of the *Daily Worker,* was a bureau informant; Quentin Reynolds, an editor at *Collier's,* also would "cooperate" with the bureau [Robins 134], and became not only a close friend of Hoover's but "a Bureau friend," as well. As a result, Hoover was able to know what articles and book reviews were as yet unassigned and thereby up for grabs, which were forthcoming, and what stories were proposed for future issues (and by whom). His insiders also supplied him with lists of office numbers and telephone extensions for employees at these publications.

William Sullivan noted in an interview with Curt Gentry that the bureau began to "develop" informants in the publishing houses after the publication of *The Federal Bureau of Investigation,* a sleepy but potentially dangerous book that highlighted Hoover's FBI. Gentry reports that Sullivan commented, "These were not necessarily lower-level employees. They included at least two publishers,

Henry Holt and Bennett Cerf" (387). Cerf, Sullivan said, sent the bureau a copy of Fred Cook's manuscript *The FBI Nobody Knows* "and may have been instrumental in delaying its publication" (387).

Equally astounding, Hoover had a "highly unusual relationship" with Morris Ernst, a lawyer with New York's Greenbaum, Wollf, and Ernst, and general counsel to the American Civil Liberties Union (A.C.L.U.). Their relationship "baffled his associates in the Civil Liberties Union" (Gordon, 261),[15] and had developed to the point that Ernst was in the habit of sending Hoover regular letters and notes, and Hoover's secretarial staff chocolates for the holidays. Hoover was grateful: "Dear Morris: My entire secretarial staff has asked me to express their appreciation for the delicious box of chocolates. It was most kind and thoughtful of you to remember them again this season. . . . Edgar" (Ernst Archive; undated letter). Their relationship was indeed bizarre. In his letters to Hoover, for example, Ernst addressed the bureau director as "dear Knight" (Oct. 18, 1950), and often invited him for dinners, lunches, or weekend visits, as in the following example:

> Dear Edgar:
>
> I am out of the hospital and am getting back on my feet, although it will take some time. I hear you are not too well. I will be in Atlantic City, I think, around May 8th. Might I hope that you will be sick enough so as to have to go to Atlantic City over some week-end to recuperate with me, at which time we can solve the affairs of the world. (Ernst Archive; Apr. 24, 1947)

Moreover, Ernst closed one of his 1948 letters to Hoover with the flourish "You are a grand guy and I am in your army" (Nov. 29, 1948). Hoover might have wondered about Ernst's loyalty: seven months earlier he received from California Senator Jack Tenney a copy of the *Fourth Report—Un-American Activities in California,*

1948. The report identified Morris Ernst "among the Communists and Communist fellow-travelers" (199).

By 1949, Ernst's peculiar relationship with the bureau director worried his associates. James Lawrence Fly warned his friend Morrie of the dangers: "[Y]our own close personal relation to Mr. Hoover has blinded you to the fairness of your critics. You appear long since to have lost your judicial poise on any issue involving this agency, and I think it is about time you were taking inventory. Without love and respect for you I could not say this; with that love and respect I cannot say less" (Ernst Archive; Nov. 10, 1949). As he did with so much of his personal correspondence, Ernst sent Fly's letter to J. Edgar Hoover, and asked him to read and return it.

Hoover kept copies of, or notes on, some of Ernst's letters to and from his associates in the bureau's file on Ernst. In a March 27, 1940, letter to Hoover, for example, Ernst enclosed a copy of a letter he wrote to John Finerty, and recommended to Hoover that Finerty be used as a bureau confidant: "Dear John, I am sending you a copy of a letter that I sent to John F. Finerty. I think you can treat Finerty as you do me by telling him such things as you care to off the record and other things on the record.* Best, Yours, [signature]." The letter ends with Ernst's handwritten, asterisked caveat: "*But make sure & def that what is off, is really off" (Ernst FBI file).

Harrison Salisbury noted in a 1984 article on the Ernst-Hoover relationship that

> When it came to his dealings with the F.B.I., Ernst was either extremely naïve or extremely trusting. He sent Hoover and Nichols scores of confidential letters written to him by friends or associates. Always he specified that the enclosures were "for your eyes alone," or that "no public use is to be made of this." Always he asked for their swift return. They were, of course, returned, though not before Hoover or Nichols had a photocopy made. It is difficult to believe Ernst overlooked this likelihood. (*Nation*, Dec. 1, 1984, vol. 239: 575-90)

Morris Ernst, of course, was the lawyer who defended Joyce's *Ulysses* for Random House in 1933. He grew to become one of Hoover's most valuable informants as well as a treasured public relations figure. Materials housed in the Ernst Archive at the Harry Ransom Humanities Research Center at the University of Texas in Austin reveal that Ernst reported to Hoover almost weekly by letter whether from his home in New York or from his travels, domestic or abroad. In these letters he disclosed private conversations and privileged lawyer-client information to Hoover. By mid-century, Ernst was meeting frequently with bureau higher-ups for what he called "our regular brief chats" (Ernst Archive). The friendship between Ernst and the bureau proved fruitful, especially in the information it yielded. For example, when the American Civil Liberties Union was battling censorship of a modern literary work, Ernst wrote to local librarians, teachers, and well-known authors asking them to write letters on the book's behalf, a tactic that proved successful when Ernst was arguing the *Ulysses* case. After he recorded them, Ernst turned the letters of support over to J. Edgar Hoover's office, where each letter was read, copied, and turned into a bureau record.

In addition to copying his private letters to Hoover, Ernst frequently tipped off the bureau director about upcoming opportunities. In the following example, an October 14, 1941 letter to Hoover, Ernst gives the director a "heads up" about an article coming out in the *New Republic,* and even offers to draft Hoover's response, something he offered to do frequently. Ernst wrote:

> I understand that the *New Republic* is getting an article written about the FBI. The editor will send it to me and I intend to send it to you. I think that you would not want to then and there answer whatever criticism there is, and in this connection, I would be honored if you would let me write you a letter containing parts of the answer, to the end that you could incorporate parts of my letter in your answer. As a matter of fact, Roger Baldwin, I think, will write the article of attack.

I am convinced that he has got nothing in the way of actual evidence to rely on. Best to you, Yours, Morris Ernst. (Ernst FBI file)

Three days later Hoover wrote to accept Ernst's offer, and added "If similar situations arise at any time, I trust it will not be an imposition if I ask for your counsel and advice" (Ernst FBI file). We can see now, based on evidence in the Ernst archive and on items gathered and collected in Ernst's bureau file, that it was not an imposition at all. In fact, just a few months later, on December 11, 1941, Ernst offered his services to Hoover as a ghost writer again, this time, drafting Hoover's counter-argument at being called a "censor": "I would like you to read the enclosed statement which I have drafted to aid you in your basic point of view, and maybe in your utterances. I have drafted it in the form of a statement to be issued by you. Bear in mind that it only hit's [*sic*] a few high spots. Yours, [signature]" (Ernst FBI file).

Hoover's successful manipulation of a network of sources close to literary modernism, especially with figures who would agree to champion him and promote his antiradical values—such as Morris Ernst, journalists, publishers, editors, book judges and reviewers—as well as his links with those who supplied inside information about articles or review essays under consideration at national magazines and journals, aided him in his mission to keep literary modernism if not at bay, at least under his watchful eye. While Frances Stonor Saunders's recent work on the CIA has revealed near-unbelievable cooperation between writers, artists, and the federal government, J. Edgar Hoover apparently was ahead of the game and used informants to his advantage in order to manage and manipulate a rapidly increasing and alarming influential movement.

I will close this chapter by making three very short points to which I will return later. First, for decades, people have been trying to imagine how the Civil Rights movement in the United States might have progressed or developed without Hoover's interference—without his racist attacks, his threatening letters, the planted evidence, the falsified testimonies, the persistent interventions, the murders, the assassinations, and so forth. I have come to think that we can also ask ourselves the same kinds of questions about modernism, and am reminded of James Baldwin's statement to the *San Francisco Examiner* that he was "in some ways" the last unassassinated Negro of his generation—"my countrymen have killed off all my friends," he told the reporter. Baldwin had threatened to expose the FBI "and its baleful role in the civil rights movement" in a book he titled *The Blood Counters,* though it was never written, James Campbell notes in his article on Baldwin and the FBI (11). Campbell notes that information about Baldwin's project shows up in his file and "crop[s] up in memo after memo" (11). David Levering Lewis even suggests that the bureau may have had something to do with an assassination attempt on Jamaican black nationalist Marcus Garvey in 1919. After discussing Hoover's persistence in trying to have Garvey deported as an "undesirable alien," Lewis notes that the bureau

> took the unusual step of appointing an Afro-American special agent to watch UNIA [Universal Negro Improvement Association] headquarters. In October of that year the Garvey "nuisance" was nearly removed when George Tyler fired two bullets at point-blank range; one creased Garvey's forehead, another pierced his leg. Tyler's motives may have been simple revenge for having been recently sacked by Garvey, but his convenient suicide while in police custody was highly suspicious. (43)

Without the political assaults on writers, without the persistent hounding and the accusations, would we have a modernism characterized primarily by stylistic innovation? Would it have taken this form if it weren't for Hoover's paranoia about its subject matter, or his fear about its power to disrupt and destabilize "Americanism," striking not only at the foundations of the growing body of nationalist discourse between the wars, but also at all that Hoover prized and benefited from in twentieth century American culture? Hoover was so eager to prosecute perversion in all of its forms (sexual, political, moral, ideological, and so forth), that we need to ask how modern literature was affected by his antiradical hysteria, by his extremist philosophy of what constituted deviant, radical, or seditious activity. In what directions might modernism have taken off without Hoover's institutional interference? As critics, we have become so used to looking at increasingly attenuated constraints on aesthetic production (the subtle influence of ideology or microeconomies of power) that we sometimes lose sight of the more powerful constraints imposed by governmental censorship, copyright laws, libel laws, and so on. An extended treatment of J. Edgar Hoover and the bureau's role as an institution managing and constraining the aesthetic production of modernists provides an essential corrective.[16]

For example, would there be the current split between the "artistically bankrupt proletarianism and artistically sophisticated modernism" that Rocco Marinaccio discusses in his work on George and Mary Oppen and their *I've Seen America* book? Marinaccio situates the Oppens' work squarely within the crux of the well-known Brecht-Lukacs exchanges on modernism, aesthetics, and ideology. Brecht argued that the experimental forms of modernism were politically neutral but aesthetically glorious, while Lukacs believed that modernism was an ideology unto itself, and one that replicated essential manifestations of bourgeois society. The polemics of such a split encourages the dialectics that continues to be present in discussions of modernism.

Michael Gold promoted drawing from "national and folk culture in the United States for the purpose of 'Americanizing' the fundamentals of the class struggle" (Wald, 30). Concerned that poetry had gone soft, or that it was beginning to uphold the status quo, he bemoaned the divergence over time of literary modernism and cultural politics, and sounded the call to arms in his 1926 essay "Poetry in America," hoping to reintroduce the notion of revolution into American poetry. Poetry, he argued, was not for the patrons or "fat cats" who were commodifying it, but for the people. Hoping to reignite a spent flame, he wrote:

> Poetry must grow dangerous again. Now only club-ladies listen to poetry, but let's have poetry to offend and frighten club-ladies. Let's have poems the Watch-and-Warders will suppress. Tom-tom poems, jazz poems, barricade poems, poems thundering like 10-ton trucks or subways or aeroplanes. Poem[s] of the Miners' Union, that every miner will want to know by heart, like a Homeric ballad. Poem[s] against Henry Ford that the police and ministers of Detroit can burn in a public *auto-da-fay*. Poems that will hurt business, poems that can be chanted by mobs. Poems that stir the stagnant waters of America's spirits. Poems of life. (*New Masses,* Dec. 1926)

As Gold advocated for more political insurgency in the art of the day, what role did J. Edgar Hoover have in preventing literature from "growing dangerous?" Llewelyn Powys wrote in January 1927 "the average man would gladly kill artists for sport, for like fleas and bugs and lice, they disturb his sleep" (*New Masses,* 6). J. Edgar Hoover shared such readiness, I think, though not "for sport" but to assuage his anxieties about American culture. His persistence in this arena and his symbolic status as the preeminent organ of the state (regarding censorship, social purity, surveillance, control, and manipulation), affected the creative lives of modern writers and thwarted the very openness and the very democratic aesthetics of the literary movement. I will return to the central question: in what directions might modernism have advanced if it were not for the persistence of Hoover's institutionalized chauvinism? In what ways did the institutional structures and systems of power represented by J. Edgar Hoover and the FBI dwarf the development of the movement?

Hoover's intervention into this movement—his attempts to quash its political manifestations by making pronouncements in pamphlets, speeches, and interviews about the profligacy and degeneracy of the literary movement—gave rise to a canonical privileging of high-modernist art, where experimentalism and style overrode content and message. The modernism that emerged to define the movement, in other words, was a modernism influenced and structured by stylistic innovation: Eliot's, Woolf's, Conrad's, Pound's, Fitzgerald's, Joyce's. It was an overtly intellectual modernism, a modernism driven by its aesthetic of complexity. As these modernists grew to define the age, those writers who eschewed flashy displays of technical and textual bravado were categorized as writers not with an aesthetic vision but as mere "proletarian writers," or "social artists," and their work would not come into its own until the emergence of a literary Left in the 1930s. That is, until recently modernism had not been defined by the content of its literature—those provocative and challenging messages championed by writers such as Langston Hughes, Clifford Odets, Edna St. Vincent Millay, Michael Gold, Hallie Flanagan, Eugene O'Neill, Mary Heaton Vorse, Carl Sandburg, Susan Glaspell, Randolph Bourne, or Louise Bryant, to name a few—who chronicled the daily rhythms and regularities of modern life using recognizable forms and familiar language. Playwright and poet Amiri Baraka, for example, was once asked in an interview why he thought W. E. B. DuBois had been so under-appreciated: "Do you think they had trouble with DuBois's rhythms or his content?" the interviewer asked. Baraka replied, "It's always the content. Always the content. Form is secondary, always" (Internet interview, "Conversation with Baraka"). For many modern writers, it was the content—always the content—that redflagged them and made them hotly pursued bureau targets while modernism's more abstract stylistic experimenters, the creators of "high" or "elite" modernism, remained of secondary interest to the bureau. This is something to think about, and it is a point to which I will return.

There are serious related issues. Whereas J. Edgar Hoover manipulated the publication and dissemination of modern literature in his first decades as director of the FBI, he continues to control the way we think about the modernist project today because files and dossiers released to scholars under the Freedom of Information Act often take years to acquire and they arrive heavily censored and blacked-out by bureau officials. The bureau claims that the censoring protects the privacy of persons living or dead (which pretty much covers *everybody,* doesn't it?), or protects national security—as if to suggest that Joyce and others have ever threatened national security. What they seemed to threaten, it is clear to me, is an Americanism fetishized by J. Edgar Hoover. The file of Theodore Dreiser, for example, advertises the typical 1920s response: "A Great American novelist, but not a great American" (Robins, 80), the file notes.

Second point: Hoover, apparently, was an avid reader. He respected Mark Twain, whose autograph he framed. He also read *G-Man* and *Tarzan* comic strips and enjoyed westerns. At his death, his library contained a complete set of Sherlock Holmes stories, and included several books on roses and on dogs, and self-help titles such as *Are your Troubles Psychosomatic?; Modern Sex Life; Health in the Later Years;* and *How to Overcome Nervous Stomach Trouble.* There was nothing in his library by James Joyce.

The third and final point: the modernist writer Sinclair Lewis said of Hoover in 1935, "Hoover is a mere infant. His best years are ahead of him" (Robins, 101). I am afraid Sinclair Lewis was right. The interoffice procedures J. Edgar Hoover regulated, the secret dossiers, the letterhead files,[17] the "DO NOT COPY" memoranda, the "DO NOT FILE" procedures, the file destruction practices, and the institutionalization of what Athan G. Theoharis calls the "non-record records"—these continue to obscure our reading of modernism and its cultural history.[18] Like Joyce's best years, I'm afraid we haven't even caught up with Hoover's yet. Joyce boasted about *Ulysses* that he had done something to keep professors busy for the next 100 years—apparently, so did Hoover.

CHAPTER TWO

Modern Literature and Hoover's Degenerist Anxieties

"Literature is one of the products of a civilization, like steel or textiles. It is not a child of eternity, but of time. It is always the mirror of its age. It is not any more mystic in its origin than a ham sandwich."
—Michael Gold, "Go Left, Young Writers!"

If we agree with Michael Gold that literature is a product of civilization, that "it is always the mirror of its age," and is "not any more mystic in its origin than a ham sandwich" (*New Masses,* Jan. 1929: 4), then we will have to agree, as well, that the age must have been pretty bad for a United States Senator to proclaim on the floor of the Senate at roughly the time Gold published his words that he'd "rather a child of [his] take opium than read one of these books" (Cleaton, 55). But such was the hyperbole and unconstrained rhetoric surrounding book criticism at this time. These exaggerated degenerist anxieties were not limited to America. James Douglas, book critic and editor for the London *Daily Express,* appealed to the common sense of the British people when he exclaimed about Radclyffe Hall's *The Well of Loneliness* that he "would rather give a healthy boy or a healthy girl a phial of prussic acid than this novel," adding to his earlier remonstration published in the *Star* that when literature "refuses to conform," it needs to be called to the nation's attention.[1] Of course, calling such filth to the nation's attention also sold newspapers. Headlines such as "Novel that Should Be Banned," "Story of Perverted Lives," and "Nauseating" in the *Sunday Express* publicized the sensation stirred up by the advanced notice of Douglas's column (Doan and Prosser, 12). As Laura Doan and Jay Prosser note, "The silencing of homosexual propaganda, it seems, was a noisy business" (12), and newspapers of the day often resorted to a kind of "stunt journalism" to maximize publicity for news items of their own making.

With the oppressive conditions of what George Bernard Shaw called "comstockery" so ubiquitous in America from 1873-1915 (when Anthony Comstock, founding secretary of the New York Society for the Suppression of Vice, reigned until his death as the nation's chief moralist), by the time literary modernism would hit full stride, writers, editors, and publishers would see their work, their lives, and the very things they stood for microscoped under the watchful eye of a new breed of modern censor, and their subject matter, in James Douglas's words, called to the nation's attention. D. H. Lawrence was fed up with the prudery, and wrote "It doesn't seem to me that it is any use altering *The Rainbow* for the Americans. Curse them, what good is it to them, altered or not" (quoted in De Grazia, 69). This pervasive campaign affected a literary movement still in flux and still seeking definition. As the movement sought to identify its supporters, it also sought to christen its heroes. So while Utah Senator Reed Smoot orated, American writers both scoffed at his rhetoric and were driven by it. Ogden Nash, whose FBI file started "late" (1941), dubbed him "Senator Smoot from Ute" (Cleaton, 61). Smoot argued of modern literature, "There cannot be a viler language. There cannot be words put together so vile and rotten as in those books. . . . I want to keep them all out. I would rather keep out a thousand, than have one mistake made" (Cleaton, 55). Such anxiety came well within reach of Hoover's own fears that America was degenerating right before his eyes. It drove him to extremes and directed his efforts to curtail the congeries of political and radical writers participating in the burgeoning literary movement.

Smoot was not alone in thinking that the new kind of literature being disseminated through books, magazines, and readers' clubs in America was filthy, politically insurgent, or both. Years before, when Theodore Dreiser's manuscript of *Sister Carrie* was picked up by Frank Nelson Doubleday's publishing house while Doubleday and his wife, Neltje, were out of the country, his wife begged him not to print the book, equating her husband's involvement with its publication with the worst, most repulsive activity she could think of: "Frank," the apocryphal story goes, "I would rather get down on my knees and scrub floors than have you publish that book." Her protestations were successful, and earned her notoriety as the woman who had turned down *Sister Carrie*. In addition to blaming his own wife, Jug, who suggested he cut some 36,000 words from the original manuscript of *Sister Carrie,* Dreiser always blamed Neltje Doubleday for "undermining his book" (De Grazia, 100).

Natalie Robins details J. Edgar Hoover's interest in Theodore Dreiser, noting that his file began the year before the devastating Sacco and Vanzetti executions, when Dreiser endorsed Workers International Relief. His file notes the various petitions Dreiser signed, his group memberships and his positions in them, and the symposia, congresses, and conventions he attended. Bizarrely, a notation in playwright Lillian Hellman's file supplements the information contained in Dreiser's. The note records goings-on at a testimonial dinner held for Dreiser: "the FBI was there," Herbert Mitgang reports (149), and they were taking names and taking notes.

An agent interviewed Dreiser in 1939, what the bureau SACs refer to as a "pretext" call or interview, and included a copy of the report in Dreiser's file. After 1939, Dreiser's biographer Lingeman notes, "Dreiser became aware of the Bureau's interest in him. . . . He complained of an FBI 'blacklist' of his books, and spoke of an 'International FBI' banning his books in South America" (quoted in Robins, 82-83). Dreiser even believed that he had been blacklisted by a conservative literary establishment, and in his typescript "Down Hill and Up," he wrote, "I suddenly found myself too nervous to concentrate. Days and weeks even went by and I accomplished nothing. Instead I walked the streets, wondering how I was to manage in the face of a situation which seemed to preclude my writing in any form" (9). In 1931 Dreiser headed with a committee of writers to Harlan County, Kentucky, a site of tremendous labor unrest. He and the other writers were there to gather materials for a report on the situation. Louis Filler reports in *American Anxieties* that "[T]here, local authorities made an extraordinary effort to discredit the aging novelist by planting a woman in his room. Dreiser confounded them by declaring, in an item which no newspaper in the country could resist, that he was not only the victim of a plot, but that he was no longer sexually potent and could have found no use for the woman" (7). It is quite interesting to see how differently the situation is represented in bureau files. An agent in an FBI field office sent a memorandum to J. Edgar Hoover reporting that Dreiser had taken a young woman from Canada to Michigan "for immoral purpose." Hearing this, Hoover considered prosecuting Dreiser under the Mann Act (White Slave Traffic Act). Natalie Robins adds that Hoover's plan to prosecute Dreiser was "a way of silencing him" (Robins, 83). Though Dreiser was a highly decorated writer, in his novels he challenged stifling national mores, social purity dogma, and the alarming growth of twentieth century capitalist greed. As such, his file notes he was "a good writer, but not a good American." In fact, one bureau agent pronounced in a 1945 memo that Dreiser was a "has-been in the literary field" (*Dangerous Dossiers*, 88). Hoover instructed bureau agents to put the writer on "censorship watch" and to monitor his mail. Clearly, it was not only Dreiser's novels but his involvement as a correspondent and national witness to the atrocities taking place in Harlan County that marked him as dangerous. That the bureau would go so far as to frame him is simply maddening. Dreiser's FBI file does note, however, that the author claimed to be impotent, but it doesn't flesh out the rest of the story or contain any of the various news articles that covered the mess.

After the fiasco in which Frank Doubleday's firm contracted to publish Dreiser's 1901 novel *Sister Carrie* but then changed its mind, sensing that the shadow of Anthony Comstock had cast itself across the pages of Dreiser's novel, the writer became depressed and almost threw himself into the East River. "No one would know," he wrote. "I would be completely forgotten" (quoted in De Grazia, 108). *Sister Carrie* would eventually be published in an expurgated version, with Dreiser cutting some 36,000 words from the original manuscript. But even the "purged" manuscript of *Sister Carrie* would draw criticism, and Dreiser would find it almost impossible to secure a publisher in America for the book.

Dreiser shopped the book around at publishing houses such as Appleton, Scribner's, Dodd, Mead, McClure-Phillips Company, Century Company, and A. S. Barnes and Company. They said the book was "vulgar" and "impossible to read" (De Grazia, 105). The writer almost went mad. It would be ten years before he would write another book, *Jennie Gerhardt*, but it, too, would stand to mixed reviews, and would be called "utterly base," for example, by a reviewer in the *Lexington Herald* (De Grazia, 109). Things didn't improve for the writer. His next book, *The Titan*, would suffer a fate similar to his first novel. Though Harper had approximately 4,000 advanced orders for the book, and had already dedicated a large budget to the book's production and advertising, the firm decided at the last minute against publication, fearing that the sexual content of the book would draw censure and legal penalties. Theodore Dreiser's work would acquire a certain fame, and would be characterized by publication upheavals and vice proceedings. Works such as *The Genius, The Financier,* and the reprobate novel *An American Tragedy* would bring his work before the legal bar on several occasions and at great personal, emotional, and creative costs to the writer. In this sense, then, and in these arenas, Dreiser and his work were drafted into current debates not only about acceptability, prurience, and literary propriety, but about the utter baseness of modern literature and its emerging aesthetic. His court battles to protect his works and his efforts to promote the aesthetic of literary realism in defense of his frank if lurid descriptions would shape public responses to modernist literature for the next two decades.

With Dreiser so successfully made a target, the social purists raged on. Harvard's Bliss Perry, a professor, argued "The American public is now facing a clear and present danger through unclean books," and Charleston's *News and Courier* played the "no decent American" card when it wrote that no one "can doubt that the food of nastiness in books is really one of the gravest problems of these times, and no decent man or woman . . . is going to try to hinder any worthwhile effort to solve that problem in so far as it can be solved" (Cleaton, 59). Even strong personalities in the publishing business joined the ranks of the vocal. Patrick Knopf spoke with Charles Scribner, Jr., about his concerns over what he called the pornographic element in fiction. Scribner recalls in his *In the Company of Writers: A Life in Publishing:* "Some of these books," he would say, "you have to pick up with a pair of tongs" (173).

Though Patrick Knopf and Charles Scribner, Jr. are a generation removed from the heyday of literary modernism, Knopf's allusion to tongs may have rung a bell with the young Scribner, since a mythology had grown around the elder Scribner's publication of F. Scott Fitzgerald's *This Side of Paradise* in 1920. In his biography of Fitzgerald's remarkable editor, Max Perkins, A. Scott Berg recounts a story told by Roger Burlingame about an early review of Fitzgerald's book:

> The bellwether at Scribners in those days . . . was an important member of the sales department. Often mistrusting his own literary judgment he spoke "advisedly" about many books, and used to take them home for an erudite sister to read. His sister was supposed to be infallible and it was true that many of the novels she had "cried over" sold prodigiously. So when it was known that he had taken *This Side of Paradise* home for the weekend, his colleagues were agog on Monday morning. "And what did your sister say?" they asked in chorus. "She picked it up with the tongs," he replied, "because she wouldn't touch it with her hands after reading it, and put it into the fire." (*Max Perkins: Editor of Genius*, 19)

It probably wasn't lost on anyone at Scribners that the sister waited until *after* reading the book to toss it into the fire. Clearly, a book that ends with the introduction of a new generation bent on defining itself against the old transgressed the boundaries of acceptable speech and thought in 1920s America, and there was something threatening about such forceful, unapologetic bravado from a young and ardent writer. Fitzgerald wrote in *This Side of Paradise* that "[h]ere was a new generation . . . a new generation dedicated more than the last to the fear of poverty and the worship of success; grown up to find all Gods dead, all wars fought, all faiths in man shaken. . . " (260, ellipsis in original). A. Scott Berg notes that "*This Side of Paradise* unfurled like a banner over an entire age" (*Max Perkins,* 19), and Mark Sullivan notes in *Our Times* that "Fitzgerald's first book has the distinction, if not of creating a generation, certainly of calling the world's attention to a generation" (386-87). That the age was not prepared to accept this new generation was another story.[2]

One of the reasons for such ill-preparation on the part of the American readership to accept Fitzgerald's novel (though it would become a mainstay on Scribner's best-seller list for years) is that, as Mark Sullivan later said of Fitzgerald's hero, "Young people found in Amory's behavior a model for their conduct—and alarmed parents found their worst apprehensions realized" (Berg, 20). Roger Burlingame noted that the novel "waked all the comfortable parents of the war's fighting generation out of the hangover of their security into the consciousness that something definite, terrible and, possibly, final, had happened to their children. And it gave their children their first proud sense of being 'lost'" (Berg, 20).

1920, the year Scribners published Fitzgerald's book, and the years that shortly followed, were extraordinary years for literary modernism. The arrest for murder in 1920 and the subsequent trials and executions of Nicola Sacco and Bartolomeo Vanzetti in 1927 gave birth to a new nation, born out of the outrage those executions incited.[3] As John Dos Passos would write in his *USA Trilogy,* in which Sacco and Vanzetti's executions serve as the climax, "all right, then, we are two nations." Powers notes of Dos Passos's "we are two nations" that "it was as much the epigraph for the generation of the thirties as Gertrude Stein's 'you are all a lost generation' was for the twenties" (*G-Men,* 95). America was a nation divided, torn apart and with a noticeable rift. Writers, publishers, and editors alike found themselves having to stand on one side or the other, caught in the throes of a powerful change sweeping across America.

With the April 1920 publication of and subsequent reaction to Fitzgerald's first novel still creating a buzz in midtown Manhattan, an important episode was unfolding in lower Manhattan's Washington Square in a bookshop run by two feminists. A vice agent posing as an unassuming customer purchased at the Washington Square Bookstore an issue of the *Little Review,* a magazine that had been serializing James Joyce's novel *Ulysses* chapter by chapter since April 1918. The New York Society for the Suppression of Vice charged the editors of the *Little Review,* Margaret Anderson and Jane Heap, with propagating obscenity. After a heady trial, the women were convicted in 1921 of distributing obscene material. William Brockman briefly rehearses the turbulent publishing history of Joyce's novel, noting that full texts of Joyce's novel were virtually impossible to obtain in the United States:

> [t]hough published by Shakespeare and Company in Paris in a number of editions throughout the 1920s, *Ulysses* was prohibited from being imported into or mailed within the United States through the remainder of the decade and into the early 1930s, and the shadow of the 1921 obscenity trial was enough to drive away any significant publishing attempts. The only publication of *Ulysses* in the United States during the 1920s was done by Samuel Roth in a bowdlerized version without the consent of Joyce. (56)

Attempted publications of Joyce's *Ulysses* in the United States were fraught with high drama. Joyce's biographer Richard Ellmann notes that with Joyce's penchant for litigation, he "dreamed of a trial of *Ulysses* as successful as that of *Madame Bovary*" (502). When the *Little Review* began to serialize Joyce's novel, for example, the U.S. Post Office refused to mail the publication on the grounds of its obscenity. In fact, the Post Office seized and burned three issues of the *Little Review* after it published the "Lestrygonians," "Scylla and Charybdis," and "Cyclops" episodes (Jan. 1919; May 1919; Jan. 1920)—the eighth, ninth, and twelfth chapters of Joyce's novel. In the fall of 1920, John S. Sumner became involved and the obscenity battles started up once more. The trial would bring Margaret Anderson and Jane Heap, not to mention James Joyce, before a national audience, and though it would satisfy Joyce's dream of a *Ulysses* trial, it would not mark his apotheosis.

When Margaret Anderson received a letter at the *Little Review* from a subscriber complaining about her publication's recent installment of a chapter from Joyce's *Ulysses,* for example, she responded, "It is not important that you dislike James Joyce. It is as it should be.

He is not writing for you. He is writing for himself and for the people who care to find out how life has offended and hurt him" (*My Thirty Years' War*, 214). Anderson notes that her response must have been an effective one, since she received an apology from the critic by return post: "The apology I received was not based upon any new under-standing of Joyce's work. It was an admission of having written without temperance and thus of having committed a grave discour-tesy" (214). Anderson said she considered that "better than nothing" (214). Paul Vanderham explains in *James Joyce and Censorship*, that in an effort to increase subscriptions, Anderson "sent an unsolicited copy of the July-August number to the daughter of a prominent New York lawyer. . . . the lawyer's daughter was so offended [that] she complained to her father, who drew the case to the attention of the District Attorney of New York County, Joseph Forrester" (2), who in turn brought the little magazine to the attention of John S. Sumner. On October 4, 1920, Anderson and her partner Jane Heap were arrested for printing and distributing the July-August 1920 issue of the *Little Review* which contained the Nausicaa episode of *Ulysses* in which Leopold Bloom masturbates on the beach while Gerty Mac-Dowell performs a laid-back sexual tease. Four months later, the trial began on February 14, 1921.

Immediately, the two women met with the irascible John Quinn,[4] a New York City lawyer who is as often described by his Irish temper as he is victim to it. When the women told him that copies of the *Little Review* had been "apprehended," for example, "Quinn told them that he 'didn't give a damn' for *The Little Review* and that 'it would serve them damnably right if it was permanently excluded from the mails'" (Vanderham, 42). Anderson writes that Quinn "fought everybody, from his office boys—who trembled visibly and were in consequence the most inefficient office boys in the world—to his friend and protégé, James Joyce, who sat calmly in Paris and ignored Quinn's cutting suggestions about how *Ulysses* ought to be written" (206). Regarding his temper, Anderson wryly points out,

"One didn't argue with John Quinn. One enjoyed his performances too much. He was better than a prima donna. No woman would throw such obvious scenes, or look around so hopefully for the applause of her audience" (215). Quinn grew to despise Anderson and Heap during the *Little Review* trial. Adam Parkes notes that "Quinn's disgust for his deviant clients colored his perception of the entire proceedings. He tried to keep Anderson and Heap out of the picture as much as possible. When he stood up to speak and found them at his side, he sent them unceremoniously back to their seats" (73). Taking the back seat was never Margaret Anderson's pleasure. In her autobiography, evocatively titled *My Thirty Years' War*, Anderson describes herself as a fighter: "This book so far may have given the impression that I have had no difficulty in making myself, that I sprang like a warrior out of the earth. If so, I have been unjust to my effort. . . .The causes I have fought for have invariably been causes that should have been gained by a delicate suggestion. Since they never were, I made myself into a fighter" (123). I knew after reading descriptions of Anderson, Heap, and Quinn that I absolutely had to see the bureau files on those three characters, on those three fighters.

I waited four long years to receive Joyce's 20-page, heavily redacted file in the mail, and spent several more years filing appeals to have parts of the file uncensored. After I received Joyce's, I sent away for the files of several others to round out my research—the files of those we could call the usual suspects—Joyce's literary friends, his modernist associates, his benefactors, editors, and cohorts. These included Margaret Anderson, Jane Heap, John Quinn, Bennett Cerf, and Morris Ernst, to name a few. What surprised me at first was that many of my strongest hunches failed to pay off.

For example, several years after I requested the files of Margaret Anderson, I received a letter noting that the FBI found "no records responsive to [my] FOIA request to indicate the subject of [my] request has ever been of investigatory interest to the FBI" (Jan. 9, 1998). I could hardly believe it. No file on Margaret Anderson?

Then I got an identical letter saying they found no records to indicate that Jane Heap had ever been of investigatory interest, either. An identical letter followed about John Quinn, too, but it also contained a badly copied flyer with the title "FBI FILE FACT SHEET," which went on to list what it is the FBI *doesn't* do: "The FBI does not issue clearances or nonclearances for anyone other than its own personnel or persons having access to FBI facilities," for example. Or "The FBI was not established until 1908 and we have very few records prior to the 1920s." Such information about what the bureau does *not* do, I thought at the time, will never prove useful. So far I've been right.

No files on Anderson, Heap *or* Quinn, though? Well, I was right not to believe it, because 16 months later I got another letter from the FBI saying that all of the bureau's records pertaining to Margaret Anderson have been destroyed.

> Please be advised that records which appear to be responsive to your Freedom of Information-Privacy Act request have been destroyed. The records destruction practices of the Federal Bureau of Investigation are regulated by and conducted in full compliance with the provisions of Title 44, United States Code, Section 3301 and Title 36, Code of Federal Regulations, Chapter 12, Subchapter B, Part 1228.

Though the letter went on to say that the "FBI Records Retention Plan and Disposition Schedules have been approved by the United States District Court for the District of Columbia and are monitored by knowledgeable representatives of the National Archives and Records Administration," there was no indication, anywhere, as to *why* they destroyed Margaret Anderson's files. Instead, the letter bombarded me with bureau-speak about the file destruction practices of the FBI. The May 26, 1999 letter ended by saying "We are required to inform you that you are entitled to file an administrative appeal if you so desire." This confused me because what exactly would I appeal? That they send me the ashes? In her autobiography, Margaret Anderson provides an anecdote that punctuates this episode with a perverse irony. Anderson explained that five simple words had changed her outlook on life, had changed her fundamentally: "Act, don't be acted upon," she wrote (269). It is chilling that after her death an institution like the FBI can continue to act upon her.

My attempts to get any FBI information on Bennett Cerf have been equally frustrating. Cerf was head publisher for Random House, and founded the publishing house in 1927 with Donald Klopfer to market the Modern Library series of classic texts and other works. "We called it Random House," Cerf wrote, "because we said we were going to publish anything under the sun that came along—if we liked it well enough" (Cerf and Klopfer, v). Already a celebrity figure by the 1930s, and later a common feature on the television game show *What's My Line?* (with which Louis Untermeyer would also be associated in the early 1950s), Cerf was an essential witness for the defense in the 1933-1934 Random House *Ulysses* obscenity trial. Several years after I requested the Bennett Cerf file, I got a letter from J. Kevin O'Brien, Chief of FOIPA Section in the Information Resources Division, informing me that the file I requested on Cerf was processed and ready for mailing. It comprised 183 pages, the letter said, but pursuant to Title 28, Code of Federal Regulations, Sections 16.10 and 16.47, I would be asked to pay copying costs at the rate of ten cents per page after the first 100 pages. The letter continued, "upon receipt of your check or money order, payable to the Federal Bureau of Investigation, these documents will be forwarded to you" (July 14, 1997). Immediately I sent off a check for $8.30 but got a letter back from one James Meyen saying that my request for Cerf's file had been denied and that I might be able to appeal his decision by writing to Judge Advocate General Code 34, Department of the Navy. I was floored. So I drafted an appeal letter, but within days I learned that my appeal to JAG #34 was denied.

I have not heard again from the FBI about those 183 pages of Bennett Cerf materials that were processed for me and made available for release. But I expect to get a letter any day now informing me that the Cerf file has been destroyed. Some weeks after my appeal to JAG #34 had been denied, I received an unaccounted-for 12-page document from the Criminal Investigation Service of the U.S. Department of the Navy about Cerf's "loyalty." The report had been prepared under Hoover's orders, who had the report made when he learned that Random House was preparing to publish Quentin Reynold's children's book *The F.B.I.* Hoover wound up writing the foreword to Reynold's book and asked Cerf to discount the book to all FBI employees. "Cerf complied," Robins reports, "and according to [Quentin Reynolds's] file, the FBI kept track of every single copy bought. Reynolds later wrote Louis Nichols that it was [his] . . . 'most popular book'" (137). A few years later, Cerf would get the chance to work with Hoover and the bureau again in bringing out a book on the FBI, Don Whitehead's 1956 *The FBI Story.*

In Cerf's book *At Random,* a memoir of his days as Random House's publishing giant, he describes the grief he went through to publish modern writers like James Joyce. Ironically, his reputation as a publisher who traded on dubious titles led him to weigh the possibilities of publishing Donald Whitehead's book on the FBI. Cerf explained that his college friend George Sokolsky had developed the nasty habit of calling Cerf a "pinko" in public. This bizarre name-calling led to Random House's agreement to publish *The FBI Story* with Hoover's introduction.

Though Cerf certainly recognized a good seller when he saw one, the way he explains this event by framing it with Sokolsky's "pinko" name-calling seems to indicate that he took on the Whitehead/J. Edgar Hoover book as a public cleansing ritual or to prove his loyalty to the bureau. In *At Random,* Cerf notes that he would run into Sokolsky at places like the Dutch Treat Club in New York, where, he explains, "publishers and suchlike meet":

> When I walked in, he sometimes greeted me with "Here comes Bennett, the pinko publisher." I didn't like it and didn't think it was justified. So one day I called him on it. I said, "Have you ever looked at our list, George? If you had, you'd realize that we print a lot of books that some people might call fascist." George immediately said, "Oh, I'm only kidding." I said, "Nevertheless, I'm going to send you our catalogue" and I did.
>
> Sokolsky called me up and said "I apologize. That's a very impressive list. I had forgotten you did *Witness* [by Whittaker Chambers]. What did your 'pinko' friends have to say about that?" I said "Plenty," and laughed.
>
> . . . Later that fall George called me and said 'Do you remember our conversation? Suppose I were to bring you a book, a story about the F.B.I., giving its good side, authorized and with an introduction by J. Edgar Hoover. Would you publish it?" (245)

Cerf details their subsequent lunch at the Stork Club with Lou Nichols—"the number three man in the FBI—right behind Hoover and Clyde Tolson" (246). The men agree to get Don Whitehead, head of the Associated Press in Washington, to write the book, giving him what Nichols said would be unprecedented clearance and access to files, etc. Cerf continues, saying that

> I became a close friend of Lou Nichols, and I went down to spend a night with him and his family at their home in Alexandria. . . . I was telling him that even though the book wasn't out yet, there was an enormous advance sale, great interest, and that it would be a great success. I said "You know something, Lou——what particularly pleases me is that your giving me this book means that I must be in pretty

good standing with the FBI. My record must be clear." Lou Nichols
said "Just, my boy, just." I never knew whether he was kidding me or
not. (246-47).

It is clear that he probably wasn't kidding. Cerf was investigated and
likely under some degree of surveillance prior to and during the time he
was ushering both FBI books into print, especially Reynolds's, which
was out of the hands of Hoover's obsessive control, unlike Whitehead's,
which he approved section by section. Without Cerf's knowledge,
agents in the U.S. Naval Department of Intelligence, Criminal Division, interviewed several of his friends and associates about his loyalty.
They reviewed his life, its patterns, and political contours. Though the
documents show that his loyalty was suspect at the beginning of the
investigation, Cerf was ultimately given the thumbs up, and was
"cleared" to cultivate the Whitehead/Hoover book project.

The FBI Story was published on November 28, 1956. More than
50,000 copies were sold in the first two weeks. The public was mad
for copies of the book. In *At Random* Cerf notes that sales of the book
were so swift that booksellers actually took copies out of store
window displays to sell, and replaced the display books with impos-
tors dressed with dummy book jackets. Copies of the book sold after
Christmas and well into the next year, Cerf noted. It was one of those
books that wouldn't stay put on the shelves. The book's immense
popularity gave rise to an amusing telephone conversation between
Cerf and "Number three man" Lou Nichols. Cerf explains:

> One morning in January the phone rang just as I arrived at my office
> and it was Lou Nichols calling from Washington. "Bennett," he said,
> "what's wrong with the book?" I said "What do you mean, what's
> wrong? It's selling as fast as we can print it." Then he said "As of this
> morning, I must tell you there are no copies of *The FBI Story* in
> Brentano's or Scribner's and none in the Doubleday Shops, or for that
> matter in any shop or department store in mid-Manhattan. None in

Penn Station; none in the Wall Street area. So I ask you: what's wrong?" I tried to explain that this wasn't bad, that the book was selling faster than the stores could reorder or we could deliver them, and I guess I convinced him.

I was so amused by this switch on the usual report about the author's aunt who couldn't find a single copy of his book in any shop in Schenectady, I couldn't wait to tell somebody. So I went to the office next to mine where Jim Michener, just back from the Austrian-Hungarian border, was putting the final touches on *The Bridge at Andau,* which we were rushing for March publication though he had finished it after our spring catalogue was already printed. When I told Jim about my phone conversation, he said "Well, with all those agents checking bookshops, this would have been a great day for somebody to rob a bank in New York." (*At Random,* 247-48)

With the book out, J. Edgar Hoover began to keep fastidious track of who did, and who did not, purchase copies. Agents and staff members of the bureau bought up copies out of pride and loyalty, but to some degree we have to assume they were motivated by fear as well. The public, hungry for the "story" of the FBI, would not let the books sit on bookstore shelves. *The FBI Story* was a popular seller, and the zeal with which it was gobbled up indicates the popularity of the bureau at the time, as well as the degree to which the public was eager to get an inside view of the enigmatic bureau, its director, and its agents. Athan Theoharis notes that

> FBI officials not only reviewed proposed publicity plans but actively promoted *The FBI Story,* including purchasing thousands of copies through FBI recreation association funds and ensuring favorable book reviews (notably by Harry Overstreet). *The FBI Story* became a best seller and was made into a popular movie, allowing Whitehead to retire as a journalist and embark on a more leisurely and lucrative freelance career. (*Secret Files,* 309)

Whitehead's book, of course, says nothing about Hoover's interest in writers, editors, and publishers, or the bureau's efforts to manage their production by bullying them with "pretext" phone calls, phone wiretaps, censorship watches, and background and loyalty checks.

Thomas Mann was another modern writer watched closely by the bureau. An internal memorandum sent to Lou Nichols in 1947 indicates that hundreds of pages were collected on the German émigré. "In the case of Thomas Mann it should be noted that there are approximately 800 references in our files to this individual" (Mann FBI file). Only 85 pages were released to me under FOIA. Sometimes bureau agents going over file material are unable to control their own cynicism. One of the pages in Mann's file copies a clipping from the New York University *Times* of June 27, 1945, describing Thomas Mann's American citizenship. In his own words, Mann said that he had "come to choose America as his permanent home." Someone in the bureau irreverently wrote across the page "This is amusing!" and signed the comment with his initials, "wsh."

Mann's literary career was stellar, and included a stint writing for Hollywood. His notoriety as a writer even earned him an appointment to the Advisory Committee of Harry Scherman's Book-of-the-Month Club, for which Mann received $1,000 per month (Lee, 111). Another item in Mann's file, clipped and copied from the *New York Times,* reports on a dinner that took place to mark the seventieth birthday of the Nobel laureate. Supreme Court Justice Felix Frankfurter, certainly no friend to Hoover, spoke at the dinner on the topic of the inseparability of art and politics. "For artists to be unpolitical," he bellowed, "is to surrender to those who reject the rights of free inquiry and of the free play of the mind, the determination of the direction of society" (Mann FBI file, 96; *New York Times,* June 26, 1945: 12). Frankfurter echoed Roosevelt's reminder that "we are all immigrants," and urged that "Americanism" should be measured by one's devotion to the Declaration of Independence and by one's pious dedication to the four freedoms. To gauge "Americanism" using any other measure—blood, for example—he said, "is to come danger-ously near the abyss into which Nazism finally fell." It is the inherent moral worth of the individual and not the accident of his birth, Frankfurter added, that is the most precious force in the American fellowship. To bureau underlings clipping and making file copies of Frankfurter's speech, the rhetoric so moving to readers today must have sounded like fingernails scraping across a blackboard. This would be especially true of the reaction by the bureau's "this-is-amusing" nationalist (Mann FBI file).

Ernest Hemingway remains a remarkable writer and a quintes-sential literary modernist. For nearly ten years, Hemingway had been sure the FBI was shadowing him, and he was not wrong. J. Edgar Hoover despised him. Hemingway knew it and suffered the atten-tion. In an August 25, 1942 letter to friend Evan Shipman, for example, Hemingway indicates that he knows he has a bureau file, and admits in the letter that he is avoiding making it too personal "because we are at war and anybody who thinks indiscreetly or criticizes in time of war adds to whatever dossiers or photostatted letters he has assimilated" (quoted in Reynolds, 67). At one time, in fact, Hemingway's main file weighed in at more than 400 pages, according to a 1974 letter describing the file to research librarian Ray Jones at the University of Florida. The University was interested in acquiring the bureau files of several writers. Twenty years later, though, following my FOIA request, Hemingway's file numbers approximately half that many pages.

Hemingway's file shows that he was under surveillance, espe-cially in the 1940s when the writer was involved in investigative work for Ambassador Braden in Cuba. J. Edgar Hoover thought him unreliable, and in a memorandum for assistant directors E. A. Tamm and D. M. Ladd on Dec 19, 1942, wrote, "I, of course realize the complete undesirability of this sort of a connection or relationship. Certainly Hemingway is the last man, in my estimation, to be used in any such capacity. His judgment is not of the best, and if his sobriety is the same as it was some years ago, that is certainly questionable" (Hemingway FBI file). Furthermore, when Hoover learned in 1943 that Hemingway was writing a book based on his experiences in intelligence activities in Cuba—Hemingway had been "acting as personal informant of Ambassador Spruille Braden in Havana"(Hemingway FBI file)—Hoover wrote of his concerns to R. G. Leddy, FBI attaché stationed at the American Embassy in Havana. "Hemingway states that all of the people whom he has known during the last year in Cuba in connection with intelligence work will appear in his book, including Ambassador Braden. We are not yet informed as to what role the representatives of the FBI will play, but in view of Hemingway's known sentiments, will probably be portrayed as the dull, heavy-footed, unimaginative professional policemen type" (August 13, 1943). To a man who would spend most of his tenure as director stylizing the image of the G-man, Hemingway's likely portraiture was irksome.

It obviously irked assistant director Edward Tamm, too, who appended the following angry note to agent C. H. Carson's ten-page memorandum report: "I do not concur with the conclusion reached in this memorandum. . . . I don't care what his [Hemingway's] contacts are or what his background is—I see no reason why we should make any effort to avoid exposing him for the phoney [sic] that he is" (Hemingway FBI file).

Hemingway never wrote the piece, though. It might be because he was plagued with tremendous writer's block, suffering through it for years. As Reynolds explains, "If the problem had been what to write next, he might have been able to face it as he had so many times before. But the problem was how to finish work waiting for an ending, always the most difficult task for him" (353). It seems as though Hemingway's own life was an unfinished work awaiting its inspired ending. He died before he would finish the autobiographical *Islands in the Stream,* for example, thereby leaving the story of his life quite literally unfinished.[5] The horrific ending would come in 1961 for the icon of what Gertrude Stein called the "lost generation"—hastened, many have argued, by bureau surveillance and persecution.

After Hemingway's wife Mary and his friend Dr. George Saviers forestalled several rounds of suicide attempts in the Hemingway farm in Ketchum, Idaho in 1960, Hemingway was sent yet again to the Mayo Clinic in Rochester, Minnesota and was receiving electroshock treatments at the rate of one every other day (Reynolds, 355-56). He signed an especially incoherent letter to Mary as "Big Kitten." Though he had been released earlier, in 1961 the suicidally depressed Hemingway checked himself into the Mayo Clinic again, this time under the assumed name of George Saviers. His wife arrived in Rochester a few days later and checked into the Kahler Hotel under the name Mrs. George Saviers. Hemingway's doctor immediately called the FBI to tell them Hemingway was there and said that he was rambling on about the FBI being after him, about the FBI following him and harassing him. The doctor asked whether he could, in fact, confirm for Hemingway that the FBI was *not* after him. The bureau gave the doctor permission to tell Hemingway not to worry. A January 13, 1961 bureau memorandum notes:

> **ERNEST HEMINGWAY,** the author, has been a patient at Mayo Clinic, Rochester, Minnesota, and is presently at St. Mary's Hospital in that city. He has been at the Clinic for several weeks and is described as a problem. He is seriously ill, both physically and mentally, and at one time the doctors were considering giving him electro-shock therapy treatments.
>
> **[CENSORED]** Mayo Clinic, advised to eliminate publicity and contacts by newsmen, the Clinic had suggested that Mr. HEMINGWAY register under the alias GEORGE SEVIER [*sic*]. **[CENSORED]** stated that Mr. HEMINGWAY is worried about his registering under an assumed name, and is concerned about an FBI investigation. **[CENSORED]** stated that inasmuch as this worry was interfering with the treatments of Mr. HEMINGWAY, he

desired authorization to tell HEMINGWAY that the FBI was not concerned with his registering under an assumed name. ▮CEN-SORED▮ was advised that there was no objection.

Hemingway's FBI file reveals that the bureau sent men immediately to Rochester, Minnesota after the doctor's call. After he was released from the Mayo Clinic, Hemingway returned to his Idaho farm on June 30. At dinner the following evening, Hemingway asked a waitress at the Christiania Restaurant to identify two men seated at another table. She told him they were salesmen. Convinced that salesmen would not be out on a Saturday night, he said "They're FBI," a recurring suspicion that his wife Mary documents in her 1976 biography, *How It Was*.[6] The next morning would be Hemingway's last. Just before 7:30 A.M. on Sunday July 2nd, he loaded two 12-gauge shells into his shotgun and shot directly into his mouth, committing suicide in the foyer on the first floor of his Ketchum home.

There is no mention whatsoever of the last days of Hemingway's life in his file—at least not in the version I received. Not even a bureau memorandum notes the sad occasion of his suicide or comments on his death. Instead, what closes the Hemingway file is a copy of Westbrook Pegler's column "As Pegler Sees It," subtitled "He Was Never A Hemingway Fan," clipped from the *New York Journal-American*. Pegler's column begins with the sentence "It has been my stubborn opinion that Ernest Hemingway was actually one of the worst writers in the English language during his time" (Jul. 17, 1961: 13). No other clipping regarding the writer's death or the magnitude of his literary stature exists in the file. Apparently, Pegler's literary assessment of Hemingway sat just fine with the bureau, and that was how it wanted to construct the American writer. The file closes with Pegler's assessment of Hemingway's filth: "He annoyed me also with profanity and vulgarity and when I pointed out that Ring Lardner had never told a dirty story and had shunned mucky stuff on paper, Hemingway's rejoinder did not dispose of Lardner. Hemingway argued that nevertheless people did speak as his characters spoke" (Hemingway FBI file). Here lies, it seems to me, the very crux of the matter. Hemingway's "dirty stories," his "profanity and vulgarity" corresponded to Hoover's anxieties about modern literature's power to corrupt. Not only did Hemingway's subversive activities mark him as an insurgent and dangerous American—such as his activities on behalf of loyalist Spain, his contributions to the literary quarterly put out by the Abraham Lincoln Brigade (ALB) titled *Among Friends,* his speeches at meetings to memorialize the men who died fighting in the ALB, his sponsorship of the Anti-Fascist Refugee Committee, his efforts to secure medical aid for hospitals in Spain (in conjunction with the North American Committee to Aid Spanish Democracy), his work with the Writers and Artists Ambulance Corps, and his "possible connections with Communist Party," listed in a section of a bureau report. These activities alone would be enough to damn the writer, not to mention his involvement with the American Committee for the Protection of the Foreign Born, the American Writers Congress, and the League of American Writers (also treated in Hemingway's file). But in addition to these, the file constructs a narrative account of a crazy man, a "phoney," paranoid, drunken, profane, and vulgar writer.

Hoover feared that the modernist writers were participating in a movement to destabilize American democracy; that modernism was seditious; that it could spoil everything that was good and clean about the nation and hasten the nation's devolution; and that it was filthy, vulgar, and radical. John Dos Passos provided the FBI director with a manifesto that played into those fears in 1927. His article in the *New Masses* "Towards a Revolutionary Theatre" outlines his radical vision, a vision that is importantly similar to the vision of Hallie Flanagan, director of the Works Progress Administration's Federal Theatre Project, discussed below. Dos Passos argued:

By revolution I mean that such a theatre must break with the present day theatrical tradition, not with the general traditions of the theatre, and that it must draw its life and ideas from the conscious sections of the industrial and white collar working classes which are out to get control of the great flabby mass of capitalist society and mould it to their own purpose. In an ideal state, it might be possible for a group to be alive and have no subversive political tendency. At present it is not possible.

. . . A play or a book or a picture has got to have bulk, toughness and violence to survive in the dense clanging traffic of twentieth century life. (Dec. 1927: 20)

A few years later, Dos Passos's notes on the revolutionary theater would come to life, transformed into the purposes of the Federal Theater Project of the 1930s. Espousing the same views as Dos Passos would jeopardize the career of Hallie Flanagan, and would land her before Senate commissions where she was asked to prove her loyalty.

In John Steinbeck's "A Primer on the 1930s," he describes the period by reflecting on the excitement generated by Flanagan's work with drama:

Meanwhile, wonderful things were going on in the country: young men were reforesting the stripped hills, painters were frescoing the walls of public buildings. Guides to the States were being compiled by writers' projects, still the best source books on America up to the time they were printed.

A fabulous character named Hallie Flanagan was creating a National Theatre. And playwrights and actors were working like mad for relief wages. Some of out best people grew to stature during that time. We might still have a National Theatre if some high-minded Senators had not killed the whole thing on the ground that *Getting Gertie's Garter* was an immoral play. (24)

Steinbeck's comments echo Mike Gold's, who poignantly eulogized 11 college students who in February of 1927 committed suicide. Gold asks, who can direct this generation?

> Eleven boys and girls have committed suicide in the colleges during the past month. They were intellectuals; they were boys and girls who ten years ago would have been fervent members of the intercollegiate socials and society, with Jack London, John Reed, and Walter Lippmann.
>
> But in today's America, there is nothing to satisfy such youth. . . . What is left for the young spirit? It must gnaw at itself and die. (*New Masses,* Mar. 1927: 5)

Both Steinbeck's and Gold's comments are important because they identify watershed moments, it seems, in American literary history when the modernism project was poised to succeed. Steinbeck points to the promising capacity of a national theatre to galvanize revolutionary action while Gold alludes to the possibilities offered by a youthful intellectual movement.

The Works Progress Administration (WPA) Federal Theatre Project was one of those close calls, and Hoover went after it in the late 1930s. He wrote several memos to Dwight Bruntley of the New York FBI who was handling the "Conspiracy to Defraud the U.S." case against Flanagan and others. Hoover suggested people Bruntley might interview to acquire damaging testimony (Flanagan FBI file). Flanagan was considered subversive, her file notes, because she boycotted restaurants that refused to serve blacks. An agent records in Flanagan's file that an informant

> first began to suspect the Federal Theatre and Adult Education Projects were communistic . . . when he noticed that MRS. HALLIE FLANAGAN and other project officials began boycotting New York City restaurants who refused to permit negroes to eat with

white people in their restaurants. Also, that they would hold
meetings behind closed doors and then began employing inexperi-
enced young women to attend their music, drama, and dancing
schools and teach them how to dance, etc., and not employing
experienced performers as intended by the project's policies; that all
sorts of communistic literature was being distributed and efforts
were being made to dominate all organizations of the WPA to form
unions to get together to spread communistic literature throughout
the U.S.; to get employees to join the Workers Alliance; distribution
of Workers Alliance literature most every day before the employees
began work, posting of such literature on bulletin boards, etc., and
all with the approval of MRS FLANAGAN and **[CENSORED]**.
(Flanagan FBI file)

The file also notes that a production of *Revolt of the Beavers* had been
"approved by MRS. FLANAGAN and her aides and shown before
children, indicating how children could smuggle guns in their lunch
boxes and to defend, if necessary, their social ideas, etc. **[CEN-
SORED]** said the project had Jewish, negro, Labor, Irish, and other
national units, even a German unit which, however, did not last very
long" (Flanagan FBI file). Through persistent efforts to link her
important theatrical work to communist dogma, especially after she
started *The Living Newspaper*—"dramatizations of the news with
living actors, light, music, movement," Flanagan explained (141)—
she was hounded right out of office, even though she was so
instrumental in developing a national theatrical consciousness.

Research for the Living Newspaper project was going well,
Flanagan explains in "Federal Theatre." The script was ready, rehears-
als were set, and the actors and dancers were prepared. "Then
something happened which was to have a profound bearing not only
on *The Living Newspaper* but on the entire history of the Federal
Theatre. The State Department heard of the play, became concerned,
and there was . . . an order that no dramatic representation could be

made upon any Federal Theatre stage of any living foreign ruler" (142). Flanagan explains that the order caused playwright Elmer Rice to quit the project altogether because "he believed that this action prophesied that we could never do any socially valuable play." Rice resigned under dramatic circumstances, in front of an audience of journalists he'd invited to see a private showing of the banned play (Flanagan, 142). Flanagan and her actors would be charged with biting the hand that fed them. But surely the situation was more complicated, and was something more like the conundrum Irish writer Samuel Beckett would semijokingly pose in his 1938 novel *Murphy:* "Shall I bite the hand that starves me," asked Murphy, only "to have it throttle me?" (19).

Beckett's novel *Murphy* constantly pokes fun at (among other things) state censorship, and several passages deliberately goad and bait the censors. One such passage concludes "The above passage is carefully calculated to deprave the cultivated reader"; another ends "this phrase is chosen with care, lest the filthy censors should lack an occasion to commit their filthy synecdoche" (118; 76). Depravity in all its forms—ideological as well as sexual—was being carefully monitored, Beckett knew. Even the opening line of his novel calls our attention to the duress: "The sun shone, having no alternative, on the nothing new" (1).

But just as there was the mundane (and for Beckett there would always be the mundane), there was plenty that was new. One such innovation was the Provincetown Playhouse. Sandra Adickes explains that the playhouse began as an adventure by Mary Heaton Vorse, Susan Glaspell, and their husbands and friends during the summer of 1915:

> One evening, as Vorse and her husband Joe O'Brien, her friend Neith
> Boyce, the novelist, and her husband Hutchins Hapgood, and Susan
> Glaspell and her husband George Cram—"Jig"—Cook, together
> with the writer Wilbur Daniel Steele and his wife, were sitting around

> a driftwood fire on the beach, Cook attacked the widespread commer-
> cialism of the American theater; the trivial quality of such Broadway
> hits as *Peg o' My Heart* would never attract the sophisticated [Green-
> wich] Villagers, nor could the Villagers, Cook believed, create works
> that would be acceptable to a Broadway audience. Even a new little
> theater in the Village had rejected *Suppressed Desires,* a play Cook and
> Glaspell had written that satirized Freudianism. Boyce had written a
> play called *Constancy* that spoofed the love affair of John Reed and
> Mabel Dodge. (165)

After venting their displeasure, Adickes notes, the group agreed to
start their own troupe and put on their two unnoticed plays
themselves. The project was an instant success. Acting the plays first
from the Hapgood home and then "in the vacant fish house on the
wharf Vorse owned" (165), the group soon expanded to include such
luminaries as Louise Bryant and John Reed, Eugene O'Neill, and
Terry Carlin. By 1916 the group had given themselves over to the
production of three short plays by O'Neill, Steele, and Bryant.
Glaspell found the summer of 1916 absolutely magical. Eventually,
Jig Cook brought the plays to New York City to play at a small stable
on MacDougal Street, Adickes reports, and shortly thereafter, with
the success of O'Neill's *The Emperor Jones,* Broadway beckoned, and
the young ambitious playwrights, actors and actresses abandoned
Provincetown for the city's bright lights.

Mary Heaton Vorse's engagement with the Provincetown Playhouse would earn her an FBI file numbering almost 200 pages.
Approximately 150 were released to me. Vorse's file has been so
heavily redacted that it is frustrating to try to go through it. I have
already quoted in chapter 1 a typically frustrating passage; here is
another heavily edited passage that thwarts any attempts to narrate
the cultural and literary climate for modern writers under Hoover's
institutional gaze:

According to [CENSORED], subject associated with individuals in the literary field, and that one of her close friends was [CENSORED], who was formerly employed by the government and was a writer. [CENSORED] stated that subject was also an associate of [CENSORED] who, in addition to being a writer, was associated with the Red Cross.

It should be noted that the indices of the Washington Field Division reflect that [CENSORED], [CENSORED], and [CENSORED] are radically inclined and believed to be Communist sympathizers. (Vorse FBI file)

Though I filed an appeal to have the names in the above passages and in other passages restored, my request was denied. I have requested the files of several people associated with the Provincetown Players— for example, Vorse, Cook, O'Neill, and Glaspell—but was told that files did not exist for the other individuals. Vorse's file incredibly includes transcripts of telephone conversations, incoming and outgoing, and handwriting and signature samples. There is also an office memorandum stating that the records of the New York City Board of Health for the boroughs of Manhattan and Brooklyn were checked under the subject's maiden and marital names. Vorse was active in the labor movement, and best-known for her novel *Strike!,* duly noted in her file along with the titles of her 15 other novels. Her association with the Provincetown Playhouse would mark her as a rebel.

The bureau would continue to monitor theater, hoping to use it to disseminate anticommunist propaganda. Ironically, they hoped Arthur Miller would participate. Miller explained in his retrospective essay, "*The Crucible* in History," that when Elia Kazan was about to direct his new work on "corruption in the gangster-ridden Brooklyn longshoremen's union," he and Kazan sent a copy of the film script to Harry Cohn, the head of Columbia Pictures. "Cohn read the script and called us to Hollywood, where he simply and casually informed us that, incredibly enough, he had first had the script vetted by the FBI and that they had seen nothing subversive in it" (*Echoes Down the Corridor,* 282-83). Miller was furious. Cohn told Miller he would produce the film if Miller would agree to make a simple change: instead of mobsters, he should make the villains communists. Miller refused and withdrew his script, which prompted Cohn to send "an indignant telegram" to Miller's Brooklyn Heights residence. It said "As soon as we try to make the script pro-American you pull out." Miller, who wrote, "I don't think I can adequately communicate the sheer density of the atmosphere of the time, for the outrageous had so suddenly become the accepted norm" (282), refused to perform Cohn's "patriotic idiocy" (283).

Charges about who was pro-American and who wasn't were common at the time. Langston Hughes was another modern literary figure Hoover had his eye on. Hughes had become an especially popular speaker and reader during the 1930s. Americans who didn't want to step on bureau toes or participate in the hiring of inappropriate speakers often wrote to Hoover to ask whether X was an appropriate enough "citizen" to address their organization, and while I go into more detail in chapter 3 about the clever ways Hoover was able to manipulate such queries, I want to dangle a tantalizing sample here as I contextualize the relationship between Hoover and Hughes.

Not limited to 1919 by any means, the "Red Scare" in America led regular law-abiding citizens to turn to the Bureau of Investigation for direction or counsel when they had questions about the appropriateness of a coworker's comment, a neighbor's activity, a teacher's instruction, a son's or daughter's reading material, or a writer's work. Thus, many of the writers' files I have looked at contain signed and unsigned letters from "regular Americans" to J. Edgar Hoover seeking his advice or counsel on delicate "loyalty" matters. More important to our purposes are the incendiary letters sent in to complain about a writer's books, articles, or interviews. In fact, there are more kinds of this sort of letter in Richard Wright's file than I ever would have imagined. One Los Angeles letter writer who claims to be black and thus, speaks on behalf of his black brethren in America, wrote several letters to Hoover denouncing Wright. An excerpt from one reads as follows: "We wish you would put him in the Purmy [?] [Pumy?] on the first line in the Pacafic [*sic*] theater of war and if a Jap kill him so we give the Jap a medil [*sic*]. And if you don't do that for god sake ban that Addle pated Sap's books for they are driveing [*sic*] us nuts. And besides he put to [*sic*] much filth in his books" (Wright FBI file). Hoover's responses acknowledge receipt, assure the writer that "the content of [his] communication has been carefully noted," and urge him to send additional material to the L.A. Field Division, should more information come his way.

So indoctrinated was the American public into Hoover's alarmist fears that American democracy was being destabilized by writers participating in communist or leftist literary activities, spreading their filth and anti-Americanism through the literary marketplace, that the public would turn, en masse, to J. Edgar Hoover for leadership, protection, and counsel.

As I discuss more fully in the next chapter, Hoover had a tactic (clever, I must admit) that when people wrote in to the bureau asking for information about whether so-and-so was an "appropriate" speaker to address their organization, Hoover would respond to their letters and would enclose what he said was some "reading material" he thought they might enjoy. He seems to have sent out most often his pamphlet "Secularism—Breeder of Crime," though "How to Fight Communism" seemed a particular favorite, too.

"Secularism—Breeder of Crime" was a pamphlet that attacked Langston Hughes's controversial poem "Goodbye Christ," and held it up as an example of the degeneracy of modern literature. In his poem, Hughes bids farewell to the iconic Jesus of Christianity (which, he argues, has done little for the oppressed workers) and embraces communism. When the Commission on Ministerial Training for the Methodist Church wrote in 1948 to say it would publish Hoover's speech but without a section of Hughes's poem "Goodbye Christ" published with it, an irate Hoover dashed off a typed memo to Tolson and Nichols that ordered, "Make certain we furnish this outfit no more material for publiciation [*sic*]. They are too squeamish about offending the commies." Hoover's reprinted speech was to be a chapter in the commission's publication *Christian Faith and Secularism.*

Acting on the understandable advice of the Abingdon-Cokesbury Press who was interested in complying with copyright laws, the Commission hoped to secure permission from Langston Hughes to have his poem quoted. Hughes adamantly refused. A letter in Hughes's file written to someone in Nashville, Tennessee whom Hughes addresses as "My dear" contains his reply. In May 1948 Hughes was completing a cross-country lecture tour. He apologizes for his hastiness ("Rushing for a train, I regret this hasty answer") and writes:

> My answer to your request is that I do *not* grant permission for the use
> of the poem, *Goodbye Christ* in the book being published by the
> Abingdon Cokesbury Press. . . . [a] poem often mutilated or cut, or
> combined with portions of other poems out of context. ["Goodbye
> Christ"] was widely misunderstood when it first appeared—irony and
> satire being difficult to use in poetry, it seems. . . . The persons who
> have put it into circulation again are hardly up to any good purpose,
> being the most anti-Negro, anti-labor, and anti-Jewish groups in our
> America. (Hughes FBI file)

The bureau's number three man, Lou Nichols, was so infuriated by the commission's refusal to include Hughes's poem in the director's reprinted speech without permission from the writer, that he penned a livid response to the commission in July 1948, criticizing them for *daring* to communicate with the likes of Langston Hughes:

> Were it not too late I would urge the Director most vigorously to
> withdraw the lecture. What is particularly heart-rending to me as a

Methodist is to observe one of the great bodies of the church performing in such an amateurish manner. I think that the quicker everybody in the Methodist Church awakens to the true mission of the church and stops palliating people like Langston Hughes our church will become more militant and more effective. (Hughes FBI file)

What Nichols meant by "the true mission of the church" is certainly unclear, and his reference to "people *like* Langston Hughes" could be an allusion to any number of things—blacks, gays, or Communists.

Hughes's bureau file dates back to 1925; but in the early 1940s, Hoover targeted the Harlem Renaissance figure and put him on Custodial Detention lists. (These were lists of persons the bureau director wanted immediately detained in the event of a national emergency.) What's worse, he instructed new agents about what to put into Hughes's files and how to write up their reports to best criminalize him. A memo from Hoover to a SAC at the New York Field Office (June 22, 1943 re: Langston Hughes, Internal Security-C, Custodial Detention) instructs: "You are requested to prepare a report in the near future summarizing the information presently in your possession concerning [Hughes] and including therein complete information as to his birth, citizenship, and Selective Service.—JEH." The report that followed read:

At Local Board No: 58, 138th Street and Broadway, it was discovered that subject's order number [was] 11931. He originally registered at Local Board Number 25, Chicago, Illinois, being there on business at the time. . . . On his registration form subject has written "I use this opportunity to regret as a citizen of the United States the dissolving of the brigade of armed forces of the United States into white and negro units thereby making colored citizens the only group so singled out for Jim Crow treatment which seems to me contrary to the letter andspirit [*sic*] of the constitution and dangerous to the moral and well being of not only the colored citizens of this country but those of our

darker allies as well." On December 21, 1942, the subject was
classified as 4-H because of his age.

On June 5, 1943, the Bureau of Criminal Identification and on
June 8, 1943 the Credit Bureau of Greater New York were checked
with negative results. (Hughes FBI file)

Hoover found the report unsatisfying. On August 28, 1943, he wrote
to New York's Special Agent in Charge to complain about the quality
of the report by one of his underlings: "Reference is made to the
closing report of SA [**CENSORED**] of your office dated Aug 9
1943. It is noted that while reference is made to this subject's alleged
membership in several Communist front organizations his Communist Party connections have not been fully developed, the principal
information in that connection being secured from 'The Red
Network' by Elizabeth Dilling." Hoover's memo continues for three
pages, instructing the SA as to what items need to go into Hughes's
file and where the SA should look to secure evidence "which would
more definitely establish his Communist connections." Hoover
includes a copy of Hughes's poem "Goodbye Christ" and asks "that
the foregoing information be incorporated in the next report submitted by your office." He adds that the SA should ascertain whether
Hughes in fact left the country in 1932 to visit Russia.

If it sounds like Hoover was scripting the report for the SA, it
seems to have worked. The SA's revised report notes "Subject of this
case is a key figure in the NY Field Division. Copy of a poem entitled
"Goodbye Christ" which was secured from the Enemy Alien Squad,
New York City Police Department, . . . is set forth," and he reprints
Hughes's entire poem. Hoover remained fixed on Langston Hughes.
In the mid-1960s, Congressman Robert Watkins sent Hoover a letter
from a constituent asking about Hughes's affiliations with the
Communist Party. Watkins copied the letter and sent it to Hoover,
hoping he would respond to the woman. Hoover replied that bureau
files "must be maintained as confidential," but added, "By way of

suggestion, a check with the House Committee on Un-American Activities or the Senate Internal Security Subcommittee might provide information which could be of assistance to your constituent." He closed his letter with a two-line post script. The first line has been censored; the second line reads "Langston Hughes is the well-known Negro poet who is known in Bufiles [short for bureau files] for communist front-type affiliations" (Hughes FBI file).

Hughes's FBI file is one of the largest I have received in the course of my many requests on modern writers, and Hoover's resolve to discredit the poet has seemed the most insistent. His unrelenting efforts worked to limit quite seriously Hughes's opportunities to publish his work and to make public appearances, thereby preventing him and "people *like* him" from practicing their livelihoods, or, more dangerous, sharpening their craft.

J. Edgar Hoover cultivated the kind of climate for writers that would lead Virginia Woolf to despair in a 1939 diary entry, "I have been thinking about Censors. . . . All books now seem to me surrounded by a circle of invisible censors" (*Diary* vol. 5, 229). An important difference between Woolf's description of the censors and Hoover is that Hoover was hardly invisible. The next chapter describes his relentless efforts to remain a public figure and a vociferous personality. That kind of persistence and agitation would lead writers to worry about their works before they even came out, while they were in production as well as during publication and circulation. Apprehensive about the fate of his book *Ulysses,* for example, Joyce predicted on November 3, 1921, a few months before its publication, "There will be a stink as soon as the damned book is published" (Joyce, *Letters* III: 27). He was right. The "stink" would come from censors and social purity vigilantes who would rally against Joyce's language and attack the modern "arsethetic."

James Joyce, Irish writer (*Dubliners; A Portrait of the Artist as a Young Man; Ulysses, Finnegans Wake*, and more). His 1922 novel *Ulysses* was believed to be a prearranged German code. Joyce told his brother that Ezra Pound had heard that British censorship suspected *Ulysses* of being a code, too.

Muriel Rukeyser, American writer and activist. Her epic poem "The Book of the Dead" documents Union Carbide's treatment of dying workers and bereaved family members in the 1930s, when hundreds of tunnel workers died after breathing silica into their lungs.

Alexander Mitchell Palmer, U.S. Attorney General. In 1920, he orchestrated with a young J. Edgar Hoover the "Palmer Raids," dragnets organized to arrest without warrants some 10,000 "subversives" nationwide in one simultaneous action. It was an operation that surpassed even the fierceness of some of the Lusk Committee (an anti-red investigative body) raids the year before.

James Baldwin, American writer (*Go Tell It on the Mountain, Another Country, The Fire Next Time,* and more). Baldwin threatened to write a book about the FBI but never did.

Erskine Caldwell, American writer (*Tobacco Road, God's Little Acre, Trouble in July,* and more). With Margaret Bourke-White, Caldwell collaborated on the moving photo-essay book *You Have Seen Their Faces* (1937). Caldwell's FBI file notes that he is "an outstanding propagandist for Communism."

John Steinbeck, American writer (*Grapes of Wrath, Of Mice and Men, Cannery Row, East of Eden,* and more). Though J. Edgar Hoover claimed not to have Steinbeck under surveillance, he kept tabs on the writer for years, monitoring his movements and bank accounts.

Poster advertising the WPA Federal Theatre Project's presentation of "Injunction Granted," a Living Newspaper performance sponsored by the Newspaper Guild of New York.

Poster advertising the Federal Theatre's presentation of Sinclair Lewis's *It Can't Happen Here.*

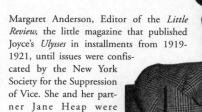

Margaret Anderson, Editor of the *Little Review*, the little magazine that published Joyce's *Ulysses* in installments from 1919-1921, until issues were confiscated by the New York Society for the Suppression of Vice. She and her partner Jane Heap were charged with propagating obscenity. John Quinn defended the women but lost the case.

Maxwell Perkins, editor at Scribner's Sons. A remarkable editor, Perkins worked diligently with modern writers such as Fitzgerald, Wolfe, Hemingway, and others, often championing their work when other in-house editors were skeptical.

Frank Nelson Doubleday, American publisher.

Dorothy Canfield Fisher. Book-of-the-Month Club judge, novelist, and educator.

Elizabeth Gurley Flynn. Irish American labor leader and organizer. Her autobiography takes its title from her work-related nickname, *The Rebel Girl*. Famed IWW songster Joe Hill wrote his song "The Rebel Girl" with Flynn in mind. She opened her house to activists, writers, and radicals of all types, and had a long friendship with James Larkin, the Irish labor leader and organizer. Hoover placed Flynn on the "Group A" custodial detention list, the list reserved for "insurgents of the most dangerous type."

Langston Hughes, American writer. Hughes is called an "alleged poet" and a "negro pornographic poet" in his FBI file. Evidence shows that J. Edgar Hoover manipulated his power and authority so as to deny Hughes reading engagements and lecture opportunities.

Alfred E. Smith, Governor of New York and one-time presidential candidate. Smith was the first Catholic to run for the presidency. That he released from prison Irish labor leader James Larkin (with full pardon) infuriated Hoover.

Theodore Dreiser, American writer (*Sister Carrie, The Genius, An American Tragedy, Jennie Gerhardt,* and more).

Thomas Mann, German writer (*Buddenbrooks, Death in Venice, The Magic Mountain,* and Hollywood screenwriter). Mann emigrated to the United States in the late 1930s. After becoming an American citizen in 1944, Mann told reporters that he "had come to choose America as his home." In his FBI file, an agent scribbled "This is amusing!" across Mann's statement. Mann was awarded the Nobel Prize for Literature in 1929.

Eugene O'Neill, American playwright (*Long Day's Journey Into Night, Emperor Jones, The Hairy Ape, Desire Under the Elms, The Iceman Cometh,* and more); member of the Provincetown Players.

F. Scott Fitzgerald, American writer (*This Side of Paradise, The Great Gatsby, Tender is the Night,* and more).

Clifford Odets, American playwright (*Waiting for Lefty, Awake and Sing!, Golden Boy, and more;* Hollywood screenwriter). A socially conscious writer. Odets's plays were noted for their attention to class issues, especially his *Waiting for Lefty,* which told the story of striking cab drivers. His FBI file identifies Odets as "the darling of the left."

Richard Wright, American writer (*Black Boy, Native Son, Uncle Tom's Children,* and more).

CHAPTER THREE

"Processed by Democracy": J. Edgar Hoover in the Age of Mechanical Reproduction

In a published eulogy for the actor John Garfield, playwright Clifford Odets bemoaned that Garfield was from that generation of Americans that had been "processed by democracy," a comment duly noted in Odets's 30-page FBI file. "In all ways," Odets wrote to the *New York Times,* "he was as pure an American product as can be seen these days, processed by democracy, knowing or caring nothing for any other culture or race" (Odets FBI file).[1] Clearly, a repellent brand of chauvinism had absorbed Odets's America, and the uniquely defiant American spirit that he so successfully captured in his 1930s plays *Waiting for Lefty, Awake and Sing, Till the Day I Die,* and *Paradise Lost* (almost single handedly making "radical theater a paying concern in New York City, and a prime medium for political expression", Norma Jenckes writes in the *Encyclopedia of the American Left* [542]), was, by 1952 he thought, a thing of the past. A number of fundamental elements accounted for such a sea change; but in this chapter I argue that J. Edgar Hoover's omnipresence and his status as a fixture in the twentieth-century American home was one of the more essential factors.

Hoover, we now know, was as obsessed with his own image as he was with his vision of the "American way of life." It is a singularly profound if not cruel irony, then, that when preparing Hoover's body for viewing after his death in 1972, undertakers at Joseph Gawler's Son's funeral home could not prevent the inevitable: "They washed his hair," one viewer told Sanford Ungar, "and all the dye had come out. His eyebrows, too. He looked like a wispy, gray-haired, tired little man. There in the coffin, all the front, all the power and the color had been taken away" (Ungar, *FBI*, 273). But while he lived, nothing could threaten the image he had so successfully constructed for himself and for the bureau. Nothing could penetrate that front or that power.

During his reign, Hoover carefully manipulated public opinion to shape the way Americans thought about crime. Claire Bond Potter argues that Hoover's "War on Crime," as it was touted, "change[d] the way Americans would come to understand crime as a national problem, police power as socially positive, and crime control as a federal responsibility" (4). Anyone who worked to degrade that image would suffer the weight of Hoover's rule. Using bureau manpower and clout, Hoover chased down authors of articles that he said "severely and unfairly discredit[ed] our American way of life" (quoted in Summers, 162). Hoover preferred instead to circulate articles that had been written by him or his various ghost writers. For instance, Hoover exerted some control over what would be published in popular magazines, and often sent DeWitt Wallace, publisher of *Reader's Digest,* pieces he had written himself or pieces he had ghost written. One count has it that *Reader's Digest* printed more than a dozen of the ghost-written articles under the Hoover byline—a figure bettered only by *American Magazine,* which published 18, and *U.S. News and World Report,* which published 25. What he didn't write himself he asked others to pen on behalf of the bureau. Morris Ernst's legendary *Reader's Digest* defense of the bureau in 1950, titled "Why I No Longer Fear the FBI," was "reprinted and distributed for years afterward" (Gentry, 387), and Hoover always kept on hand reprints of his speeches and pamphlets.

Hoover, in fact, had come up with a handy little trick he used to re-disseminate copies of his articles, speeches, and pamphlets. To those "good" Americans who would write to the FBI to supply information or to ask a question, Hoover responded by distributing reprinted copies of his essays, speeches, articles, and so forth. After acknowledging a writer's letter and thanking him or her for the information sent in, or after responding in some way to the query posted by the writer, Hoover often closed his letters with a characteristic flourish, as the following example illustrates. When the Springfield Urban League wrote to Hoover in December 1947 asking whether the bureau could "approve" Langston Hughes as a speaker for their group (one has to be careful whom one invites these days, the writer noted, and asked Hoover to send the league any relevant items from the Hughes file), Hoover wrote back saying

> Your letter dated December 23, 1947, has been received. The information contained in the files of the Bureau is confidential and available for official use only. I am sure you will draw no inference whatsoever from my inability to comply with your request. I am enclosing some material I thought you might enjoy reading.
>
> Sincerely yours,
>
> John Edgar Hoover, Director.
>
> Enclosure
>
> Secularism—Breeder of Crime
>
> Questions and Answers on Loyalty Program

Red Fascism

How to Fight Communism

Dir. Testimony. (Hughes FBI file)

Of the enclosed pamphlets, the first one Hoover lists, "Secularism—Breeder of Crime," reprints Hughes's controversial poem "Goodbye Christ." Furthermore, a handwritten note at the bottom of his letter to the Urban League incriminates the Harlem Renaissance poet: "Note: Bureau files contain numerous references reflecting Hughes to be a Communist. He is the author of the sacrilegious poem which was utilized in the speech, "Secularism—Breeder of Crime" (Hughes FBI file).

A similar episode is documented a year later in Hughes's file, and testifies again to Hoover's persistent redistribution of his opinions. A telegram from the Inter Veteran's Council of Springfield, Illinois, dated January 24, 1948, asks a similar question, noting that Hughes is scheduled to speak in the State Building on March 11 of that year. "Is he a communist?" the sender of the telegram asks. Hoover responds almost identically, and adds at the bottom of the letter, "Hughes authored the sacrilegious poem alluded to in 'Secularism—Breeder of Crime' pamphlet (enclosed)."

I am using Langston Hughes's file to illustrate Hoover's media blitz, his constant efforts to reinforce his own dogma, and his brutally narrow nationalist ideology and antiradical propaganda. Important to our understanding of the success of such a campaign is that in Hughes's file, letters from outside parties seeking information about the poet's communism are usually followed by three things: 1) a response from Hoover acknowledging the letter but saying he cannot help the writer due to secrecy regulations, 2) an indication that reading materials such as those listed above had been enclosed with the Director's response, and 3) a notice of the subsequent cancellation of the event. Cancellations transpired, for example, following Hoover's responses to queries from organizations in Springfield, Illinois, Kankakee, Illinois, and Tempe, Arizona (Hughes FBI file).

Hoover's practice of speechmaking, reinforced by his rather smart second-round pamphleteering, allowed him to reinforce bureau doctrine; to circulate his own anxieties about the speedy degeneration of the country; and to rearticulate his dread that America was being dismantled not only by the outside forces of radicalism, anarchy, and communism, but by blasphemous and sexually degenerate modern writers like Langston Hughes. Hughes's realistic portrayals of American life and his use of familiar dialects and slang (or "street") expressions opened him to charges of filth and vulgarity and earned him the derisive title of the "poet low-rate" (rather than "poet laureate") of Harlem. As the Hughes examples show, Hoover seized opportunities to sermonize and proselytize when he could. The American public certainly thought of him as a censor and morality "expert," as their inquiry letters demonstrate. Once cultivated and indoctrinated into Hoover's civilian network, this army of citizens could be mobilized to support the institutionalized practices he concocted and sustained while director.

Hoover's moralizing tracts appeared in more than just the pamphlet form. He also controlled and distributed popular culture representations of the bureau and its G-men. Some of these include his "development" of bureau friendlies such as Courtney Ryley Cooper. Cooper was a Kansas City journalist specializing in crime stories. His 24 stories, 3 books, and 4 movies on the bureau "gave the Bureau something more valuable than publicity," Richard Gid Powers notes in *Secrecy* (197); Cooper "was the man most responsible for the Bureau's new image," he argues. His features on the FBI painted the bureau as an efficient crime-fighting machine whose highly skilled agents were hand-picked and trained by Hoover himself. They were sharply dressed, clean cut, trim men—what Powers calls "stereotypical square-jawed special agent[s] with the . . . characteristic fedora" (204)—and they were as incorrigibly dedicated to fighting crime as they were incorruptible about bringing its offenders to justice, an asset during the crime-ridden years of Prohibition America. To be sure, it was in Hoover's best interest to revamp the public's understanding of his G-men. "Unlike old-fashioned detectives who simply found clues, federal investigators were activist policemen and skilled scientists who *produced* clues from the seemingly random information that littered the world," Claire Bond Potter explains in *War on Crime* (132). Cooper's stories tell a similar narrative, and describe "miracles of crime lab wizardry" and suspenseful criminal convictions—all turning on the genius of Cooper's master detective, Hoover, who "pulled all the wires, shuffled his agents' assignments, barked orders over the telephone, and flashed signals over the teletype" (Powers, 197-98). Working with Hoover, even, incredibly, turning over his bylines to the bureau director,[2] Cooper was able to participate in the campaign to make Hoover America's "top cop," her "Public Hero Number One," her favorite son. Hoover reproduced these flattering images of himself as often as he could; he reinforced the images with speeches and public appearances where he spoke against crime, Communism, and manifestations of anti-American literature and speech; and he circulated and re-circulated texts of his speeches and articles. This system allowed Hoover to sponsor and certainly profit from (in all the senses of the word) a carefully constructed media presence. By the mid-1930s, with the addition of Rex Collier's Hoover-approved radio scripts for the program *G-Men,* which aired 13 episodes starting in July 1935, Hoover had practically saturated the market with endorsements of himself, his work, and his bureau. His involvement with media representations of the FBI took numerous forms, William Beverley notes (53), and would in effect serve to lionize him. In the late 1950s, postal meters at the publishing firm of Henry Holt and Company, Inc., carried and stamped the message "Read this book now! *Masters of Deceit* by J. Edgar Hoover" on all outgoing mail. Hoover pointed this out to his partner Clyde Tolson in a memo that was subsequently placed in Holt's 230-page bureau file (Holt FBI file).

Hoover was not new to media manipulations of this kind. Even at a young age, he was interested in using media to his advantage. By the time he was 11 years old, he was writing, publishing, and distributing a small neighborhood newspaper, a two-page bulletin called *The Weekly Review.* His name was on the masthead as editor, Powers reports, and not surprising, the "news" centered on family events: "'The Weekly Review' was the world seen through the eyes of the eleven-year-old J. Edgar Hoover, a world that revolved around his family" (*Secrecy,* 20). The examples Powers furnishes focus on family trips ("Mr. D. N. Hoover . . . will leave on Sunday . . . on some business for the government") and household catastrophes: "Wanted. A servant at No. 413 Seward Square," and "Escaped from death. On Friday, about 12:15 o'clock, Mrs. Hoover, of 413 Seward Square, S.E. came near losing her life. She was frying some eggs for lunch, and the blaze caught to her back, but she managed to put the fire out on her arm, and someone in the kitchen put out the fire on the back." Issues of the *Review* also contained tidbits of gossip, information about his Washington, D.C. Seward Square neighborhood, moral proverbs, and amusing if not blunt "advertisements": "Eat Potatoes," for example, or "Drink Swiss Dairy Milk" (Powers, 20). These early publications, circa 1906, demonstrate if nothing, else Hoover's interest in collecting and distributing information. Eleven years later, by 1917, Hoover would rise to prominence at the Justice Department, where his interest in collecting, organizing, and distributing information would develop into what Natalie Robins calls an obsession (33).

Hoover's media manipulation, his obsessive organization of information and his efforts to disseminate his image, his opinions, and his dogma were aided by growing technologies that were available to the bureau. Hoover aspired, I think, to become what FDR would eventually become: "that grand old pal of the airways," as he was nicknamed by songwriter George S. Kaufman. Roosevelt had become utterly recognizable to the nation through his fireside chats, which allowed FDR to reproduce himself countless times and to insert himself almost magically into the nation's collective living rooms. In fact, it is a singular irony of FDR's fireside chats that through a scheme proposed to hide his disability from the American public, FDR earned notoriety as one of the presidents best-known to the American public, the very public he was fooling with what biographer Hugh Gregory Gallagher has called his "splendid deception." FDR took the new radio technologies seriously. With voice lessons, he was able to learn and practice different ways to use his voice. Gallagher explains "FDR was able to dominate the news media from the White House throughout the presidency. With his magnificent radio voice and his artfully crafted talks, FDR was able to project his presence into every living room. When FDR took up the complicated subject of banking, said Will Rogers, he 'made everyone understand it, even the bankers'" (*FDR's Splendid Deception*, 92-93). J. Edgar Hoover practiced his voice, too, especially to rid himself of a pesky stutter in adolescence. He used emerging radio technology to his advantage, too, and even ordered a copy of Dale Carnegie's book, *Public Speaking and Influencing Men in Business.*[3]

In addition to being on the radio himself, Hoover tried to have his name on the airwaves as frequently as possible. His friendship with radio comedian Fred Allen offered Hoover an unusual opportunity. In 1938, Allen asked his friend for permission to use his name in two slapstick-type radio skits on his program *Town Hall.* Hoover agreed. Robins describes the skits: "In one, an Indian accuses someone of taking a porcupine from his gift shop and says, 'Chief want porcupine, call J. Edgar Hoover'" (415). In the second skit, some G-men arrive on the scene to assist a man and woman who have been burgled. The man, surprised to see that J. Edgar himself has been dispatched along with his men to work on the case, says apologetically "But this is hardly a case for the G-Man," to which the woman replies, "It sure is. The thieves stole my radio, Mr. Hoover, and it's Town Hall Tonight." Robins adds that Allen inserted references to Hoover into more shows, once he saw how it delighted him.

Hoover obviously took advantage of a phenomenon new to the 1920s, what Ann Douglas calls the "first age of the media": "This was the first age of the media, of book clubs, best sellers, and record charts, of radios and talking pictures and phonographs; by the end of the decade, one of every three Americans owned a radio, three out of four went to the movies at least once a week, and virtually no one was out of reach of advertising's voice" (20). Years later, his name would blare from phonographs, too. In 1937 Harold Rome penned and subsequently copyrighted a song titled "When I Grow Up," ("The G-man Song"), quoted in Powers's book:

> Gee, but I'd like to be a G-Man
> And go Bang! Bang! Bang! Bang!
> Just like Dick Tracy, what a "he-man"
> And go Bang! Bang! Bang! Bang!
> I'd do as I please, act high-handed and regal
> 'Cause when you're a G-Man, there's nothing illegal.
>
> I'd be known in all the best spots of New York
> Like Twenty-One and Eighteen and The Stork.
> To all the smartest nightclubs I would go
> To find out all the things that a G-Man ought to know. (*Secrecy*, 179)

Interestingly, this song has nothing to do with crime or its prosecution but everything to do with the allure of the G-man image, which clearly by the mid-1930s, as the nation was gripped by the Depression, had obsessed a generation of youths eager to enter into the "high life" evidenced frequently in the press in photographs of J. Edgar Hoover and his companion Clyde Tolson living large. The song's "Bang! Bang! Bang! Bang!" refrain indicates the cops-and-robbers mentality of the song's narrator/fan. By the time this song was published and circulated, Hoover already had orchestrated a successful publicity campaign that exalted him to godlike status. Ex-agent Hank Messick opens his book on Hoover not merely with the line "Unlike God, John Edgar Hoover admits no mistakes" (1), but with an epigraph by Alex de Tocqueville that reads, "Besides, what is to be feared is not so much the immorality of the great as the fact that immorality may lead to greatness."

Part of his greatness came from magazines and newspapers that featured him on their covers or in their feature stories. Powers notes that "a few heretics, including Jack Alexander in the *New Yorker* and Kenneth Crawford in the *Nation,* cast a skeptical eye on Hoover's towering public relations image" (234)," but other media agencies scampered to get Hoover materials, especially during World War II, when he had become such an important symbol of security in wartime. Powers explains that Hoover's image was so popular that "even the comics used him in their adventures. He was 'J. Arthur Grover,' whose FBI laboratories produced the serum that turned a 4-F weakling into Captain America; he was also the boss of 'The Shield' (known as 'the G-Man Extraordinary'), and the Washington contact for the Justice Society of America" (257). Moreover, in 1936 the backs of Post Toasties cereal boxes offered drawings of "Mickey Mouse the G-Man!" solving crimes like the Great Diamond Robbery for breakfasters hungry for Hoover and FBI crime-solving souvenirs. As these examples show, Hoover's presence in the culture prolifer-ated. Equally important, it was exalted.

When he could, Hoover even helped to exaggerate the bureau's presence in the media, and the media's interest in the bureau. In his "Foreword" to Don Whitehead's *The FBI Story,* Hoover asserts that his office has been in the world's eye constantly for the past three decades. Surely that was not true; nonetheless, Hoover mythologizes: "For more than thirty years, as the FBI's director, I have watched the story of the bureau being reported on a day-to-day basis by the press, radio and, now, television" (xiii). It is precisely the proliferation of Hoover's image in popular as well as in high-brow culture that allowed him to cultivate the kind of America "processed by democracy" that Clifford Odets characterized in his 1952 eulogy of John Garfield.

Just as technologies served to replicate Hoover's image and make him a key figure in the American home and national consciousness, those same technologies served the bureau's interest, too. Hoover prided himself on how his anticrime enterprise used state-of-the-art technologies to collect and process information on its citizens. Some bureau employees were stationed next to radios, for example, in order to record in shorthand interviews with targeted radicals or subversives as they came over the radio. The file for labor organizer and leader Elizabeth Gurley Flynn, for example, contains a shorthand transcript of a 1943 interview in Salt Lake City over radio station KLO. A note on the transcript indicates that it was "taken by a stenographer in [the] office as it came over the radio" (Flynn FBI file). The bureau's use of sophisticated forensic technologies and its exploitation of sophisticated media technologies played important roles in the evolving image of Hoover and bureau. As such, it was a media operation and marketing campaign with terrifyingly measurable results. Hoover would claim in his foreword to the Whitehead book, for example, that his influence and reach extended to the crossroads of America: "The fact that some 7,000 young people, their parents and other visitors call at our headquarters each week throughout the year is a source of pride to us. . . . The FBI is a very human organization. It is never very far from the crossroads of America, either spiritually or physically. Our agents are always as close to you, the reader, as your telephone" (xi). Looking at the FBI files of some modern writers, we now know this to be true.

Hoover's Immigration Battlegrounds: Alien Radicals, Intellectuals, and Provocateurs in the Labor Movement

James Larkin (1874-1947), a man whom George Bernard Shaw called "the greatest Irishman since Parnell" was, with his comrade James Connolly, one of the most celebrated labor leaders of the twentieth century. He had successfully organized thousands of Irish workers into his Irish Transport and General Workers' Union (ITGWU) in January 1909, and with Connolly had directed thousands more during the workers' struggle against the Employers' Federation in the infamous 1913 Dublin Lock-out.[1] Disheartened by the failure of 1913, Larkin abandoned Ireland later that year and sailed for the United States on the *St. Louis,* hoping to rally support for his Irish workers and to raise funds to resurrect the ITGWU. Even before his arrival in the United States,

Jim Larkin was a name recognized by radical Americans. In fact, an article on "Larkinism" had been published in a January number of the radical newspaper the *Masses* that year. Larkin remained for a decade in the United States, where he continued his work as a labor organizer and quickly earned a reputation for stirring up and organizing underpaid, overworked, and half-starved workers in American cities as diverse as New York, Butte, Oakland, and Chicago. In fact, when eulogizing his father in 1947, James Larkin, Jr. was careful to remind an American audience that "There is hardly a state in the Union in which Jim Larkin did not lie in jail either because of participation in and leadership of some union fight, either of Irishmen or Germans or Italians or of Poles, or any other race on God's sod, and in every quarter of these United States they fought" (O'Riordan, 64). Larkin's absorption in labor activities eventually would land him in 1920 in the dreaded Clinton Prison in Dannemora, New York (at the time, one of the worst prisons in the United States), and then in Sing Sing Prison on charges of criminal anarchy and criminal syndicalism;[2] his celebrated presence in the American and Irish labor movements would even nearly cost him his life. This I have learned from reading the 490 pages that were released to me after I requested James Larkin's FBI file.[3] Larkin's activism in the United States quickly attracted the attention of a young J. Edgar Hoover. With the industrious and youthful Hoover in charge, the General Intelligence Division of the Justice Department collected files "on hundreds of thousands of 'radicals,' infiltrated lawful organizations, and fanned the red scare by supplying sensationalized charges to the press," Bud and Ruth Schultz explain in *It Did Happen Here: Recollections of Political Repression in America* (159).

Deportation grew to become "the greatest menace that the American labor movement [had] ever faced," according to a full back-page ad in the *Liberator* sponsored by the Deportees Defense and Relief Committee. "The reactionary forces here are aiming to prohibit foreigners from joining or retaining membership in political or industrial organizations of the working-class. . . . The hysterical guardians of privilege and wealth seek to outlaw every movement which challenges their autocratic rule. The present frenzied attacks override every tradition of civil freedom in America," the ad continues (*Liberator*, Feb. 1920).

Stanley and Margaret Nowak recalled the Palmer Raids and their effect on workers in an interview for Judith Stepan-Norris and Maurice Zeitlin's oral history collection *Talking Union*, in which the couple remembered and described the aggression of the raiding police:

Stanley Nowak: [I was a kid when I saw] the Palmer Raids in my own neighborhood. . . . Russian, Polish, Lithuanian . . . social clubs raided by the police. They used these tactics that on Sunday, Saturday night, Christmas Eve—

Margaret Nowak: New Year's Eve.

Stanley Nowak: New Year's Eve party. That's right. As the people went into the halls to celebrate their New Year's eve, they would raid them and stay there, and arrest everyone who came into the hall, and take them to the police headquarters. And then from there, for a time, for weeks, the families could not locate their sons or their husbands, at what station they were kept, because even the police department didn't know. They were not prepared for these kind[s] of raids. There was something like ten thousand people—so-called Reds and radicals—arrested throughout the country. How many of them were in Chicago, I don't know. But that was my introduction to it. And later on—

Margaret Nowak: What made it more impressive for him, he told me—as we tried to write his book, he had to dig into his memory— is that many of these people who were arrested were people who had come from his village, his community. He knew them. And to a boy

who had been educated in American schools about our great traditions and so on, and he saw these things happening to these people
who had never done anything to anybody and it disturbed him.
(Stepan-Norris and Zeitlin, 200)

Just as there were thousands of victims, there are thousands of stories
like the one the Nowaks recall.

Sonia Karoos, for example, was the daughter of a Lithuanian
immigrant who became naturalized so that he could vote for Eugene
Debs, the Socialist candidate for Congress in 1916. Sonia Karoos lost
the American citizenship her father had given his children when she
married a Russian immigrant in 1918. Karoos and her husband were
arrested in the middle of the night during Palmer Raids in Philadelphia on January 2, 1920, the largest night of the recurring raids, one
in which 6,000 foreign-born labor "anarchists" were netted for
deportation (Murray, 153). In a 1989 interview Sonia Karoos
recalled her experiences:

> One o'clock, there was banging on the doors. It woke up the whole
> building. There were police cars and all kinds of detectives all over the
> street. They came in and took all my books, all my letters, whatever
> they found. They took everything, every little paper they could get
> hold of. They threw it all into big bags like the post office has. They
> just threw everything in there and took them away, and I could never
> get anything back.
>
> Then they took my husband and me away. I was almost seven
> months pregnant. The police threw me in the wagon. . . . I got sick
> from all the excitement. . . . Before the ambulance came it was
> morning, and the baby was dead.
>
> After the baby died, I was in the hospital for three or four days, and
> then they brought me back to jail. I was held there until somebody
> brought bail. My husband was in jail for about two weeks. . . . We were
> charged with being undesirable. (*It Did Happen Here*, 162-63)

Marked as foreign agitators, Sonia Karoos and her husband were "undesirable" because their activism, and the activism of those of their ilk, threatened to destabilize American capitalism.

Because of his noticeable activism in the labor movement, James Larkin also was considered "undesirable," and he did not escape the kind of brutality associated with Hoover's antiradical division. As Louise Bryant would argue in 1920, "Jim Larkin went to prison because he is a champion of labor" (*Liberator*, June 1920: 16). Most likely, Larkin attracted the attention of the Department of Justice immediately after his arrival in the United States. Here less than a week, Larkin was invited to address a crowd of some 15,000 people gathered in New York City's Madison Square Garden to celebrate the election of the socialist candidate Meyer London to Congress. "Echoing an uncompromising poem of [James] Connolly's," Manus O'Riordan writes, "Larkin told his audience: 'We Socialists want more than a dollar increase for the workers. We want the earth'" (O'Riordan, 64). A year later, to another rally of thousands, Larkin eulogized Joe Hill, the legendary organizer, singer, and songwriter for the Industrial Workers of the World. Hill, whom Larkin called "one of the Ishmaelites of the industrial world," had been framed on murder charges and was executed in Salt Lake City in 1915. Larkin spent the next few years speaking at more high-profile gatherings, sermonizing workers in no fewer than 18 states by his own count: New York, Connecticut, Rhode Island, Massachusetts, Maine, Illinois, Montana, Idaho, Washington, Oregon, California, Arizona, Nevada, Pennsylvania, New Jersey, Delaware, Texas, and Alaska. Because of the conspicuousness of his fearless activism, Larkin was one of the alien radicals targeted early in Red Scare raids. His was one of 73 headquarters ransacked in New York City during the first night of the November raids coordinated by the Lusk Committee in 1919, and he was one of the first prisoners brought in by the New York State Constabulary.[4] The *New York Times* in fact reported that Larkin, "Irish agitator and strike leader," was one of "the two most

prominent prisoners caught in the raids by the Lusk Committee" and
was "one of the most dangerous of the agitators in this country"
(Nevin, "The *New York Times* and Larkin," 276). He was charged
with criminal sedition and anarchy.

Larkin liked to brag about the radicalism in his family: "[He] was
the nephew of one of the Manchester martyrs, hanged by the British
government in 1867. He boasted of his family tree, amid cheers of
approval from Irish audiences, that 'a man was hung in every one of
four generations, as a rebel,'" his long-time friend and fellow
organizer Elizabeth Gurley Flynn notes in her autobiography, *The
Rebel Girl* (187). Larkin's prominence in the labor movement led J.
Edgar Hoover to take what we now know to be a classic interest in
Larkin's trial. He appeared to be consumed by his interest in Larkin.

Hoover was eager to see Larkin convicted, and was no doubt just
as eager to be part of that political triumph. On April 15, 1920 he
wrote to prosecutor Alexander Rorke and offered to hand-deliver
incriminating materials from the Department of Justice in Washington, D.C. to Rorke's office in New York City. Hoover wrote that he
was about to receive from Britain the birth certificate and criminal
record of James Larkin, adding, "I am culling the files of this
Department for any information relative to the activities of Larkin.
As I expect to be in New York the early part of next week, I will bring
this material with me and give it to you for your use. With best wishes
I remain sincerely yours, J. E. Hoover, Special Assistant to the
Attorney General" (Larkin FBI file). Hoover never got the chance to
deliver the records to Rorke because the trial ended before any
documents arrived from Britain.

Such initiative on Hoover's part was not unusual, and there are
several examples in the Larkin file of his eagerness to be involved in
the case not only during the proceedings but well afterwards. A
letter sent on April 21, for example, begins "Dear Mr. Rorke: I take
pleasure in inclosing herewith a memorandum prepared by me
upon a speech made by JIM LARKIN at Yorkville Casino, New

York, April 6, 1920, which contains certain statements of pertinency [*sic*]to his activities. Very truly yours [unsigned carbon], Special Assistant to the Attorney General" (Larkin FBI file). Five months later Hoover was still obsessed with the case, even though Larkin was already in jail, and wrote "Dear Mr. Rorke: I have just come across the inclosed clipping dealing with JAMES LARKIN whose pernicious influences you so successfully curbed; however, he seems to be engaging again from behind prison walls in his usual propaganda. I thought the same might be of personal interest to you. Very truly yours, J. E. Hoover, Special Assistant to the Attorney General" (Larkin FBI file). It is important to acknowledge Hoover's behavior during the Larkin investigation because while it was not the only case to capture the future director of the FBI's imagination, it represents exactly the kind of case that did. This sort of calculated ambition on Hoover's part is important because it indicates early on in his career the degree to which he would attack other cases within the purview of the Justice Department, and later, within the Bureau of Investigation. His acute interest in the Larkin matter, and his indisputable frustration after Larkin's pardon and release (which I discuss below), yield considerable information about the man who would come to hold so much sway over American political, literary, and cultural matters for the next half century. Hoover's singularity of purpose during post-World War I antiradical hysteria would soon be rewarded, and the prominent role he played throughout the Red Scare, especially his audacious part in the Palmer Raids, would earn him striking recognition. Hoover had made James Larkin's arrest and conviction a Justice Department priority, and as Larkin's FBI file shows, Hoover would not desist until he saw the radical deported to Ireland.

The numbers of labor leaders, union organizers, rabble-rousers, and malcontents were growing among the immigrant and alien population, especially among the Irish. The end of the second decade of the twentieth century was a time of tremendous upheaval at work sites all over the United States; notably strident and vocal among labor agitators were the Irish. Historian David Doyle notes, "only British and Russian Jewish immigrants produced more foreign-born labor leaders than did the Irish" (193). Whether coming to America in the wake of the devastating group of famines in 1845-1849, escaping the near-famines of 1879-1880, 1890, and 1898-1899, or availing themselves of short-lived but magnanimous *fin de siècle* emigration assistance sponsored by Irish grants or individuals' benevolence,[5] the immigrant and alien Irish soon produced an unusual number of sons and daughters who grew up to be notable union officers, union leaders, or union presidents in the succeeding century.[6] They turned their attention to the coal, iron, and steel industries, and James Larkin was right there with them, one of those Irish radicals who, like Mother Jones before him, agitated to organize workers into the Western Federation of Miners and the Amalgamated Steel Workers Union.

The presence of the Irish in the labor movement, especially in the anthracite coal regions of Pennsylvania, likely triggered bureau fears about a possible return to late 1860s and 1870s Molly Maguire terrorizing strategies. The Molly Maguires were a secret society imported from Ireland whose members countered work site injustices using a variety of violent responses such as beatings and industrial sabotage. Some episodes escalated to murder. Kevin Kenny's fine work *Making Sense of the Molly Maguires* struggles to redefine those workers, and reminds us that we "need to understand American labor history in transatlantic perspective, and to examine the impact of repeated waves of immigration on American class formation" (Kenny, 5). To be sure, Hoover from the Justice Department and William Burns from the Bureau of Investigation tracked those waves, and monitored Larkin as he moved from Butte to Bethlehem, from Donora to Duquesne, from McKees Rock to Milwaukee, agitating on behalf of organized labor. While his struggle to organize workers took him across the United States, Larkin focused his efforts in industries where concentrations of Irish workers were highest: mining, iron, and steel. It is his association with Irish workers that is consistently noted in Department of Justice memoranda, in FBI files, and in sensationalized press releases. Larkin is always described in racial terms; he is always the Irish agitator, always the Irish alien radical.

Much of the information in Larkin's FBI file bores the average reader. I remember reading through Larkin's file one hot summer and coming across such mundane surveillance notes that I thought I would die from the tedium. "Subject bought a stamp," "Subject mailed a letter," "Subject ate a cheese sandwich"—these notes reveal close but drearily uneventful observations. In fact, reading the notes I almost felt sorry for the SAs assigned to the duty. Then I read a notation that said something to the effect of "Subject JAMES LARKIN is known to hang out at Fitzgerald's pub in Chicago but since there are three Fitzgerald's pubs in the city, we will spend a week hanging about each one." At that point, I remember thinking, "Nice work if you can get it." Less than a week later, after forcing myself to stick with the file, I stumbled onto something remarkable.

Certainly the most interesting item in Larkin's massive file is a Special Report filed in 1919 by a New York Special Agent in Charge (SAC) that contains information about an assassination plot against the labor leader's life. Though the bureau and the Attorney General's Office were warned about the plot, there is no evidence in Larkin's file to suggest that either office did anything to avert or to prevent the assassination plot from being carried out. The agent warned Headquarters of the conspiracy on December 2, 1919, after learning of a meeting held in the city on November 24 at which four men met to discuss the best way to murder Larkin.

The Special Report deserves to be quoted in full, and reads as follows:

SPECIAL REPORT

Date when made: 2 DEC 1919

Period for which made: 24 Nov 1919

At a meeting held last night in this city (location known to the writer), the decision that Jim Larkin must be assassinated for the good of the Irish Republic was arrived at by the following:

Brian McGann   Shaun Kavanaugh

'Pat' Quinlan   ___?___ Redmond

This "necessity" is due to the following expressed belief of the above mentioned "committee of disposal"; they have been informed that Larkin intends to "jump bail" or to stay and defeat the case against him, or "jump bail" after conviction, and flee to Ireland in time for the January elections; that his presence in Ireland will mean that he will do all possible to arouse the Irish Socialist vote against the Sinn Fein, whose policies, according to Larkin, are capitalistic and not in accord with good Socialist doctrines; that every means will be taken to prevent Larkin's presence in Ireland, and one of the methods suggested was the use of cyanide of potassium (suggestion coming from Quinlan); that all of the aforementioned plotters are men of the type who will not hesitate at violence of any sort to attain their ends.

I am further advised from the same source that a man named Fawcett[7] who is "consul general to the Irish Republic" in the City of New York, is charged with the duty of protecting an individual (whose name is at present unknown to the informant) who bears a striking resemblance to "Jim" Larkin; that this individual is to be kept under cover until such time as Larkin is disposed and then he will journey to Ireland and, impersonating Larkin, will take steps to influence the Irish Socialist forces to line up with the Sinn Fein. This individual is a stoker, and in the words of one of the plotters, "is coming over or going that way now," (informant could secure no explanation of this remark).

I respectfully suggest that this information be treated with utmost secrecy, inasmuch as the circumstances surrounding the acquisition of this information prevent the use of this information as it stands at present. Disclosure of this information at present would reveal its source and absolutely ruin the chances of our informant to secure further information in connection with this matter. May I therefore suggest that this information be addressed personally to Assistant Director and Chief, Mr. Burke, who is familiar with the services of this informant and the reliability of information secured?

Informant advises that there is no doubt that the men involved are sincere in their intent to murder Larkin, as they have decided that he must be put out of the way completely to avoid the possibility of his "come-back."

I have instructed informant to keep in touch with the progress of this plot and I will forward information as secured as promptly as developments occur. (Larkin FBI file)[8]

The men who plotted Larkin's assassination at the November meeting in New York City were referred to as the "committee of disposal" in the report prepared by the special agent. Pat Quinlan, who suggested they use potassium cyanide (KCN) to kill Larkin, may be the same Quinlan of IWW fame, whom Larkin appointed lieutenant of the Connolly Club (Larkin's workers' club) in early 1918. If this is the same Pat Quinlan, it is unclear why he would have been involved in this murder plot, especially since Larkin was such good friends with Big Bill Haywood, cofounder of the IWW. Quinlan's association with the IWW and Haywood would put him in Paterson, where, in 1915, he was arrested for inciting a riot. He was sentenced to jail for two to seven years but did not serve the full term.

Though warned by the special agent in charge of the severity of the committee's intention, and cautioned about the four men's history of violent aggression, there is no evidence that the bureau did anything to prevent the assassination conspiracy from reaching its likely end; and I have come to suspect that only Larkin's imprisonment "saved" him from this treachery.

Hoover, who received a copy of the report on the meeting of the "committee of disposal," regarded Larkin and many foreign-born agitators like him as troublemakers. They had come over to the United States not only to stir things up and to force crises at the workplace but also to challenge American capitalism directly, hoping to supplant it with socialist or communist models. Labor leaders like James Larkin, acting in the wake of the 1917 Russian Revolution and buttressed by the support they received in American workers' circles, were seen by the Justice Department as firebrands, agitators, and provocateurs of the worst kind, whether their work involved labor organizing, political radicalism, or both. They were thought to be dangerous and understandably so, since their efforts to organize laborers and to raise workers' consciousness at this time were meeting with unanticipated success in America.

In 1919, just months after the First World War ended and Lenin wrote his first "Letter to American Workers," millions of American workers—some 20 percent of the nation's work force—participated in the largest strike wave in United States history. During the First World War, strikes had been prohibited. Attitudes persisted even after the war that any kind of work stoppage was disloyal (Powers, 58). Powers notes that "[t]he media had little difficulty frightening the country when some 4 million American workers went out on 3,600 strikes in 1919" (58). Robert Asher explains in his essay on the massive strike activity that in 1919 American workers were "emboldened by tight wartime labor markets, increased personal savings, and ample union strike funds [that had] accumulated during World War I's full-employment economy" (*American Left*, 532). He suggests that the workers struck to protect their and their union's newly won power and privilege. They sought to "consolidate and extend their wartime gains while employers sought to reverse them," Joshua Freeman notes (633).

January 1919 was marked by tugboat workers' strikes in New York City and shipyard workers' strikes in Seattle over the denial of a wage hike that had been promised to them after the war. When 35,000 Seattle shipyard workers walked off the job on January 21, members of the Seattle Central Labor Council voted on February 6 to add their 60,000 workers to the walkout in support. Schools, public transportation, businesses, and stores closed, bringing the great city of the Pacific Northwest to its knees. "Convinced that the shipyard strike was the opening battle against the open-shop offensive of the employers, overwhelming majorities in each of the more than one hundred constituent unions of the Central Labor Council voted to 'shut it down' in solidarity with the shipyard workers" (Rosenthal, *American Left*, 687). What followed in that city for the next five days was a nothing short of amazing. Seattle's "transportation, service, and craft workers, including Japanese barbers and restaurant workers, came out in a general strike to support the city's shipyard workers' strike for equitable pay increases" (533). Individual unions carried out necessary tasks such as feeding the workers and policing the city. "It was this decision to run the city that made the general strike one of the most radical events in U.S. labor history" (687).

In Seattle, the general strike nearly paralyzed the city for five days, lasting from February 6 through noon on February 11 when workers returned to their jobs. Effectively organized and executed, the Seattle general strike cut across contracts, across international union constitutions, and across charters. One eyewitness reporter in her "When is a Revolution Not a Revolution: Reflections on the Seattle General Strike by a Woman Who Was There" noted the efforts that went into sustaining and magnifying the general strike, and praised the workers' efforts:

[This was] a General Strike in which the strikers served 30,000 meals a day, in which the Milk Wagon Drivers established milk stations all over town to care for the babies, in which city garbage wagons went to and fro marked "Exempt by Strike Committee," a General Strike in which 300 Labor Guards without arms or authority went to and fro preserving order; in which the Strike Committee, sitting in almost continuous session, decided what activities should and should not be exempted from strike in the interests of public safety and health, and even forced the Mayor to come to the Labor Temple to make arrangements for lighting the city. . . . It was a show of sympathy and solidarity for our brothers in the shipyards. (*Liberator*, Apr. 1919: 23)

When the strike was over, workers realized that they had "done something bigger" than win recognition for shipyard workers, an unsigned writer reported in the *Liberator*. They had educated the city of Seattle on its dependence on labor, and "had had intimate contact with the intrarelation of the city's industries and the city's life." To boot, "they had done it all quietly, without a touch of violence, without an arrest" (*Liberator*, Apr. 1919: 25).

On the first day of the Seattle strike, the Immigration Bureau of the Labor Department rounded up three dozen immigrant strikers and members of the IWW and sent them from Seattle to Ellis Island for deportation on the *Red Special*. "After the Seattle strike," Powers notes, "every picket sign looked like a red flag to alarmists, and picket signs were everywhere" (19). The following month saw a series of strikes (now notorious) by workers in textile mills in Lawrence, Massachusetts and Paterson, New Jersey, and by miners in Butte, Montana. Nearly 2,000 more strikes would occur by mid-year: "there were 175 more strikes across the country in March, 248 in April, 388 in May, 303 in June, 360 in July, and 373 in August" (19).

A series of workers' strikes rippled throughout the nation and made effective waves. In May, electrical workers in Toledo, Ohio went on strike and forced the deployment of federal troops to stave off what the *New York Times* said would be a "union takeover of the city" (*American Left*, 533). August saw Chicago railroad shopmen and New York City subway workers strike, as well as sympathy strikes and job action slowdowns on California's railroads. In October, 60,000 steelworkers in San Francisco went on strike, and by November, to prevent the transportation of "scab" coal, railroad switchmen all over the United States staged brief sympathy strikes to support a 400,000-strong national coal miners' strike that defied a federal court injunction (533). So crippling were the effects of the 1919 strike wave that federal troops and tanks were sent to several cities across the nation to force workers back into coal mines, back onto tugboats, back into subway tunnels, and back to jobs in electrical work, the steel industry, transportation, the garment industry, and textile mills. Tension and aggression escalated. In April there were bomb scares across the nation, and in May, brutal beatings of May Day demonstrators. Simultaneous explosions followed in eight American cities that May.

September of that year brought with it the nation's first police strike (Boston), and at mid-month ushered in the beginnings of what would come to be known as the Great Steel Strike, a job action participated in by more than 300,000 striking workers. Mary Heaton Vorse reported on the steel strike for the *Liberator* in January 1920:

> People talk of the steel strike as if it were one single thing. In point of
> fact, there are 50 steel strikes. Literally there are 50 towns and
> communities where there to-day exists a strike. . . . This is something
> new in the history of strikes—50 towns acting together. Pueblo acting
> in concert with Gary; Birmingham, Alahama [*sic*] keeping step with
> Rankin and Bruddock, Pennsylvania.

By February 1920, an advertisement for the 1919 edition of the *Labor Year Book* identified 1919 as "the greatest year in Labor's History" (*Liberator*, Feb. 1920: 50). All of these strikes—taken as evidence of "worker militancy"—gave rise to a counteroffensive against unions and radical union leaders; this counteroffensive would continue into the following year and displayed the brute force and capitalist aggression that would characterize the raids that Hoover coordinated for the Justice Department.

By the end of the year 1919, institutionalized aggression had successfully curbed worker militancy, robbing workers of union-won postwar workplace advantages. "Vigilante action by businessmen, the revived Ku Klux Klan, the courts, and the military power of the State combined to roll back virtually all the gains unionized American workers had made during the World War I era," Robert Asher notes (533). Though touted as "the greatest year in Labor's History," with millions of American workers straitjacketed by federal, local or regional counteroffensives, 1919 would become a nightmare year for the post-World War American working class and would mark the dawn of one of the most powerful campaigns against the rise of unionization in America.

With Larkin's success in organizing workers, then, he was an obvious target for Hoover's antiradical push. Within a year of his arrival in America, Larkin had successfully organized a half-dozen groups of American workers into unions and was equally success-ful in rallying workers to the strike. Larkin's FBI file shows that as early as 1917 he was branded a criminal syndicalist by the bureau, and it is clear that bogus evidence was being collected to connect the Irish labor leader to a July 22, 1916 bombing that took place in San Francisco during the Preparedness Day Parade, a parade sponsored by industrialists to goad Woodrow Wilson (and Amer-ica) into the war. The parade allowed the nation's capitalists to flex America's industrial muscle and to demonstrate industry's readi-ness to direct factory and industry workers to the war effort. Thomas J. Mooney and Warren K. Billings, labor organizers who spent the better part of 1916 trying to unionize the car men of the United Railroads of San Francisco, would be named as central figures in the Preparedness Parade bombing, and the case would become one of the most notorious labor frame-ups in the early half of the twentieth century, Dan Georgakas argues (485).[9] Mooney's "actual offense," Georgakas notes, "was that he had been *de facto* leader of the Left wing of the California Federation of Labor and his activities had alarmed some of the most powerful forces in the state" (485). Mooney and Billings would come to be viewed as labor martyrs, and would remain in prison on falsified charges for more than two decades.

Revealingly, Larkin's FBI file shows that federal agents were trying to implicate *him* in the 1916 Preparedness Day Parade bombing as well, though their attempts were unsuccessful. Labor leaders such as Mooney, Billings, and Larkin were obvious targets on whom to pin these criminal charges, since the labor movement openly reviled the notion of a "Preparedness Parade," insisting that it was propaganda to fuel the "Open Shop" wars being fought in San Francisco at the time. One writer for the *Masses* noted that the parade "was more a demonstration of scab workmen being forced into line by their employers than anything else, but also belligerently symbolized the Open Shop to the great mass of Union Labor who opposed the impudent propaganda of the captains of industry" (15).

Though Larkin was never charged with having a role in the Preparedness Parade bombings, it is nonetheless maddening to watch the distortion of "evidence" in the FBI files. For example, what begins as a simple "Concerning Jim Larkin: I am advised by Special Agent [CENSORED] that Larkin called to see [CENSORED] at the Fresno Hotel about the time of the Preparedness Day Parade, July 22, 1916," becomes "[Larkin] was in San Francisco shortly before preparedness parade, in which city he was visited at the Fresno Hotel by [CENSORED]," only to evolve into a further, more sinister distortion: "He visited nearly every day with [CENSORED] who has since been convicted and sentenced in *Preparedness Bomb Plot* in San Francisco." Also collected as evidence, though spurious indeed, are several sworn affidavits from special agents in the Department of Justice who testify that Larkin is an anarchist who "advocates the overthrow by force or violence of the Government of the United States."

Linking Larkin to the 1916 Preparedness Day Parade bombing was one of the early operations on the part of the Justice Department to muster enough "evidence" to secure Larkin's deportation or to assure his arrest and conviction, because by that year his involvement in the American labor movement already had become alarming. Larkin was well aware that he was under Bureau of Investigation surveillance at the time; in fact, he noted it years later in a 1934 affidavit recorded in Ireland, saying of his first two or three years in America that "there were agents in the Department of Justice who had made good reports on me and that they could not get anything on me although they felt I was engaged in sabotage" (quoted in Nevin, 307). Larkin's 1934 testimony explained that his business in America involved working with leaders in the American labor movement to organize longshoremen, seamen, and industrial workers to gain control over the workplace through strength in numbers and not necessarily by brute force. He testified:

> Shortly after landing in the United States I set up an organisation known as the "Four Winds" Fellowship, which was open only to trade unionists and socialists. . . . I also made contact with the American Labour movement, undertaking organising work for the Western Federation of Miners, International Longshoremen's Association, Coastwise Seamen's Union and the Amalgamated Steel Workers Union, also other unions throughout the forty eight states. . . . The "Four Winds" Fellowship was to be used as a means to getting entrance into the trade unions with a view to control, particularly among longshoremen and seamen. Subsequently, it was the intention to get into the basic industries such as steel and copper. (Nevin, 299-300)

Larkin's work organizing laborers in a number of American cities brought him to the top of the Justice Department's list of wanted anarchists and agitators.

Known variously as "Big Jim," the "Lion of Labor," "the Irish agitator," and the "archangel of anarchy," as prosecutor Alexander I. Rorke referred to him during his trial summation, Larkin had come to the United States in 1914 on a lecture tour but soon found himself fully engaged with the American labor movement. He established his "Four Winds Fellowship" and spent some time initially working with the Industrial Workers of the World. After being picked up in the November 1919 Lusk Committee raids, Larkin was convicted of criminal anarchy for having a hand in writing and distributing material confiscated during the raid, and in particular, a manifesto published in *The Revolutionary Age*. His jury decided that the manifesto advocated the overthrow of the government by force, although Larkin insisted it merely advocated a change of government by peaceful means. New York Governor Al Smith pardoned him in 1923, having recently taken gubernatorial office, and argued that Larkin's conviction interfered with the freedom of political discussion. Christopher Finan notes that at this time, "there was no more powerful spokesman for liberalism in the United States than Al Smith" (4). The pardon angered and frustrated J. Edgar Hoover, Larkin's file shows, and he instantly animated a swift and brutal campaign to deport Larkin using evidence taken from Department of Labor reports, FBI reports, New York arrest reports, and a series of statements falsely attributed to Larkin by bureau special agents in charge.

In an important memo to bureau Director William J. Burns dated February 7, 1923, only weeks after Larkin's pardon and release, Hoover recommended to Burns that deportation proceedings against Larkin start immediately. (Importantly, some essential information has been blacked out in the file by bureau censors, information that might confirm a pattern of misconduct, as we shall see.) In this

February letter, Hoover tickles Burns' institutional memory, alluding to a case that previously was handled through Hoover's office. He suggests they handle Larkin's case similarly:

> You have noted the report that Jim Larkin has been released from prison in New York by Governor Smith. It is very likely that a deportation case could be made upon Larkin and I am calling it to your attention in order that you may indicate if it is your wish to proceed with the preparation of this case and present the same to the Department of Labor.
>
> I understand that there was a warrant issued for Larkin when he was convicted under the New York State laws and this warrant, of course, will still hold good. It would require that the case be prepared in this office and be submitted and followed through as was done in the case of [CENSORED]
>
> Respectfully,
> J. E. H.

One week after Burns received Hoover's memo, he asked for and received a copy of the Department of Labor's (DOL) file on Larkin. Afterward, Burns wrote to Robe Carl White, Second Assistant Secretary of Labor, and informed him that although the DOL file on Larkin was practically identical to the FBI file on Larkin, "certain details concerning the meeting at Odd Fellows Hall, NYC, on Feb. 16, 1919" had been left out of the Department of Labor report—specifically, that Larkin asked the audience to pledge allegiance to the communist flag, that he preached violence at the meeting, and that he advocated the overthrow the government. Burns wrote on March 5, 1923:

> My dear Mr. White:
> I am returning to you herewith the Department of Labor file upon James Larkin which you were kind enough to transmit to me under the date of February 14, 1923.

In the examination of this file I find that it contains practically all the information upon Larkin which is in the files of the Bureau of Investigation with the exception of certain details concerning the meeting at Odd Fellows Hall, New York City, on February 16, 1919, at which Larkin commanded his audience to rise and swear allegiance to the Red flag. At this meeting, according to our records, Larkin made an appeal for money, using such slogans as "Every Dollar Kills the Capitalist" and "Give now or the Boss will Take it Away Later."

After very careful examination of all the information in our files, it is very evident that James Larkin is a person who fully comes within the provisions of the immigration law providing for deportation of an alien who advocates the overthrow of the Government of the United States by force or violence. It would be very desirable to effect his deportation at an early date for, as you no doubt have noted, he has been upon a speaking tour throughout the country in the interest of radicalism. I would appreciate being advised as to the prospects for an early deportation of this undesirable alien.

Very truly yours,

W J B [initials]

Director

The collusion to attribute anarchist statements to Larkin in an effort to mount a deportation case against him began when Burns started comparing files from field offices and government agencies around the country. Burns wrote to New York SAC Edward J. Brennan on January 29, 1923 that "certain statements are quoted and attributed to Larkin but copies of the reports in which the statements appear cannot be located. One of these reports is that of Agent [CENSORED] for June 24, 1919. Kindly forward to me copy of this report and advise me whether the quoted statement of Larkin appearing therein can be proven to have been made by subject." Burns quickly received this response from Brennan:

In the report of **[CENSORED]** mentioned above, and which covered this particular meeting, I fail to find any statement of this kind which could be held against Subject. It does, however, claim in the report that the speakers urged the overthrow of the Government (Larkin FBI file).

Burns and Hoover went ahead with the case nonetheless, even though agents present at the Odd Fellows Hall meeting could not attribute the statements expressly to Larkin. Taken together, these letters between Hoover, Burns, White, and Brennan suggest that at Hoover's initial prodding, Burns fabricated the case that led to Larkin's deportation, apparently using as his model the same methods employed in the case Hoover referred to in his heavily censored January 1923 letter.

Ultimately, Hoover's and Burns's work was successful, and within three months, Larkin was deported to Ireland. From his Washington office Hoover insisted that two New York special agents go down to the pier to watch and subsequently verify by private letter the departure of the *S.S. Majestic* and Larkin's presence on board. Edward J. Brennan was one of the federal agents who obliged. A carbon copy of his letter, sent to bureau director W. J. Burns, remains part of the bureau record and testifies to the frenzy that characterized Hoover's obsession with the Larkin case.

Such activity on the part of the Justice Department begs the question, just how dangerous *was* James Larkin? In what ways did he threaten America? Like many other labor leaders at the time, Larkin was identified as a threat to capitalism. Though Larkin was not the only activist who sought to organize American workers during the first and second decades of the twentieth century, nor was he the only alien radical involved in the labor movement to be pursued by Hoover and the Justice Department during those decades, the Larkin case remains symptomatic of Hoover's growing distrust of alien radicals, his mounting hysteria in the face of the burgeoning immigrant and alien populations in America's cities, his increasing frustration over their involvement in the labor movement, and his anxiety over the rise of unionization among the American workforce.

It is important to remember that the 1910s and 1920s were particularly important decades for American labor organizations; their numbers were growing at what would seem to their detractors an alarming rate, providing the working classes not only with economic gains but with political power and clout as well. Whereas before the First World War roughly 10 percent of the American labor force was unionized, by the end of the Second World War, more than 12 million workers belonged to unions, and by the 1950s, more than a third of American wage earners were organized. While labor organizations were gaining popularity and political savvy, the bureau considered their tactical maneuverings insurgent and dangerous, and characteristically yoked their "un-American" philosophies with communist doctrine. James Larkin's hand in successfully organizing some of the nation's largest essential workers—the Western Federation of Miners, the International Longshoremen's Association, the Coastwise Seamen's Union, the Amalgamated Steel Workers Union, and other workers throughout America—garnered the attention of the Justice Department and marked him as one of those alien radicals whose militancy needed to be checked.

At a time when the labor movement steadily was gaining currency—through the popular IWW, the American Federation of Labor (AFL), the United Mine Workers (UMW), and in the 1930s, the Congress of Industrial Organizations (CIO)—anti-union sentiment allowed government and big business to swoop in and curb the labor movement in an effort to neutralize the power of the unions. These efforts manifested themselves in a number of violent massacres, such as the 1918 Centralia Massacre, discussed above, that ended with the lynching, shooting, and castration of IWW member

Wesley Everett—an inquest jury interpreted the evidence as a "suicide." Several violent labor disputes occurred, such as the notorious Battle of Matewan (1920), where organizing coal miners clashed with strike-breaking detectives from the Baldwin-Felts Corporation. A year later, anti-union violence would erupt there again, "setting off an armed rebellion of 10,000 West Virginia miners at the so-called Battle of Blair Mountain, dubbed by a local newspaper as 'the largest insurrection this country has had since the Civil War.' Army troops had to be called in to put down the uprising" (Murray, 114). Calling attention to the recurring violence, a wry one-liner in a special Christmas number of the *Masses* announced "The murdering of strikers is in Colorado this week" (Dec 1913: 20). The hiring of "professional" informants and labor spies from the Pinkerton or Burns agencies also contributed to carefully planned efforts to break labor unions just when their membership and collective powers were growing. One of the most obvious anti-union strategies was known as the American Plan, "a slogan of antilabor employers during the 1920s Red scare, equating a nonunion workplace with patriotism and a union shop with disloyalty" (Murray, 15). The American Plan developed its roots a decade earlier in the aftermath of the bloody 1914 Ludlow Strike at Rockefeller-owned coal mines (158). Given the widespread unrest at worksites and the overwrought antiworker bias, it can hardly be a coincidence that a "committee of disposal" was discussing and strategizing its assassination plot against labor leader James Larkin's life at the end of a year of great worker turbulence.

A decade after America produced some of the richest men in the world by crushing unions in the coal, iron, and steel industries (where Henry Clay Frick, Andrew Carnegie, John D. Rockefeller, Jr., Charles Schwab, and J. P. Morgan, for example, made their millions), these men, whose anti-union animus and opposition were so powerful that they inspired the laws that would govern labor throughout the twentieth century, would tolerate neither amalgamation nor agitation. While the "open shop" policies instituted in many factories after the bloody Ludlow Strike of 1914 at the Rockefeller-owned coal mines did not prevent workers from joining unions, "dismissals without cause were easy enough to explain away," David Brody explains in *Labor in Crisis: the Steel Strike of 1919*, and more likely than not, often resulted in blacklisting. For example, U.S. Steel officials emphasized "We don't discharge a man for belonging to a union . . . but of course we discharge men for agitating in the mills" (89). Agitation, in other words, became synonymous with anti-Americanism, since it worked to dismantle the American Plan, a plan that equated organized labor with anti-Americanism and non union attitudes with patriotism. The very name of the "American Plan" indicates the widespread hysteria in America over the growing immigrant work force.

How eager was "America" to uphold the "American Plan," to crush not only nascent but long-established unions, to cripple workers with ten-hour work days and six-day work weeks, and so on? It seems there was a growing assembly of people who were very eager to comply, even if it required physical violence and brute force, as the events that occurred at Ludlow, Matewan, Centralia, Blair Mountain, and in so many other sites across our land show.

While the occurrence of job actions remained high after the postwar strike wave in 1919, and though direct action continued through the 1920s, labor's "postwar offensive" was curbed by government restraint, and gave rise to a Red scare that "equated labor militancy with foreign radicalism" (Freeman, 633).[10] Larkin was an obvious victim of the Justice Department's singular vision, its either/or binary. David Levering Lewis provides a nice image when he notes, "According to the Attorney General's alarming report on subversion, released in November, the country was honeycombed with anarchists and Bolsheviks" (16). To extend his metaphor, things were about to get sticky for American workers.

Larkin was immensely popular with American workers. When he was brought to trial, people lined the streets along the courthouse

eight- and nine-deep just to get a look at him, the Irish writer Lady
Gregory recorded in her diary. "They thought of him as a god," she
wrote (Nevin, 473). This sort of popularity alarmed Hoover, who
thought Larkin was dangerous to American democracy and capitalism. Larkin's FBI file clearly shows this. I believe that if Hoover hadn't
been successful in mounting a case against the Irish labor organizer,
seeing him thrown into jail on a five- to ten-year criminal anarchy
sentence, and subsequently deported to Ireland after his gubernatorial pardon, then Larkin's involvement in the American labor movement might have cost him his life,[11] as it had so many others during
the tumultuous, antilabor decades of the 1910s and 1920s.

Compounding the Department of Justice's anxieties about the
growing labor movement was its alignment with the modernist
literary movement. Years before Mike Gold extolled in "Go Left,
Young Writers" the virtues of writers' creative involvement with left
politics, writers already were "going" there. They engaged at all levels
with the growing labor movement, first by organizing their own
union in 1913, the Authors League of America, and then by investing
their energies and talents in cooperative efforts within the labor
movement. The alignment manifested itself in several ways. In the
1920s writers participated in protests against the arrest and subsequent execution of workers Nicola Sacco and Bartolomeo Vanzetti,
for example. Cast as a "watershed moment" in almost every history
of the radical twenties, and seen as a defining moment for the left, the
Sacco and Vanzetti case brought together labor and literary activists
and galvanized their political action. The files of many modern
writers contain paperwork outlining their involvement in agitating
for the release and pardon of the men.

Writers such as Katherine Anne Porter (on whom no file exists,
I was told after I made a FOIA request) have files incriminating them
for their activism and engagement in current political issues. Porter's
11-page file, which I have not seen but Natalie Robins describes in
Alien Ink, began after she was named in a newspaper article about the

Citizens National Committee for Sacco and Vanzetti. A report in poet Edna St. Vincent Millay's FBI file indicates that she signed a petition to ask FDR to reverse the Attorney General's decision to deport Harry Bridges, the Australian-born West Coast labor leader. Bridges entered the United States in 1920 by "jumping ship," Murray notes in his short biographical sketch of the labor organizer (28-29). Bridges founded the International Longshoremen's and Warehousemen's Union in 1933 and led a major West Coast dock strike in 1934. The federal government, including Hoover, Bridges's "nemesis" (Murray, 29), tried to have him deported as a communist sympathizer. Bureau strategies for sniffing out labor sympathies among writers often included mail interception. Ella Winter and Donald Stewart, for example, close friends of Bridges, had their mail monitored for decades (Robins, 93).

Many writers aligned themselves with workers and with worker struggles in the early twentieth century. Carl Sandburg, famously pro-labor and ardent in his poetry about class consciousness and the abuses of poverty, had his FBI file, too. Mitgang reports that "Carl Sandburg had an Army intelligence file of six pages, dating back to 1918, and an FBI file of twenty-three pages" (94a). When Sandburg returned from the Philippine campaign with Company C in 1900 after serving five months in Puerto Rico (he preferred to call himself Charlie—"it sounded more American"), he entered Lombard College and there he began reading Walt Whitman's *Leaves of Grass* (Crichton, 41). "I had wondering and hopes," he said, "but they were vague and foggy" (Crichton, 41). Sandburg would come to translate those "vague and foggy" hopes into a poetry that was distinctively American and notoriously working class. Like Whitman, whom Larkin quoted as he departed the United States on the S.S. *Majestic*, and whom he credited with bringing him to class consciousness, Carl Sandburg's early initiation with *Leaves of Grass* would affect not only the rhythms of his poetry but the cadences of his politics. Archibald MacLeish was a big fan of Sandburg. Though he argued in 1934 that poetry and politics did not mix, he would sing to Sandburg in 1936 a different song: "We must now become pamphleteers, propagandists—you by your own right, I as one who can aid you somewhat. Well?" (quoted in Segall, 64).

Readers of the *Liberator* and other radical newspapers and magazines of the time were fed regularly by poetry and political rhetoric, urged to become the kind of pamphleteers and propagandists MacLeish advocated. A 1919 article "What Are You Doing Out There?" reminded readers of the crucial coalition between writers and activists:

> This magazine goes to two classes of readers: those who are in jail, and those who are out. This particular article is intended for the latter class. . . . The relation between these two classes of people is embarrassingly like that in the old anecdote about Emerson and Thoreau. Thoreau refused to obey some law which he considered unjust and was sent to jail. Emerson went to visit him. "What are you doing in here, Henry?" asked Emerson.
>
> "What are you doing out there?" returned Thoreau grimly.
> (*Liberator*, Jan. 1919: 12)

At the appointment of J. Edgar Hoover to bureau director in 1924, attorney general Harlan Fiske Stone announced that from then on, the bureau would not be "concerned with political or other opinions of individuals. It is concerned only with their conduct and then only with such conduct as is forbidden by the laws of the United States" (Robins 56-57). Robins explains that "despite Stone's mandate not to investigate what was on American minds, Hoover never stopped keeping track of American writers" (57) or international writers who were out there "doing something," as I have shown.

FOIA officials responded that there was no main file on British poet W. H. Auden after they received my request (this, despite the fact that other researchers have seen and reported on its contents).

Although W. H. Auden would write in his moving February 1939 elegy "In Memory of W. B. Yeats" that "poetry makes nothing happen," Hoover couldn't risk the possibility of Auden's being wrong. Where Auden's poem advises future poets to lift their "unconstraining voice," to "sing of human unsuccess / In a rapture of distress," and to "teach the free man how to praise" (Auden, 743), Hoover would have preferred something a little less prescriptive.

By pursuing labor leaders, union agitators, cultural workers, intellectuals, and modern writers who were involved in workers demonstrations, committed to class equality, eager to wipe out workplace violence, and unsympathetic to industrialist greed, Hoover's manipulation of modernism carried on.

CHAPTER FIVE

"Trade Papers for Revolutionaries": Modernism's Newspapers and Little Magazines

When Joseph Kalar voiced his frustration over the shifting direction taken by the *New Masses* in 1929 after he realized it had been publishing "far too many manifestoes on the desirability and significance of proletarian art" than it had been publishing proletarian art, he may not have been aware that he was opening the proverbial lid-tight can of worms (Aug. 1929: 22). Kalar wanted to know for whom the magazine was written: "It is time that we knew who we wanted to read this magazine—embryo artists, or the people who sweat. Is this to be a workers magazine or a potential writers' magazine? That's what I want to know" (Aug. 1929: 22).

A letter to the editor published two months later in the *New Masses* supported Kalar's position. Detroit subscriber Arthur Clifford lectured, "You are getting too damn literary. . . . Now this poetry you're printing. It makes me suspect, like Joseph Kalar, that you're using the magazine as a training ground for writers. No good. No, what you've got to do is to make the *New Masses* a sort of trade paper——a trade paper for revolutionaries. Give us all the dope on the progress of labor, communism, and what not" (Oct. 1929: 30). Kalar's and Clifford's demand that the *New Masses* identify more clearly its aims, and either fish or cut bait when it came to articulating the paper's political aims, fit squarely within the parameters of the investigations being carried on by Hoover's bureau. It, too, wondered on which side of the political divide newspapers and little magazines identified themselves. Were they organs of revolution or were they arts magazines? The *New Masses,* for example, carried on its masthead that it was a "revolutionary magazine of art and literature." To provide comprehensive answers to such questions of allegiance, then, special agents and special agents in charge would open files for many of the writers and editors associated with modernism's newspapers and little magazines, and clippings of their editorials, fiction, poetry, and art would fill their dossiers.

Among many editors of the little magazines and newspapers that were so fundamental to circulating modern literature among the masses and educating readers about essential elements of the new modern aesthetic, there was often internal tension about the reach or the vision of such projects. Should little magazines and newspapers serve as organs to distribute and circulate modern literature and art, or should they work to raise the political awareness of their readers and provide forums for the interesting exchange of ideas? Were the papers to pursue literary genius and creative innovation or track and probe social issues? If they were trade papers, in other words, the question was, what trade were they in?

Most little magazines and newspapers helped to launch the literary movement of modernism, and cultivated an avant-garde sensibility that would nurture and sustain modernism through the end of the Second World War. With names as varied as *Dial, Egoist,* the *Masses, New Masses, Liberator, Blast, Crisis, Seven Arts, English Review,* the *Little Review,* the *Freewoman,* the *New Freewoman, Fire!!, New Age,* and *Wheels,* to name a few, the newspapers and little magazines responded in dynamic ways to technological and aesthetic changes in modern culture.

Judging by the topics covered in the short-lived history of the *Masses,* for example (a radical newspaper that ran 1911-1917), such magazines tried to strike a balance between social and literary topics. While the *Masses* dealt with issues of censorship, race, class struggle, feminism, suffrage, industrial wars and labor strikes, "preparedness" and war, they also featured fiction writers Sherwood Anderson, Floyd Dell, Richard Wright, and Upton Sinclair, poetry by Dorothy Day, Floyd Dell, William Carlos Williams, Carl Sandburg, Federico García Lorca, Amy Lowell, Rose Pastor Stokes, Joel Spingarn, and Upton Sinclair, and artwork by their very own talented group of artists including Stuart Davis, John Sloan, Art Young, Boardman Robinson, Henry Glintenkamp, Maurice Becker, and Robert Minor, even publishing a Picasso sketch once. The news, features, reviews, and political cartoons of the *Masses* were "too naked and true for the money-making press," the masthead proudly announced:

> A free magazine. This magazine is owned and published co-operatively by its editors. It has no dividends to pay, and nobody is trying to make money out of it. A revolutionary and not a reform magazine; a magazine with a sense of humor and no respect for the respectable; frank; arrogant; impertinent; searching for the true causes; a magazine directed against rigidity and dogma wherever it is found; printing what is too naked or true for a money-making press; a magazine whose final policy is to do as it pleases and conciliate nobody, not even its readers—there is a field for this publication in America. Help us to find it.

William O'Neill writes of the *Masses* that "since the *Masses* was the boldest journal of its time, it frequently ran afoul of the censor.

By successfully maintaining its attitude of gay defiance and by constantly pressing against the outer limits of community tolerance, it substantially increased the editorial freedom of all periodicals" (39). It often engaged in discussions about its own plight with the censor. In an October 1916 article "Some Recent Workings of the Censorship," the editor wrote:

> In the past six month six radical periodicals have been suppressed by the Post Office Department without the formality of a trial and without the possibility of redress: *Revolt,* of New York; *Alarm,* of Chicago; *The Blast,* of San Francisco; *Voluntad* (Spanish); *Volni Listy* (Bohemian); and *Regeneración* (English-Spanish). All of these papers, except the last one, were denied the privileges of the mails on the grounds that the Post Office Department "did not like the tone of the paper."

The article goes on to itemize several examples of censorship throughout the country, including the suppression in Cincinnati of Dreiser's novel *The Genius* and the censorship in New York of the Russian Ballet. It criticized "the stupid suppression of serious plays in Boston, Philadelphia and Chicago," noting that "undisturbed, the silly and lascivious burlesque show, musical comedy and vaudeville act go on. The moral is, of course: 'As long as you are vulgar you are safe'" (O'Neill, 44, 46).

Actually, the moral would be closer to something like "If you've got money, we'll leave you alone." The reason vaudeville and burlesque theaters went "undisturbed" while Dreiser's *The Genius,* performances by the Russian Ballet, and serious plays in large American cities were victimized likely stemmed from the relative commercial unimportance of the latter enterprises. That is, these were not vast commercial concerns run by families with big money and big city political clout like those involved with vaudeville and burlesque circuits in New York City, whose theaters played to an astonishing 1.5 million customers or more a week. In his 1911 study of the influence commercial culture held over New Yorkers, for example, Michael Davis noted in *The Exploitation of Pleasure* that in Manhattan alone,

> there were seven burlesque theaters with an estimated weekly atten-
> dance of almost 1.4 million, and 30 "high priced" theaters that were
> patronized by about 160,000 people a week. [T]here were approxi-
> mately 400 motion picture theaters in the city as a whole, drawing
> hundreds of thousands of customers every day. No other city in the
> nation came close to the variety and abundance of commercial culture
> offered by New York.
>
> New York's position as the nation's cultural mecca, and the
> important role played by entertainment industries in the city's
> economy, made the conflicts over obscenity that occurred there
> unique in their importance to municipal life. Furthermore, the
> demography of NY shaped these debates in particular ways. One
> scholar has estimated that in 1900 NYC's population was 47%
> Catholic, 39% Protestant, and 12% Jewish. (quoted in Friedman, 11)

Though the above description covers the beginning of the second decade of the twentieth century, the following image captures the magnitude (and cultural capital) of the same theaters a few short years later. Robert Snyder asks us to begin by imagining an aerial photograph of the New York City vaudeville scene taken during its prime, sometime around 1915. Snyder helps us to imagine the photo, saying, it is

> a picture of a cultural nerve system, with vibrant centers of activity
> located throughout the city and vigorous messages pulsating between
> them. The hub is at Times Square in Manhattan, site of the famous
> Palace Theater and the major booking offices. Secondary centers
> appear in the major business districts of other boroughs: 149th Street

in the Bronx, home of the Royal and National Theaters. The Fulton area of downtown Brooklyn, home of the Orpheum. Farther afield in the most localized business districts of the city, often in working-class or immigrant quarters, are neighborhood, small-time theaters such as Loew's Avenue B on the Lower East Side of Manhattan and Fox's Folly Theatre in Williamsburg, Brooklyn. On the city's fringe at the seaside cluster [lie] summertime vaudeville houses that cater to resort and amusement park crowds: the Brighton Beach Music Hall in Brooklyn; the Terminal Music Hall in North Beach, Queens; Nunley's Casino in South Beach, Staten Island. (Snyder, 118-19)

Snyder adds that once transit lines were spread uptown and to the far reaches of the Bronx, for example, urban sprawl took over—but so, too, did the commercial development of theaters across the vast city: "Major circuits hurried to open vaudeville and combination vaudeville-film houses. From around 1910-1920, the Loew, Keith, and Fox interests built or acquired at least 12 Bronx theaters, each seating more than 1000" (127). These are impressive numbers indeed. Why would city vice squads not want to interfere with these commercial enterprises? The *Masses* writer correctly calls his readers' attention to the anomaly, and challenges the inconsistency and the irregularity with which police and vice censors applied the laws of legal constraint.

Editors of the *Masses* suffered from this kind of disproportionate application of the law, and knew it all too well. Just months earlier, issues of the *Masses* were pulled from newspaper and magazine stands in New York City subway and elevated train stations by its distributors, Ward and Gow, following the publication of an anti-enlistment pledge. The magazine quickly was banned from Columbia University's main library and bookstore, suppressed by the Magazine Distribution Company in Boston, quashed by the United News Company of Philadelphia, and kicked out of Canada by the government (May 1916, "The Latest," 23). *Masses* editors claimed that the

Ward and Gow action led to a loss of some 3,000-4,000 readers per month (March 1916). Others followed with condemnation: "The editors of the *New York Globe* honored us with a public denunciation for offering to our readers an anti-enlistment pledge. They seem to think we are almost as bad as Christ," a *Masses* article "As to Patriotism" read (13). In May, the newspaper reported that yet another college had quashed the sale of the *Masses* and that Ward and Gow's sensationalized application of censorship affected the free speech of other radical magazines at New York City's Hunter College:

> Hunter College is the latest to adopt the Ward and Gow censorship, having threatened with expulsion two students who were selling the radical intercollegiate magazine, "Challenge." Why not shake an advertisement out of it?
>
> > "Send your girl to Hunter College.
> > We're a highly moral crowd,
> > For all the good ones are Warded
> > And the naughty ones are Gowed." (7)

In September, frustrated but still with their senses of humor intact, *Masses* editors would report that

> The *Masses* is on the reading tables of the New York Public Library, the Library of Barnard College, the Library of the School of Journalism at Columbia. It is strange the number of respectable people in this community who pay $1 a year for this monthly installment of blasphemy and indecency. I might pause to say that John D. Rockefeller, Jr., has personally subscribed to the *Masses,* though we try to make it as unpleasant reading for him as we possibly can. (Sept. 1916: 5)

Just as Rockefeller couldn't keep away from the *Masses,* newspapers like it, as well as new literary magazines, were being noticed and subscribed to by American readers. None was more impressive than the little magazine *transition*. Founded in 1927 by Eugene Jolas, Maria Jolas, and Elliot Paul, *transition* published work by avant-garde modernists Gertrude Stein, Dylan Thomas, Franz Kafka, e. e. cummings, and James Joyce, whose *Finnegans Wake* it serialized over a period of ten years in 17 installments (Fargnoli and Gillespie, 217).[1] A writer in the *New Masses* attested to the quality of the publication in a review, saying,

> Indeed, it is my sincere belief that *transition* is the most alive and important literary force in our transition civilization: it voices the beginning of epical melodrama on earth, and is ready for great things. But the esoteric whose delight it is to astound the yokelry, in Mencken fashion, is merely serving the cynical bourgeois "liberal" tradition; and plays the role of the opportunist in art.
>
> To get the record straight, it should be clearly understood that James Joyce is a master artist, and Gertrude Stein an occasionally interesting one. Cummings, too, has a biting fine talent. It is the colloquial influence that they exert, and the general "esotericizing" trend of their Method-over-Literature that we find so odious. (18-19)

Another writer praised *transition,* noting in September 1929 that "I always read the magazine *transition* faithfully. . . . The world is our workshop; that is what the Social Revolution means: collective arts shaping the world. It is coming fast; it will change empires, cities, workers, artists, gangsters, children, machines, rivers, cows, and geniuses" (12). Such was the power and scope of the newspapers and little magazines of modernism. It is this very attitude—the "it-is-coming-fast-it-will-change-empires" attitude—that made these organs of avant-garde modernism and proletarian discourse so potentially dangerous and insurgent.

Mark Morrison notes that papers like the *Masses* and its two successors, the *Liberator* and the *New Masses,* allowed modernist writers to identify and retain an audience for their literary and cultural work. Even though Max Eastman and Claude McKay expressed their hesitancy about the literary movement, Morrison notes, both knew that the *Masses* and the *Liberator*

> were also venues through which modernist authors and artists sought audiences. . . . [N]ot only did modernists desire mass audiences, but the impulses of modernism and the very idea of a counterpublic sphere animated each other. *The Little Review* in America, and British little magazines like the *Egoist* and its predecessors the *Freewoman* and *New Freewoman,* tried to foster a broadly based oppositional counterpublic sphere in which aesthetic modernism could be discussed alongside anarchism, sex, radicalism, suffragism, syndicalism, and other such concerns. (169-70)

Like the *Masses,* and the *New Masses,* other little magazines and newspapers of the age contained assortments of avant-garde literature and art mixed with good political soapboxing. To that end, many editors and their publishers suffered protracted legal difficulties. The *Masses,* for example, was forced to cease publication in 1917 because of bankruptcy.

Soon after the United States entered World War I, Congress passed the Espionage Act of June 15, 1917. Not since the eighteenth century could words as well as actions be deemed treasonous. At this time, Postmaster General Albert Burleson was targeting the radical presses, trying to find reasons to suppress their publications. In fact, the laws that Postmaster Burleson invoked against the *Masses* eventually cost almost every socialist publication its mailing license. When the August 1917 issue of the *Masses* was ready for publication, the newspaper's business manager, Merrill Rogers, took an issue to censor George Creel for preview. He was given the go-ahead to mail the issue. When a copy of the same issue was presented to New York City Postmaster Thomas Patten, he sent a copy to Washington. "Unmailable" was the verdict returned, and the *Masses* was denied use of the mails. Though the editors agreed to delete any offending material, the post office would not specify which particular parts of the issue were treasonous, only that the *Masses* had "conspired to obstruct enlistment and recruitment" of soldiers during the first world war (Fishbein, 26). Since the editors could not mail out to subscribers copies of their August issue, they had to sustain the publication of their magazine with revenue only from newsstand sales.

The following month, when the editors presented to the censor and postmaster a copy of their September issue, they were denied second-class mailing privileges because they had failed to mail out an August issue: the postmaster reasoned that because editors were unable to mail out the previous month's issue, the *Masses* could no longer be considered a "monthly" periodical! Stripped of their second-class mailing rights (much less expensive than first-class mail rates), eventually the *Masses* fell into bankruptcy. Unable to sustain itself without unobstructed access to the mails, the *Masses* went out of business in December 1917. Furious, and certain that their rights had been violated, the editors decided to sue, and after a notorious trial, they won. Judge Learned Hand passed down a landmark decision and argued that "to [equate] agitation, legitimate as such, with direct incitement to violent resistance, is to disregard the tolerance of all methods of political agitation which in normal times is a safeguard of free government. The distinction is not a scholastic one, but a hard-bought acquisition in the fight for freedom" (Zurier, 61). Hand's decision, clearly ahead of its time, was appealed and was overturned in a counter-suit, *United States v. Eastman et al.,* in 1918. By this time the journal had ceased publication, having been bankrupted by censorship restrictions. In the second trial, the jury split and the judge declared a mistrial. Another conspiracy trial against the *Masses* was initiated in October 1918. This time, the jury handed down a divided verdict—eight for acquittal, four for conviction. The defendants went free but the effects of the long struggle left an indelible mark not only on editors and readers of the *Masses,* but on writers and artists whose work united expression and activism. American culture and the history of political radicalism would never be the same following these years of radicalism, censorship, governmental intervention, and the use of brute force and legal muscle to squash dissent.

It is not as if the *Masses'* editors in particular were hounded; in fact, most little magazines and newspapers daring to tread the waters of political insurgency and revolutionary aesthetics were not safe. Nor was Dreiser's novel *The Genius,* the Russian Ballet, or serious theater safe, as the October 1916 article that opens this chapter attests.

J. Edgar Hoover's FBI had a hand in manipulating the pressure put on these organizations. He not only collected information about editors and writers associated with modernism's newspapers and little magazines, but he targeted especially the African American papers and journals. In *Terrible Honesty: Mongrel Manhattan in the 1920s,* Ann Douglas notes that the Department of Justice harassed with equal vehemence editors and writers associated with black publications: "The Justice Department, investigating black newspapers and journals at this time, concluded that they were 'antagonistic to the white race and openly, defiantly assertive of [their] own equality and even superiority.'" J. Edgar Hoover, she continues, "singled out *The Messenger* as 'by long odds the most able and most dangerous of all Negro publications'" (325).[2]

Wallace Thurman was one of the African American writers associated with *The Messenger,* but left it in October 1926 for the position of circulation manager at a white magazine called *World Tomorrow* (Lewis, 194). The dream that motivated Thurman in these years was that of starting his own literary magazine, one that was distinct from the NAACP's *Crisis* and the Urban League's *Opportunity.* He imagined a fiery publication that didn't do "literature on the side," as he thought the others treated African American literature;

his magazine would be devoted to literature and art. Thurman would devote countless hours toward the fulfillment of his dream. David Levering Lewis explains:

> [Wallace Thurman] spent every spare moment he had in raising funds to support what he hoped would be his forthcoming venture, the publication of a magazine devoted to showcasing the art and writing of African Americans. He, Richard Bruce Nugent, Zora Neale Hurston, and Aaron Douglas met regularly to discuss the venture. Thurman almost went broke. When the first issue finally did come out, it was printed against Thurman's marker, an IOU to Service Bell, the refined Harlem printer. (Lewis, 194)

The November publication of *Fire!!* took its readers and supporters by surprise but it also caught them off guard. Lewis notes, for example "Professor Brawley found it so disgusting that he predicted, 'If Uncle Sam ever finds out about it, it will be debarred from the mails. . . . Vulgarity has been mistaken for art'" (194). He did not appreciate what he saw as the quarterly's blunt treatment of unseemly and inappropriate topics. Lewis also reports that one of Countee Cullen's friends told him that simply mentioning *Fire!!* to W. E. B. DuBois, who edited *Crisis,* "hurt [his] feelings so much that he would hardly talk" to him; moreover, even local friends and cronies joined in the censure—editors of *Fire!!* were given the silent treatment when they went out to Craig's, a high-end restaurant of the Harlem literati. A critic for the Baltimore *Afro-American* boasted, "I have just tossed the first issue of *Fire!!* into the fire" (194). When the remaining stacks of the magazine burned by accident, the continuation of the enterprise seemed unlikely. A year later, though, the same group would try again with a new review called *Harlem.*

The little magazines and radical newspapers of modernism were essential to the dissemination of modern literary talents looking to publish short stories, poetry, or excerpts of longer works, especially at a time (as we shall see in the next chapter) when modern literature was developing a reputation for being obscene. But more important than providing publication opportunities for writers, these newspapers and magazines served to heighten the social consciousness of readers. And it is in this capacity, I argue, that writers and editors associated with some of the magazines and newspapers discussed above drew the attention of J. Edgar Hoover and the bureau.

Writers and editors of little magazines and newspapers educated readers about the issues of the day, encouraging them to act like engaged citizens. Tackling head-on issues such as class struggle, the unthinkable rise in the number of lynchings after World War I and the absence of anti-lynching legislation, the rise in poverty, police brutality, racial stereotyping, suffragism, free speech and censorship, war and protest, feminism, industrialist's greed, and so on, weekly articles assailed readers with up-to-the-minute protestations about American and global injustices. These publications were important for galvanizing political action and winning supporters to causes as varied as workers' strikes across America, the Sacco and Vanzetti arrests and subsequent executions, the Scottsboro Boys' arrests and notorious trials, the Ludlow Strike, the Centralia Massacre, the Harlan County murders, the Mooney-Billings frame-up, the Gauley Bridge disaster, and countless other events that wanted political action. These little magazines and newspapers also contained eyewitness accounts of the young century's most formative events: the Russian Revolution; the Palmer Raids; the 1919 race riots across the nation, leading to what Claude McKay would call the "Red Summer"; and the General Strike of 1919. The publications reinforced an activist ideology, and not only brought together a collective readership but helped to construct and invent one, by encouraging readers to engage in public (and published) debates about the issues raised in their pages; by inviting them into the memorable kinds of conversations Margaret Anderson and Jane Heap would carry on in the *Little Review;* by organizing readers' balls and workers' outings; and by encouraging a counterrevolution to dethrone repressive forces in America. As such, they were indeed trade papers for revolutionaries.

CHAPTER SIX

Modernism, Obscenity, and Social Purity Discourse

In several of James Joyce's letters to friends, editors, publishers, and associates, he complains of his fate at the hands of dutiful censors. On Christmas Day 1912, for example, he wrote W. B. Yeats of his "unfortunate book *Dubliners*" and asked Yeats if he would "intervene in its favour" (*Selected Letters,* 206). Almost a year later he wrote to publisher Grant Richards about his continued exasperation, and outlined the history of his "luckless book":

> Dear Sir,
>
> I sent you two years ago a copy of a letter which I sent to the press concerning my book *Dubliners.* Since then the book has had a still more eventful career. It was printed completely and the entire edition of 1000 copies was burned by the publisher. A complete set of printed proofs is in my possession. In view of the very strange history of the book—its acceptance and refusal by two houses, my letter to the present king, his reply, my letter to the press, my negotiations with the second publisher—negotiations which ended in malicious burning of

the whole first edition—and furthermore in view of the fact that
Dublin, of which the book treats so uncompromisingly, is at present
the centre of general interest, I think that perhaps the time has come
for my luckless book to appear. (November 23, 1913; *Selected Letters,*
207-08)

Joyce enclosed to Grant Richards a copy of his open letter, published
under the title "A Curious History" in *The Egoist.* The title puns, I
think, on the word *curiosa,* a code word used in advertisements to sell
erotica or to mark restricted-access sections in bookstores. First
published in the January 15, 1914 issue of one of modernism's new
little magazines, *Egoist,* "A Curious History" alludes to an earlier
letter to the editor Joyce sent to several publishers on August 17,
1911, which was published in *Sinn Fein* on September 2, 1911
(Dublin) and the *Northern Whig* on August 26, 1911 (Belfast).[1]

Though Joyce sounds mournful, he actually may have exploited
the attention that playing the *artiste manqué* afforded him, and may
have encouraged more of the publicity in order to hasten his own
celebrity. This is not to say that Joyce enjoyed having the publication
of his works forestalled by watchful censors or social purity zealots
who insisted that because his work was lewd, indecent, or obscene, it
could not be disseminated without corrupting the moral senses of the
average person. These accusations certainly frustrated Joyce, brought
him real grief, and threatened to compromise his aesthetic. But I am
suggesting that he saw in this unfolding pantomime a very specific
role he could play. Since he knew he had to endure the censors, he
likely thought he might as well try to promote his hardships
(recirculating his open letter, for example), and to comment on their
assessments of his work in his writings.

Joyce's work was entering the literary marketplace at a time when
censorship regulations in Britain and the United States were affecting
the dissemination of modernist art. The rhetoric of social purity was
shaping the discourses of the day, especially when it came to

discussions of literature and decency. As Joyce shopped his collection of 15 short stories (*Dubliners*) around to publishers in Britain and France between the years 1904 and 1914, several of them refused to have anything to do with his book. Grant Richards, for example, the English publisher who eventually would issue the collection after some ten years of back-and-forth negotiations with the author regarding suggested expurgations and emendations, feared the attacks on his press that would follow from the publication of such questionable material. His firm had recently suffered grievous financial difficulties and bankruptcy. Richards insisted that Joyce "leave out altogether" the collection's second story, "An Encounter," where two young Dublin boys skip school for the day and encounter a licentious man in the park. After initiating a sinister conversation with the young unnamed narrator about how he enjoys whipping young boys who have young girl for sweethearts, the man leaves to go off to the edge of the field to masturbate. "I say. Look what he's doing!" the young Mahony cries out to the unnamed narrator. "He's a queer old josser" (*Dubliners*, 26).

Joyce's queer old josser certainly would catch the attention of England's censors and social purists, Grant Richards knew, though surely no one could deny the existence of such a universal degenerate. Richards went so far as to recommend other publishers to Joyce, biographer Richard Ellmann notes, and even though he had already contracted the collection of stories under his own imprint, Richards "knew too well how a successful vice prosecution might lead to punitive fines, imprisonment and a second bankruptcy" (Mullin, 14).

Joyce's subsequent negotiations with publisher George Roberts to bring the collection out in Dublin under the name Maunsel and Co. similarly perished when Roberts panicked; his printer John Falconer panicked with him, and refused to surrender to Joyce the already typeset sheets of the collection in the event that his work on the book would provide grounds for implicating him in a vice prosecution, too. Mullin notes that Joyce's early experiences with social purity crusades and publishers' panic attacks indicate the degree to which his works were open to charges of lewdness, and made issuing Joyce's books too risky a venture for commercial publishers.

One consequence of the sexual suggestiveness of his works was that his books would come out from small, unestablished presses:

> [A]ccordingly *A Portrait of the Artist as a Young Man* and *Ulysses* would issue from presses which, like Joyce's own proposed "Liffey Press," were peripheral to the mainstream publishing industry and dedicated to evading the strictures imposed by "comstockery." These were the little magazines and hastily assembled private publishing houses of avant-garde Modernism, and their interest in Joyce was initially piqued by his open letter on the *Dubliners* travails, "A Curious History," which appeared in January 1914 in place of Ezra Pound's usual column on the arts in *The Egoist.* (Mullin, 15)

When Ezra Pound contacted Joyce and offered to assist getting him into print and circulated, Joyce had just come off what Joseph Kelly explains as "enormous difficulties because of the frank themes and languages of *Dubliners,* [and he] must have been heartened by Pound's candor. And to have his work solicited, after so many disappointments, must have been a tonic to Joyce's injured pride" (*Our Joyce,* 63). A bit over-the-top (but understandably so), Kelly identifies Joyce's initial encounter with Pound as "the most influential event in Joyce's literary career" (63). Joyce was likely unaware that *Egoist* was facing financial difficulties and had been predicted by Pound to fold within a few months. In Joyce's private battle with censorship and prudishness, Pound saw a public "cause" that might save his little magazine.

Joyce responded to Pound's offer by scripting the open letter "A Curious History" for *Egoist.* His letter decried his victimization by the institutions of "interminable and familiar censorship" (Mullin,

15), and brought Joyce the attention he desired. In 1914, Grant Richards published *Dubliners* and *Egoist* began to serialize Joyce's novel *A Portrait of the Artist as a Young Man.* The publications of these works, however, were not without duress. Printers involved with *Egoist* quickly protested their involvement with Joyce's work, and publishing Joyce's novel about the development of a young male artist in Edwardian Dublin proved just as troublesome.

Modernism's little magazines and smaller presses regularly published notices of the difficulties that the little-known Joyce was braving as he tried to place his work in public circulation. Joyce became a symbol, a *cause célèbre,* attracting the attention of, and being championed by, the voices of a unified avant-garde set against Victorian and Edwardian squeamishness as represented by the censors and other state apparatuses. Bolstered by the attention and support his open letter in *Egoist* brought, unafraid to tell the world his tale of woe, and spurred on by the martyrdom such self-dramatized victimization narratives offered him, Joyce was unafraid to make noise about his experiences with censorship and to alert fellow writers and artists to its growing presence in the industry. In fact, Richard Ellmann pointed to this penchant in the writer for display, and described Joyce's life as moving from crisis to crisis, exacerbation to exacerbation. Though he argued on behalf of no one but himself in his letters to the editor and his open letter, Joyce tacitly became the symbol of repressionist attacks on writers by social purity crusades. He succeeded in raising a battle cry against such forces; that is, editorials and notices followed in little magazines and newspapers promoting free speech and decrying the censors' small-mindedness. These published statements were circulated to a robust crowd of like-minded readers, many of whom were participating in the project of modernism as writers, artists, or cultural workers ready to rally around yet another manifestation of the state's desire to influence control and exert authority over writers. They responded publicly and in print to Joyce's difficult affairs. Katherine Mullin notes that

"to read these exhilarated, often passionate, invariably defiant bulletins from Modernism's little magazines is to participate in a heady
atmosphere of anticipation, frustration, triumph, disappointment
and, above all, ideological mission." (18)

From the beginning, then, Joyce's work was subject to the reserva-
tions of editors, the uneasiness of print setters, and the uncertainties of
publishers, all responding in advance to what they imagined would be
the pronouncements of state censors. Even the solicitors with whom
Joyce met to discuss his publication hardships were squeamish about
working with him, and refused to allow their names to be connected to
Joyce's book in any way. Confounded by the inconsistencies in
publishers' objections, Joyce cited as an example that one publisher did
not object to a passage about Edward VII while the king was alive but
that another publisher identified the same passage as offensive after the
king had already "passed into history" (*Selected Letters,* 198; August 17,
1911). Even Edward's successor, his son George V, would not get
himself entangled, and commanded his private secretary to respond to
Joyce's letter of August 1, 1911 to say that it was "inconsistent with rule
for His Majesty to express his opinion in such cases" (*Selected Letters,*
198). Thus, Katherine Mullin is right to open her study of Joyce and
social purity with the assertion that "Joyce's publication history is a
history of censorship" (1).

The story of modernism is the story of censorship, too. Writers
as diverse as James Joyce, James Baldwin, Claude McKay, Theodore
Dreiser, Thomas Wolfe, Djuna Barnes, Sherwood Anderson, Zora
Neale Hurston, D. H. Lawrence, Richard Bruce Nugent, Max
Eastman, John Dos Passos, Floyd Dell, Ernest Hemingway, Langston
Hughes, Radclyffe Hall, and countless others were at some point in
their careers tormented by their unsuccessful efforts to see their work
published. The notoriously precise Comstock Law, invoked in
indecency disputes, prohibited "every obscene, lewd, lascivious,
indecent, filthy, or vile article, matter, thing, device, or substance;
and . . . [e]very article . . . which is advertised or described in a

manner calculated to lead another to use or apply it for preventing conception or producing abortion, or for any indecent or immoral use." What modern writer could successfully pass through such a shrimp net?

In 1922, Jay Gertzman reports, John Sumner formed a special committee to "decide if erotically explicit manuscripts (by D. H. Lawrence, James Branch Cabell, Sinclair Lewis, Ben Hecht, or Theodore Dreiser, to name a few targets) should be published" (113). The *New York Times* reported on the new committee in an article titled "Plans Laid to Censor All New Literature." Sumner is quoted as arguing the following position:

> Everyone knows that many of the authors of the "younger school" are lacking in literary merit and have made cheap reputations by turning to salacity after failing to command attention by legitimate work. Their vogue is largely the result of a conspiracy on the part of salacious writers of the new school to praise one another, and they have enlisted many critics in the log-rolling. (Aug. 4, 1922: 1, 7; Gertzman, 113)

In a climate such as this, where a network of modernist writers who share a bank of artistic principles and methodological aesthetics can so easily and without reprimand be compared to a back-slapping group of corrupt logrollers, where lies the hope?

For many modernists, their work lay dormant on publishers' desks, awaiting the bravery of an intrepid or just plain resolute editor. Maxwell Perkins, who worked as an editor at Charles Scribner's Sons in New York City, was one of those kind of editors who didn't necessarily fear the censor's intrusive eye, though he did suffer the vicissitudes of getting something past his boss, "Old Scribner." A. Scott Berg explains in his biography of Perkins, *Max Perkins: Editor of Genius,* that when he was new to the business, Perkins "had discovered great new talents—such as F. Scott Fitzgerald, Ernest Hemingway, and Thomas Wolfe—and had staked his career on them, defying the established tastes of the earlier generation and revolutionizing American literature. He had been associated with one firm, Charles Scribner's Sons, for thirty-six years and during this time, no editor at any house even approached his record for finding gifted authors and getting them into print" (3-4). Perkins wasn't ruled by squeamishness for the language or subject matter so new to modern literature, and in fact, championed its innovations. Numerous legends had sprung up about Perkins after 36 years in the business. One such story was that he agreed to publish Hemingway's first novel, *The Sun Also Rises,* "sight unseen, then had to fight to keep his job when the manuscript arrived because it contained off-color language" (Berg, 4). Berg also reports that

> Another favorite Perkins story concerned his confrontation with ultraconservative publisher, Charles Scribner, over the four-letter words in Hemingway's second novel, *A Farewell to Arms.* Perkins was said to have jotted down the troublesome words he wanted to discuss—*shit, fuck,* and *piss*—on his desk calendar, without regard to the calendar's heading: "Things to Do Today." Old Scribner purportedly noticed the list and remarked to Perkins that he was in great trouble if he needed to remind himself to do these things. (4-5)

When Perkins tried a third time to convince colleagues at Scribners to publish Fitzgerald's *This Side of Paradise,* he circulated the author's completed revision and prepared to present it at the editors' meeting. The older editors spoke first. William Brownell pronounced the book "frivolous." "Old CS" [Charles Scribner] said "I am proud of my imprint. I cannot publish fiction that is without literary value" (15). The matter, Berg notes, seemed closed, until Old CS asked Perkins what *he* thought.

> Perkins stood and began to pace the room. "My feeling," he explained, "is that a publisher's first allegiance is to talent. And if

we aren't going to publish a talent like this, it is a very serious thing." He contended that the ambitious Fitzgerald would be able to find another publisher for this novel and young authors would follow him: "Then we might as well go out of business. . . . If we're going to turn down the likes of Fitzgerald, I will lose all interest in publishing books." The vote of hands was taken. The young editors tied the old. There was a silence. Then Scribner said he wanted more time to think it over. (15-16)

The rest, as they say, is history. Scribner's Sons published Fitzgerald's *This Side of Paradise* in 1920 and launched Fitzgerald's career.

One thing that distinguished Scribner's Sons from some of the other publishing houses in the city after the First World War is that it had not yet suffered protracted prosecutions by the New York Society for the Suppression of Vice, as many of the other publishing houses had. "Its books never transgressed the bounds of 'decency,'" Berg explains. "There were none of the newer writers who were attracting attention—Theodore Dreiser, Sinclair Lewis, Sherwood Anderson" (13). With Perkins's signing of modern talents such as Fitzgerald, Hemingway, Erskine Caldwell, and Thomas Wolfe— writers who at one time or another would become embroiled in debates about the degeneracy of their work—things would change, and fast, at Scribner's Sons.

Always at the forefront of the struggles between modern litera- ture and indecency was the hand-picked successor to Anthony Comstock as secretary to the New York Society for the Suppression of Vice, John S. Sumner. Jay Gertzman notes in his study of the trade in erotica from 1920 to 1940, that "It was Sumner's lot in the Roaring Twenties to help lead a doomed ideological struggle in days when the winds of change were the only constant in the moral climate" (114). Sumner had filed charges against Margaret Anderson and Jane Heap, which led to the notorious *Little Review* trial, and was responsible for "hounding" Dreiser (*The Genius*), D. H. Lawrence

(*Lady Chatterley's Lover*), Radclyffe Hall (*The Well of Loneliness*), and others.

Gertzman notes that Sumner "kept his ears and eyes trained on the Gotham Book Mart, but not because the store specialized in erotica" (154). Instead, he knew that the shop carried works published by New York's younger publishers such as Seltzer, Liveright, and Charles and Albert Boni, who

> published avant-garde European writers in America, [and] the Gotham brought them to the attention of New Yorkers by carrying as wide a range of their work as possible, especially including the little magazines they wrote for. Expatriate American poets and novelists made it a point to visit Frances Steloff when they returned to the United States; her kindness to them and her respect for their accomplishments is well known. Since the sexual frankness of these writers, and their American contemporaries, was integral to their work, the Gotham would have been a bookstore in which readers could find daring and intelligently conceived erotic materials and still exhibit respectable tastes. (154)

After Steloff became the owner of the Gotham Book Mart, "the younger school of modernist writers was Gotham's special interest" (154), Gertzman adds. Given this, Sumner kept close tabs on the place and staked out shops like the Gotham that negotiated the thin line between modern literature and obscenity.

The Gotham Book Mart was singled out for Sumner's vigilance, Gertzman notes, and Frances Steloff became one of his favorite rogues to pursue. Gertzman explains that

> Steloff's commitment to literary excellence included distributing works by some writers with erotic sensibilities. Not only boldly outspoken modernists, however, made this bookseller one of Sumner's most closely watched suspects. Like other upscale bookstores,

the Gotham stocked various kinds of literary and scientific erotica. Moralists also had reason to suspect Steloff's New York colleagues Harry F. Marks and the Holliday Book Shop. (90)

Interestingly, vice squads usually left alone what were called "high hat" (that is, Fifth Avenue) stores that risked selling obscene material, since "the more secure the community status of a bookstore, the smaller the chance of what the anti-vice societies would call 'fair' media coverage" (90).

In 1935, Sumner brought charges against Steloff for carrying André Gide's volume *If It Die*. (This is the episode Christopher Morley defended in a 1936 column in the *Saturday Review of Literature* as discussed in chapter 1.) Morris Ernst defended the Gotham Book Mart after Sumner and his men raided the bookstore looking for obscene materials. They found and confiscated, among other examples of pornography, the book *Hsi Men Ching*. In a brief defending the bookstore as well as the book, Ernst "described in detail the historical and literary importance of *Hsi Men Ching*, [calling it] 'a veritable source book of Chinese manners and customs,' whose illustrations were not only appropriate to the text but 'decorative, not realistic'" (Gertzman, 165). The whole "test," it seems to me of what was considered "appropriate" for the average reader, then, was this question of realism. If the illustrations were "decorative," they were not pornographic. If they were representational, then they were. The same standards of decency seemed to apply as a test to modern literature. If a novel or collection of stories was what Ernst would call "decorative"—that is, highly stylized, full of stylistic flourishes, narrative experimentation, neologisms, experimental chronology, polyvocal and multilingual aspects (characteristics that have come to describe elements of "high" or "elite" modernism in order to distinguish it from other modernisms)—these works made it past the censors because they didn't threaten to destabilize anything. They were decorative. On the other hand, if the literature leaned more towards realism, as Dreiser's surely did, and spoke of struggle in real terms and not as an abstraction, then it was accused either of being base or of being artless. Joyce's uncompromising treatment of Dublin, his scrupulously mean attention to detail and his fidelity to verisimilitude, seem in part greatly responsible for the book's having taken so long to come into print. As Joyce was engaged in these extended battles from Trieste to get his work published, other artists, in particularly those participating in the "scandalous" International Exhibition of Modern Art mounted for an elite audience in 1913 on Manhattan's East Side, were fighting against similar ideologies about art and representation. They found their work received, reviewed and ridiculed along the lines of the same polemic.[2]

After I requested the FBI file of John S. Sumner, I received a response from the Record/Information Dissemination Section of the Records Management Division of the US Department of Justice. The letter informed me that material had been located on John S. Sumner but "this material is unavailable and has been placed on 'special locate'" (Dec. 20, 2003). I have filed an administrative appeal with the Office of Information and Privacy. Like J. Edgar Hoover, Sumner exerted such a reckonable force over publishers that many of them, to eliminate the threat of a vice prosecution, exercised auto-censorship in anticipation of legal nastiness, and would decide not to publish something because they feared a protracted and costly legal entanglement. Such was the case with Jonathan Cape's rejection of Beckett's novel *Dream of Fair to Middling Women*. In a biography of the publisher and his eponymous firm, Michael Howard notes that one of the firm's editors, Edward Garnett, missed a "sure thing" when he passed on Beckett's novel because he thought it was indecent. It had already been rejected by another publishing house (Chatto) on those grounds. Howard explains:

> During the summer heat wave of 1932 Garnett perhaps dropped a
> catch, just before he went on holiday in August. Taking a pile of

manuscripts with him to Land's End he reported on a novel called *Dream of Fair-to-Middling Women.* Jonathan had told him it was by a young Irishman who had already published a short critical biography of Proust with Chatto and they had turned the novel down, "believing that the Censor would object to one chapter in it." Garnett wrote:

> "I wouldn't touch this with a barge-pole. Beckett probably is a clever fellow, but here he has elaborated a slavish and rather incoherent imitation of Joyce, most eccentric in language and full of disgustingly affected passages—also *indecent:* this school is damned—and you wouldn't sell the book even on its title. Chatto was right to turn it down."

> Samuel Beckett was then twenty-six. His novel was not accepted, but after two years Chatto published him again: And 35 years later, as "the most respected and influential innovator of the English language since Joyce," he was awarded the Nobel Prize. (Howard, 137)

By 1938 Beckett had become so frustrated with the anxieties of censors—whether vice prosecutors or publishers—that he directed willful comments to them in his novel *Murphy,* as I have shown in chapter 2. Though Garnett's pronouncement on Beckett's and his contemporaries' indecency—"this school is damned"—thankfully was wrong, it sums up the spirit that prevailed at the time when modernism's most innovative authors were trying to place their work.

Joyce's struggle with the censors was a symptom of culture that pervaded early twentieth century attitudes and practices, affecting not only the publishing industry but the reading public, too, determining the public's intellectual life at this crucial juncture between Victorianism and modernism. Joyce and his fiction, Mullin notes, were "conscripted into Modernism's war on social purity" (11).

Joyce responded to the censors in a number of interesting ways, and grew to become an agent provocateur where censorship was concerned. For example, he incorporated the titles of censored books into his stories, flaunting his understanding of the history of censorship and commenting at the same time that at least *his* characters were allowed to own and read the censored titles. The narrator of "Araby," one of the more seemingly innocuous stories in *Dubliners,* for example, tells of a priest whose reading included *The Memoirs of Vidocq* (29), episodes of police and detective stories written to entice readers. Francois-Jules Vidocq was "a master of disguises and duplicities, one who . . . (with *sang froid)* experienced every possible escapade on both sides of the law" (Gifford, 43). Vidocq's *Memoirs* provided narratives of vice as well as stories of its reprimand. First a criminal, then an informer, later a detective, Vidocq could provoke crimes, enact them, describe them in rich and titillating detail for his readers, and discuss the disciplining of its criminals. Such was the all-around allure of the *Memoirs,* which Gifford notes had been bowdlerized by publishers and censors. In Joyce's story, *The Memoirs of Vidocq* appears as just a simple book title in a list of books a previous tenant left in someone else's home; but its presence in the narrative exposes (and thereby taunts) the vagaries of censorship.

A result of heightened social purity campaigns, the fear of protracted episodes with censors began to affect publishers in Britain, Ireland, and the United States, and led to the bizarre practice of self-censorship, as we have seen in the Jonathan Cape example above. Mullin describes self-censorship as "a natural response by publishers and printers not only to the legal threat posed by vigilantes, but to the considerable popular support their campaign attracted" (Mullin, 8). Praise for high-profile national campaigns against licentiousness in literature began to appear in newspapers, which in turn spawned their own social purity campaigns in which they crusaded against vice publications and collected large funds for its prosecution. "The Guarantee Fund" established by Britain's newspaper *The Spectator,* for example, eventually raised the considerable sum of £720 18*s* to combat sordid fiction (9).

Affected by the abstemiousness of groups like the New York Society for the Suppression of Vice and other censoring agents, the bureau's J. Edgar Hoover seized opportunities to monitor writers and publishers and to curb the dissemination of their work. In FBI files, modern writers were described as manufacturing filth, vulgarity, and/ or anti-American sentiment, and Hoover feared that through their filth, they could win their bewildered audiences to communism, socialism, or some other form of the Red menace. He also was concerned about the frank sexuality in the literature, and feared that a generation of readers would be lost to unnamable perversions. Edward De Grazia says that "Hoover subscribed to a 'monkey-see, monkey-do' theory of the evils of pornography" (564). If one young mind were corrupted, then his friends would succumb and the moral fabric of Americanism would start to unravel, one dirty book at a time.

A disturbing offshoot of the discourse about modern literature's perversions affected writers not only in the prepublication stage but also after publication. Often, public libraries would bend to the wills of the censors, and ban books of a certain fame: "To be boycotted by the libraries was a heavy blow to any author, since their purchasing power permitted them to cover the publishing costs of a novel" (Mullin, 9). What with the publishing industry, the booksellers, the New York Society for the Suppression of Vice, the FBI, the newspapers, and now the libraries participating in the censorship wars, it is no wonder that Dreiser would cry out in utter exasperation, "A literary reign of terror is being attempted. Where will it end?"

Hoover's role in the literary reign of terror included, as we have learned, attempts on his agents' part to discredit Dreiser and others, to silence them, and to dissuade them from participating *as writers* in politicized events. Hoover also placed bureau-developed insiders in some of the nation's largest and most influential publishing firms, as I have discussed in chapter 1 (Doubleday, Holt, Scribner's, and William Sloane Associates) or he cultivated as "Friendlies" workers who already were on the payrolls at these firms. Hoover also had insiders on the staffs of magazines, who alerted him to the sorts of stories that were being considered or drafted for forthcoming issues; they also mentioned what books were up for review and who was being assigned the job, and they supplied him with the names of poets or fiction writers who would be featured in their magazines.

Athan Theoharis explains in *Secret Files* that from the beginning of Hoover's career as acting director of the FBI, the bureau chief realized the importance of maintaining information about obscene or indecent activities. He notes that

> [Hoover] found pornography personally distasteful and feared its impact on the morals of his fellow citizens; but he also recognized that an influential constituency of religious and civic leaders shared his attitudes. In March 1925, shortly after his appointment to the Directorship, Hoover authorized creation of a discrete Obscene File and devised a special submission procedure to ensure that "obscene or indecent" materials would be routed to this centrally maintained source. (295)

Theoharis adds that the creation of this file promoted Hoover's interests in several ways, not least among them that the bureau's prosecutions for obscenity could secure for the FBI some very favorable publicity (295). Though Hoover took over the directorship of the bureau after Anthony Comstock's death and almost a decade into John S. Sumner's work since 1915 as secretary of the Society for the Suppression of Vice, Hoover had to bear the same kinds of criticism aimed at those two social purists, since his bureau supported, ideologically at least, "comstockery" and the suppression of obscene materials.

Like J. Edgar Hoover, John S. Sumner tried to change the image of his organization after he inherited it, especially after frequent lampoons in the press. Andrea Friedman observes in *Prurient Interests: Gender, Democracy, and Obscenity in NYC, 1909-1945* that

Sumner tried to change the makeup of the New York Society for the Suppression of Vice by recruiting "prominent Catholics to join its Board of Managers . . . to make the board more representative, and also solicited a wide range of child-saving organizations 'to accept the public duty of directorship in this Society'" (131-32).[3] Another effort to educate the public about the new makeup of the Society took place in 1923, the year that marked the fiftieth anniversary of the society: a brochure announcing the Society's anniversary fundraising scheme featured a statement detailing "what [the Society] is" and "what it is not." Friedman reports that the statement stressed the New York Society for the Suppression of Vice is not "'narrow, prudish nor puritanical.' It does not seek the right to censor nor has it any 'rights or powers of oppression'" (132).[4] Sumner's attempts to reinvent the society failed. Regardless of iterating what it *didn't* do, or the rights it *didn't* have, the public, especially modern writers, were more concerned about what the Society *could* and *would* do.

When F. Scott Fitzgerald penned the apocalyptic statement "culture follows money," he was not writing about the pornography industry but he might well have been. As Allison Pease notes in *Modernism, Mass Culture, and the Aesthetics of Obscenity*, objections to pornography and obscenity can be traced as far back as the 1600s, and they developed not because the content of the material was objectionable but because the producers of pornography were able to evade licensing and taxing fees, thereby keeping all of their profits themselves and lawfully skirting taxes and tariffs. The conflicts between pornography and culture, obscenity and decency, lewdness and morality, in other words, have always had their genesis in skirmishes over money. The motives for banning obscene or lascivious work, Pease argues, stem from commercial as well as moral concerns.

A similar phenomenon occurred in the art world, centering on modern art and the problem of taxing nonrepresentational works of art. *Brancusi vs. United States* (1927-28) focused attention on the work of sculptor Constantin Brancusi and called into question whether the label "work of art" could be applied appropriately to a nonrepresentational work. If it were considered "art," it would not be subject to import duty (40 percent of its declared value), since art was considered a concept, an idea. At the time of the 1927 trial, an art object was tariff-free under U.S. Customs regulations, which is where the Brancusi "problem" started. Painter and photographer Edward Steichen, owner of the piece and a friend of the artist's, was required to pay the tariff of $240 to retrieve the sculpture *Bird in Space* if he wished to keep it.[5] As Margit Rowell suggests, "It goes without saying that for all those involved—lawyers, artists, critics, collectors, art dealers—the issue at stake went far beyond the concrete case of the piece of sculpture serving as an example. The battle was purely and simply about the free circulation of art" (9). As in early battles over the definition of pornography, commercial interests also initiated the important *Brancusi vs. United States* debates.

Striking similarities exist between the discourses of social purity and the discourses of anticommunism. Not only are both couched in the language of the "crusade," but antivice and anticommunism draw on the rhetoric of war. Just as J. Edgar Hoover labeled communism the "fifth column," New York's Archbishop Spellman borrowed the phrase to label *obscenity* a "'fifth column' that represented the most dangerous sort of subversion from within" (Friedman, 184). Moreover, both Sumner and Hoover argued that the corrupting forces came from outside of the United States, and were efforts to destabilize America and the strength of her forces. War, in fact, served as one of the excuses for beefing up antivice crusades. Sumner wrote in response to a letter from the Authors League protesting the suppression of Dreiser's *The Genius* in 1916 that "we need to uphold our standards of decency more than ever in face of this foreign and imitation foreign invasion rather than to make those things which are vicious and indecent so familiar as to become common and representative of American life and manners" (quoted in Gertzman, 114).

Hoover, too, thought that vice was funded and disseminated by foreign interests, that profits from Japanese and Russian pornography sales in the United States, for example, funded anti-American propaganda. Because Hoover and Sumner shared similar concerns, I am eager to read Sumner's bureau file, now that I know that one exists and that it has been placed on "special locate"—a nebulous bureau term. I am curious to learn how he is depicted in his file, and how his ideological mission (what Gertzman called Sumner's "doomed ideological struggle in days when the winds of change were the only constant in the moral climate," 114) survived the vagaries of the modern era.

Ironically, then, at the same time that modernists were rallying around Joyce, who was making himself out to be the poster child of dispossessed writers, a victim alienated and prevented from seeing his writings put in circulation because of outmoded social purity discourses and institutionalized paradigms of propriety, J. Edgar Hoover and his men were beginning to pay attention to modernist writers who, in his opinion, were hastening the devolution of the institutions Hoover and his men endorsed, sanctioned, and protected at all costs. By making noise to whoever would listen (even contacting the king, he told Grant Richards in his November 1913 letter), Joyce succeeded in calling attention to himself and to his work.

Joyce's self-promotional campaign attracted the attention of Sumner and his men, who would propel *Ulysses* into the limelight in 1920 with the *Little Review* trial, which would set other things in motion—the bureau's now destroyed file on Margaret Anderson (as discussed in chapter 2), for example. While Joyce was constructing his "poor little me" narrative—and it was certainly one that would work for him—Sumner may have wondered what all of the commotion was about. When the *Little Review* began to reprint Joyce's novel *Ulysses* serially, beginning with the Spring 1918 number, it was only a matter of time before Anderson and Jane Heap would have someone walk into their Greenwich Village bookstore and serve them with papers for their arrest. As Anderson proudly noted, "We were the first to publish this masterpiece and the first to be arrested for it" (De Grazia, 9). Though the more important trial would take place more than a decade later, the questions raised by the book and its writer continue to remain important ones, and continue to be essential to our understanding of twentieth century censorship history in the United States. Though Judge John M. Woolsey found that Joyce's 1922 novel *Ulysses* was *not* obscene—thereby lifting the US ban and releasing the book for its American publication with Random House—Woolsey couldn't help but add that the book was "somewhat emetic," as well. Thus, Joyce is both endorsed and abandoned by the same pronouncement of the judge. Joyce's modernist "arsethetic" once more gets the better of him.

Ironically, it would get the better of Samuel Roth, too, that notorious publisher and erotica dealer. Heavily investigated by J. Edgar Hoover and his bureau, Roth had to bear the brunt of social purity protest just as much as the next guy, but irony and not impudence would land him in jail. A bizarre twist occurred in 1928 when Roth was prosecuted and sent to jail for publishing pirated chapters of *Ulysses*—but not because Joyce or his publishers complained, or because the New York Society for the Suppression of Vice brought charges against Roth's publication *Two Worlds Monthly*. Instead, the jailing occurred "at the insistence of the Clean Books Committee of the Federation of Hungarian Jews in America. The committee was . . . fed up with Roth because it believed his publication of Joyce's portrayal of Leopold Bloom 'defamed' Hungarian Jews" (De Grazia, 277). While imprisoned at the Lewisburg Penitentiary, Roth would send Hoover a five-page letter that outlined his victimization and martyrdom, and he would offer, in exchange for a comprehensive presidential pardon, whatever information Hoover wanted to learn about communist activities outside of the United States. But Roth would also discuss James Joyce in that letter, and would argue that the notorious "*Ulysses* trials" propelled the yet-unknown artist into the public arena and a magisterial career. What closes the FBI file on Roth, then, that venal scoundrel, is his assertion that *he* paved the way for James Joyce's apotheosis. Talk about perverse.

CHAPTER SEVEN

Epilogue

"A good artist is a deadly enemy of society."
—James Agee, *Let Us Now Praise Famous Men*

"There is only one difference between a madman and me," Salvador Dali once said. "I am not mad." He was probably right. But what was it that drove J. Edgar Hoover? After looking at Hoover's interventions into modernism, his management and manipulation of its key texts, main figures, and significant publication ventures, I have concluded that his persistent intrusions into the lives and careers of modernist writers, editors, and publishers was not only a factor that structured the important literary movement of modernism but one that also, unthinkably, steered it.

Bureau files make clear not only Hoover's efforts to monitor writers who had begun to fasten themselves to emerging political as well as literary aesthetics; they reveal that the culture Hoover developed and the character he presented to the bureau gave rise to generations of special agents and bureau underlings who learned from and modeled his example. File evidence makes it manifestly clear that the bureau worked to discredit writers, editors, and publishers; to harass and beleaguer them; to incriminate them; and to limit their access to publication, their nomination for awards and prizes, and their opportunities to present their work in public arenas, all at precisely the time when literary modernism was gaining strength and strengthening its morale. Countermanding this, Hoover stepped up his own public relations campaign, hoping to foil if not to supplant their careers. He did this not covertly but in a fury of publication, by mass-producing essays, magazine articles, pamphlets, books, movies, and anything else he might think of to promote the bureau and to justify his importance to it. In doing so, he thrust his image as well as his principles onto the American panorama.

These abuses included sending FBI agents to strong-arm publishing firms into rejecting manuscripts from "undesirable" writers.[1] Hoover's bureau kept files on several publishers, as I already have noted (Benjamin Huebsch, Bennett Cerf, Horace Liveright, Henry Hold, Albert Boni, etc.) and we know of his inside sources at many downtown publishing houses, not to mention his bureau's likely influence over book club selections. He not only cultivated files on writers, editors, and publishers, but maintained files on their literary agents, too. (I never got Katherine Anne Porter' file but I did get her agent's 66-page file.) Moreover, friends such as Morris Ernst, who was prominent in legal circles and championed as a giant of civil liberties, would "work both sides" of a censorship case by providing Hoover with damaging testimony about writers and their works, especially when he was involved in notable, high-profile cases. Hoover would use the information to demonstrate a writer's degeneracy and to hasten his or her ruin—or to try to, at least. Equally bad, he would turn around and use the information Ernst supplied to start files on many of the writer's supporters.

J. Edgar Hoover's investigations into the editors and writers involved in the explosion of little magazines and newspapers during the second and third decades of the twentieth century reveal his interest in manipulating sites of literary modernism. His files on writers and editors associated with these publications remained open for years, and came to define these writers and activists for succeeding generations. Max Eastman, Michael Gold, Mary Heaton Vorse, Langston Hughes, Elizabeth Gurley Flynn, W. E. B. DuBois, John Reed, Louise Bryant, Claude McKay, and many others had to bear the brunt of Hoover's institutional disapproval. Working in harmony with vice suppression squads, social purity censors, and post office regulators, Hoover used modern literature against itself, as manifest evidence of a writer's obscene mind and corrupt morality. As I have argued, modern literature, more than any other twentieth-century art form, excited Hoover's anxieties and was a particular lightning rod for his paranoia and anti-intellectualism.

Where have Hoover's exploits led us? What result did Hoover's crusades have on the creative life of modern writers? What effect did the impact of the bureau's regulation, monitoring, and bullying of writers have on the shape and character of modern literature? How did the bureau's involvement in publishing affect the industry itself, and how did it influence the lives and career trajectories of writers, booksellers, publishers, and distributors? The measure of Hoover's brawn and his capacity to shape and structure American experience while he directed the bureau (1924-1972) continues to reveal itself more than 80 years after his appointment as acting director of the Bureau of Investigation.

We now know, for example, that Hoover's persistence quite bothered the novelist James Baldwin, and kept him from his work. Biographer James Campbell writes that the FBI's surveillance of Baldwin grew to affect his work, and "greatly contributed to his own private state of emergency. Between 1963 and 1972, he published only one novel, *Tell Me How Long the Train's Been Gone,* a book far less organized than any other he had written up to that time, and—probably to compensate—more strident in its tone" (11). Steinbeck, too, felt the pressure, and found it tiresome, as noted here in an earlier chapter. If Hoover's efforts kept Baldwin from writing, wore

Steinbeck out, exacerbated Hemingway's paranoia and depression, convinced Edna St. Vincent Millay that she was under constant surveillance, shamed Dreiser into admitting his impotence, short-leashed Hughes, and pressured others associated with promoting and circulating modernist work, it seems important to ask whether these results were ever *enough* for J. Edgar Hoover, or whether he wanted more for his manipulative efforts?

Sometimes Hoover's early investigations of writers affected the development of their careers years later. In 1943, for example, Hoover recommended that Steinbeck *not* receive a commission in the United States Army. Army intelligence agents disagreed, calling Steinbeck a "candid and powerful writer." In the end, a lieutenant who said he was swayed by Hoover's negative assessment overturned the positive recommendations of the army intelligence agents, and Steinbeck did not get the commission (Robins, 97). In another case, the application of William Carlos Williams for the position of Consultant in Poetry to the Library of Congress was denied in 1954 because the committee had been supplied with an unfavorable report on the writer, furnished by the FBI. I have also demonstrated how Langston Hughes's career was straightjacketed by bureau concerns over his communistic bent. Hoover deliberately worked to bar Hughes from speaking engagements. A final example centers on Archibald MacLeish. Herbert Mitgang reports that in 1962, MacLeish was being considered for a minor post as arts advisor to the Kennedy administration.

> This resulted in an alert by Hoover to FBI offices all over the United States to dig up any useful information on him: "Determine from persons interviewed their opinion concerning appointee's loyalty from his written works," Hoover advised. (Here was a case where the FBI specifically sought to determine an author's loyalty by examining his writings even though then, and later, bureau officials have said that they do not interfere with freedom of expression.) . . . [T]he bureau's

efforts to discredit MacLeish [involved] scores of interviews and a rehash of old accusations. (*Dangerous Dossiers,* 164-65)

We will never know what may have happened to MacLeish's nomination because Kennedy's assassination ended the Advisory Committee on the Arts. As in these examples, full of negative evidence, where things have failed to happen or failed to transpire, we are left to measure the effects of Hoover's institutionalized oppression by what we cannot see or by taking note of things that did not happen.

Cartha "Deke" DeLoach, who served the bureau for nearly thirty years and rose to its #3 position, understands the usefulness of such a conundrum. Championing Hoover, DeLoach wrote in 1995,

> In the final analysis, no one can prove that potential "secret blackmail" files did not exist. You can't prove that leprechauns don't exist, either. With no Irish blood in me, I'm more willing to believe in the Little People than the idea that J. Edgar Hoover kept clandestine records. Unlike Mr. Kessler and Mr. Summers [two of Hoover's biographers], I was there during those years and—I know what I didn't see. (45)

Hoover was such a fan of Sherlock Holmes stories that he might have smiled to hear DeLoach's argument, since it would recall for Hoover one of the most popular Arthur Conan Doyle cases, and would focus on another of Hoover's passions, racehorses.[2] In "Silver Blaze," the eponymous racehorse who was expected to win the Wessex Cup has gone missing, and Holmes is called in to solve the case. The horse's trainer Mr. Straker was found dead at the stables, killed by a blow to the head. Holmes solves the crime by looking at "the curious incident of the dog in the night time." A conversation initiated by the Inspector reveals that Holmes solves the case using negative evidence:

> "Is there any point to which you would wish to draw my attention?"
> "To the curious incident of the dog in the night-time."

"The dog did nothing in the night-time."

"That was the curious incident," remarked Sherlock Holmes. (*The Complete Sherlock Holmes*, 347)

Focusing attention on the evidence that is not there, Holmes deduces that because the dog did not bark it must have known the intruder. The case of *Silver Blaze* provides an especially fascinating way to read DeLoach's comment about the lack of evidence being turned into evidence.

As readers of modern literature and culture, we find ourselves in the same paradoxical predicament. How do we postulate about something that failed to happen, failed to transpire? It seems that the only reasonable way to draw conclusions about the results of Hoover's manipulation of modernism would be to discover a pile of evidence from which to make claims: books that were never published; medals and prizes that went unawarded to certain kinds of writers; essays that never made it past censors; little magazines that were barred from the U.S. mail system; pamphlets judged obscene or lewd; postcards deemed too lascivious to dispatch; book club selections that never made it to readers; announcements of readings or speaking engagements that had been cancelled, and so forth. Presuming we could amass such mountainous evidence, what about its darker twin, those books that were halted in the gestation process and never even written? Or the manuscripts abandoned by writers and tucked deep into dresser drawers? What of the little magazines or trade papers that were never started up? The poems or articles that were never penned? The news columns that were nixed before the journalist even sent the story in? How do you measure what is not there? That has been one of the vexing questions of this project.

Of course, one way to measure Hoover's presence in the midst of all of this absence is to look for its half-life, to look at the present state of affairs and to identify ghosts and shadows, vestiges of J. Edgar Hoover and his now-familiar tactics lurking in the Federal Building, in the White House, in the press room, or equally as terrifying, in the army, the police force, the university, the church. What aspects of the Hoover personality refused to die with him in 1972?

As J. Edgar Hoover's preoccupation with political radicalism, especially communism, became a feature of the Hoover bureau, and the strength of its force affected writers, intellectuals, activists, and artists during an era that shaped modern literary tastes and modern art styles, its standards were upheld and preserved by the deportation from America of alien radicals, intellectuals, and provocateurs; by the criminal trials of "anarchists," "spies," and "subversives"; and by the legal battles forced upon writers, booksellers, editors, and publishers of radical books, journals, and magazines. If the reality of any period lay in its battles, then some of this period's headiest battles were fought against the oppressive restrictions of J. Edgar Hoover's FBI, an institution that grew to structure modern experience, shape it, and thereby affect the literature that defined it.

In a moving though brief memoir published in the *New Masses,* Martin Russak, a weaver, recalled that when he asked his father why there weren't many books in the New York Free Public Library about strikes and revolutions, about workers and factories, his father laughed aloud. "Then the old man he spoke thoughtfully: 'Books are slow. We workers are way ahead of them'" (May 1929, 6). This I think was part of Hoover's fears: that the revolution would come with the union of workers and writers. As I hope I have shown, Hoover spent a great deal of energy trying to keep those two constituencies apart, afraid, and discredited; he feared an amalgamation of workers' strength and writers' metaphors. There is no doubt in my mind that J. Edgar Hoover worked very hard to shape and maintain his fetishized version of Americanism as he continued to lead the bureau until his death at the age of 77. Of course he did. Hegemony is hard work.

Notes

Introduction

1. Rita Felski suggests in *Doing Time: Feminist Theory and Postmodern Culture* (New York University Press, 2000) that the new interest in modernity was sparked by widespread debates around postmodernism in the 1970s and 1980s. "Many though not all of these debates defined the postmodern against the modern. Modernity stood for the logic of assimilation and the tyranny of sameness, the domination of 'grand narrative,' the belief in the redemptive power of great art" (60). Janet Lyon provides an interesting corrective to recent attempts to define modernity in *Manifestoes: Provocations of the Modern* (Cornell University Press, 1999):

> modernity is not a seamless temporal entity characterized by period, progress, and development, though its narratives often prefer that plotline. It is, indeed, subject to the very discontinu- ities of time that its narratives seek to disguise: different "times" co-exist within the same discrete historical moment, just as surely as homologous "times" exist across centuries. (203)

2. Two years is unusually long. "Each agency is required to determine within 10 days (excluding Saturdays, Sundays and legal holidays) after the receipt of a request whether to comply with the request" (*A Citizen's Guide on Using the Freedom of Information Act and the Privacy Act of 1974 to Request Government Records* [Washington: U.S. Government Printing Office, 1993], p. 10). While the FOIA permits extensions in unusual circumstances—"the need to collect records from remote locations, review large numbers of records, and consult with other agencies" (11)—

agencies sometimes take more than 10 days to respond, and do not notify the requester that an extension has been invoked (11 *n*).

To be sure, the waiting is the hardest part. The biggest difficulty about writing a book such as this is that at some point you have to stop requesting and waiting for bureau files and start writing about them. Invariably, in the middle of a sentence, a new file will arrive that changes the contours of a chapter or argument. Some files take so long to get that one gives up on them. I waited so long to receive George Orwell's bureau file that I gave up waiting for it.

After this book had gone into production, I received 79 pages of Orwell's 90-page file. Not only is the file almost entirely blacked out, but a handwritten scrawl at the bottom of more than half of the pages reads "There is no mention of or reference to George Orwell or any AKAs on this page." Why send it to me, then? Adding to the absurdity, everything *but* the phrases "informed," "pointed out that," "added that," "further related that," "stated that," "said," "indicated," "declared that," "remarked at this time," and "recalled that" is blacked out on several of the reports that make up the Orwell file. I guess all we can know for sure, given this sort of erratic documentation, is that somebody was doing some serious talking. Unfortunately, we'll never know what was said, or by whom, though.

3. Executive order 12356 slowed down the declassification process and limited public access to information available under the FOIA. Moreover, in 1986 Reagan further restricted access under the FOIA, and gave government agencies the authority to refuse to confirm or deny that certain records exist at all—that a main file exists, for example. Reagan's executive order continues to cripple the process and compromise the integrity of the FOIA. Herbert Mitgang, for example, describes the infelicitous restrictions in his book *Dangerous Dossiers: Exposing the Secret War Against America's Greatest Authors* (New York: Donald I. Fine, 1988), noting that he sent away in the 1970s for Thomas Wolfe's file and received 42 pages of almost entirely blacked out material. He was told that there were an additional 82 pages in the Wolfe file that would not be released to him, and his subsequent appeal was denied. More than a decade later, and after Reagan tightened the FOIA, biographer David Donald requested Wolfe's files but received a statement from the FBI indicating that no file on Wolfe existed (99). See also information

regarding *Rubin v. Central Intelligence Agency* in "CIA's Refusal to Confirm or Deny Existence of Writers' Records Does Not Violate FOIA," *New York Law Journal,* December 17, 2001. I am grateful to Kiki Culleton for bringing this to my attention.

Chapter One

1. James Joyce, too, was a mapmaker. Edna O'Brien notes in her biography that his penchant for detail developed out of necessity at an early age:

   > Over the years [the Joyces] moved to less and less salubrious districts, from south Dublin with its semblance of respectability, to the seaside at Bray, then back to Dublin to a small terraced house and then to humbler abodes on the north side of the city; near slums with cracked fanlights in the doorways and women in the nearby streets behind their barrows selling cabbages and potatoes. As they pitched tent in different quarters James drew a skeleton map of the city in his mind, his father predicting that if that young lad was set down in the Sahara he would draw a map of it. (9)

2. I'm not sure whether the *z* on "nutz" is a typo or the SAC's orthographical indication of the exponential degree to which the Vorses, per the bureau informant, were nuts.

3. Art Young, "Inspecting the Qualifications," *Liberator,* March 1920, 14-15. In this political cartoon, a man named "Old King Capital" sits on a throne covered with jewels that were paid for by "lumber," "coal," "steel," "railroads," "banks," and "gold," their price tags reveal. Lined up for inspection before Old King Capital are ten men; each carries a placard that advertises his qualifications. Ole Hanson's reads, "150% American"; Pershing's, "I Shoot"; Palmer's, "Leave it to Me"; Lodge's, "I Put a Lot of New Jokers in the League of Nations"; Johnson's, "I Know How to Talk About Liberty"; Bryan's, "W. J. B."; Borah's, "A Little Apparent Opposition Helps"; Hoover's, "I Never Fed a Red"; McAdoo's, "You Know Me, Cap!"; and Wood's, "I Broke the Strike at Gary."

Art Young, born in Illinois, studied in Paris. He spoke about his art in the premiere issue of the *Masses* in 1911: "I would rather draw political cartoons than anything else," he said. "I believe in the picture with a purpose. There must be a vital idea back of every drawing that is really worthwhile." Young continued: "Real art is, in the last analysis, simply self expression. Socialism always has been and I suppose always will be the keynote of my work. To me it is the culmination of all radicalism and the thought back of most of my drawings" (11). Indicted with other *Masses* editors in 1918 for "conspiracy to obstruct recruiting and enlistment," Young went on to work for the *Liberator,* a magazine founded in 1918 "on Lincoln's birthday" (*Liberator* 1:1, 3) once the *Masses* suspended publication.

After criticism flooded in about the unthinkable breaches of civil rights and rights to privacy (not to mention due process), Hoover tried to deflect attention from his role in the Palmer raids. "Hoover lies when he denies responsibility for the Red Raids," Felix Frankfurter told his law clerk Joseph Rauh. "He was in it—up to his ass" (Summers, 39). Summers notes that Hoover kept files on Frankfurter for half a century, "referring to him privately as 'the most dangerous man in the United States,'" and that in 1921 he identified the future Supreme Court Justice as a "disseminator of Bolshevik propaganda" (38).

4. David Levering Lewis, *When Harlem Was in Vogue,* 16.

5. A cartoon by I. Klein in the *New Masses* illustrates the unprecedented support: it shows a bloodhound with a big sack of money on its back "sniffing out" Communists. Uncle Sam leads the bloodhound around (July 1930: 18).

6. Whitman was a favorite of leftist radicals who endorsed and adulated him. Alan Wald notes "Whitman's work embodies not only facets of classic romantic ideology but also a robust proletarianism and perhaps even a proto-modernism indicated by his free verse catalogues and use of common speech. [Genevieve] Taggard was exceptional in her questioning of Whitman's rightful presence at the 'christening' of a new revolutionary poetry. From the beginning to the denouement of the Communist cultural tradition, most Communist poets would invoke Whitman as a model. When Meridel Le Sueur published *Annunciation* in 1935, she was

hailed in the *New Masses* as 'something of a female Walt Whitman'" (*Exiles From a Future Time,* 36).

7. See Sarah Wilson's "Picasso: Public Enemy" in *Tate* (Spring 1994), and Blake Eskin's "Featherman File" in the *Yiddish Forward* (Apr. 30, 1999: 2). Hoover didn't like rock and roll, either: emblazoned on the wall of Cleveland's Rock and Roll Hall of Fame is Hoover's 1968 pronouncement: "Rock and Roll is repulsive to right thinking people."

8. Granville Hicks was one of the professors called to testify in Hearings before the 1953 House Committee on Un-American Activities. More than 100 pages of testimony are copied in Hicks's FBI File. When questioned by Mr. Walter about the extent of the Communist "menace," Hicks stated with exasperation "Well, for some reason, the emphasis in all these investigating committees always falls on the fact of how much communism there is and never on how little there is. . . . It seems to me I have been sitting around here for 2 days in which it has been demonstrated that there were 10 or 12 Communists at Harvard 14 years ago and that perhaps there is one still there. Now, I would honestly think if you could just say to the public, 'Look, that's all,' instead of saying, 'Look how much that is; isn't that terrible?' you might do a good deal to allay the fear that is sweeping over this country" (Hicks FBI file). Though he had been an editor of the *New Masses,* Hicks surprised his friends by testifying that the publication was "a Communist magazine" (Hicks FBI file).

9. Hoover also enjoyed being seen attending championship prize fights, being photographed at exclusive Miami Beach resorts, or being mentioned in the press as a guest at the home of wealthy friends (Powers, *Secrecy,* 180). He also enjoyed weekly Saturday trips to the racetrack, where photographers eagerly awaited his arrival. So into publicity, Hoover even expressed in 1936 a marked interest in writer Sinclair Lewis's visit to tour bureau headquarters. Though he didn't trust the writer, "he wasn't going to let politics totally interfere with the publicity that a Nobel Prize visitor could bring to him" (Robins, 100).

10. In 1919, A. Mitchell Palmer warned, "The Negro is 'seeing red'" (quoted in Maxwell, 13). Palmer was alarmed about the rise in the number of African Americans in the Communist movement. William Maxwell notes in *New Negro, Old Left* that "Howard 'Stretch' Johnson, a charismatic Harlemite who graduated from Cotton Club dancer to Communist youth leader, once claimed that in late 1930s New York, '75% of

black cultural figures had [Communist] Party membership or maintained a regular meaningful contact with the Party'" (1). Early developments in race relations, what Hoover would call "unrest," can be traced in the United States to communist-led efforts to educate blacks about America's systemic oppression. A recent article in the Cleveland *Plain Dealer,* for example, noted that papers stored in Siberia since America's Red Scare describe the efforts of the Communist Party to educate blacks about their oppression to win their membership. The papers

> detail the efforts of the Communist Party to recruit blacks in Harlem . . . and organize sharecroppers. . . . Other materials highlight communist attempts to organize sharecroppers in the South in 1934 and blacks, other minorities and even children in Harlem. . . . From the party's perspective, blacks were the most oppressed section of the U.S. population and therefore were prospective recruits. The party's Harlem organizer in 1934 reported on efforts to "develop a proletarian backbone in the broad movement for Negro liberation." . . . He said 20 children in Harlem were being brought into the cause and party officials were looking into getting them uniforms. Working with children "has possibilities of development into a mass movement," he wrote. ("Retrieved papers shed light on Red activities in the U.S." Jan. 31, 2001: A1).

11. Charles Lee writes in *The Hidden Public: The Story of the Book-of-the-Month Club* that

> the board membership had about it the touch of magic: its chairman Henry Seidel Canby, distinguished teacher (Yale), biographer, and journalist (a founder and first editor of *The Saturday Review*); William Allen White, author, editor, politician and symbol of the Middle West; Dorothy Canfield Fisher, novelist and voice of Vermont; Heywood Broun, intense individualist and one of the best-known newsmen of his time; and Christopher Morley, a risen literary star, glowing with

charm and sophistication, twinkling with wit. Almost at once
the judges were the subject of attack. (107)

As ill health or death took the original judges they were replaced:
"Broun died in 1939. White in 1944. Marquand and Fadiman became
judges in 1944. Mrs. Fisher retired on the advice of oculists in 1951 and
was succeeded by Amy Loveman. Dr. Canby retired in 1954 and was
succeeded by Gilbert Highet. Following the deaths of Miss Loveman and
Mr. Morley, John Mason Brown and Basil Davenport were appointed [in
1956] to the board" (Lee, 223).

I was surprised to learn after a FOIA request that the bureau did
not have a file on Book-of-the-Month-Club judge Dorothy Canfield
Fisher, since so many of the files I have reviewed contain references to her.
In these, her name is underlined, check marked, or x'ed—notations that
usually indicate a systematic indexing. Herbert Mitgang notes that
Dorothy Canfield Fisher's name appears on a 1944 internal memo
written in response to Hoover's request for information about the Writers
War Board. She is listed as one of the writers affiliated with Communist
groups. Also named are Pearl Buck, Clifton Fadiman, Carl Van Doren,
and Clifford Odets (*Dangerous Dossiers,* 228).

12. Anthony Summers suggests in *Official and Confidential: The Secret Life of
J. Edgar Hoover* that following a tip that William Sloane Associates "was
shortly to publish a book on the FBI by Max Lowenthal, a personal friend
of President Truman's . . . [who] had been squirreling away documentation of the FBI and its Director since the late twenties," J. Edgar Hoover
immediately stepped up efforts to crush the book and its author (175).
He invited Morris Ernst's help to sabotage the book. (Letters I have read
from the Ernst Archive housed at the University of Texas Humanities
Research Center support this.) Incredibly, however, Summers contends
that Hoover had a hand in orchestrating a break-in at the Lowenthal
home in order to get an advanced copy of the manuscript: "Lowenthal's
son, John, believes he knows how Edgar knew of his father's book before
it came out. The family home, he says, was raided by burglars who
'seemed more interested in going through [his] father's papers than in his
possessions'" (175).

13. Dardis adds that before 1917 the choices of most American book
publishers were on the conservative side, politically speaking:

> Most U.S. firms ignored the feverish wave of literary experi-
> mentation taking place in Europe. It is for this reason that so
> many of the major works of the 20th century modernists were
> published by the Jewish firms in the late teens and twenties.
> This was to be true of all of Joyce's works [Huebsch and
> Random House] . . . D. H. Lawrence's *Women in Love* and *The
> Rainbow* [Seltzer], Ezra Pound, Eliot [Boni and Liveright],
> Sherwood Anderson [Huebsch], Hemingway and Faulkner
> [Boni and Liveright]. It was [Liveright] who published all of
> O'Neill's plays, all of Hart Crane and Djuna Barnes and e. e.
> cummings. (Dardis, 51).

14. Paul Vanderham describes Ernst's and Cerf's strategies to initiate a *Ulysses*
    trial in order to test the U.S. ban on the work in his 1998 *James Joyce and
    Censorship: The Trials of "Ulysses"* (87-91). See also Robert Spoo's essay on
    this topic. Both outline the extreme measures to which lawyer and
    publisher went to get a copy of Joyce's novel smuggled from France into
    New York with a specific battery of critical materials pasted inside the
    covers of the book. Cerf wrote to Paul Leon in France, "It is important
    that this . . . be actually pasted into the book, as if it is separate we may
    not be able to use it as evidence when the trial comes up, but if these
    opinions of respected people are actually pasted in the book, they
    become, for legal purposes, a part of the book, and can be introduced as
    evidence" (*Trials of "Ulysses,"* 88). Vanderham notes that the importance
    of such a strategy "cannot be overemphasized. By virtue of the fact that
    the imported copy of *Ulysses* was destined to be the sole piece of evidence
    in the upcoming proceedings, Ernst's decision to have the opinion of
    literary critics pasted therein was clearly motivated by his desire to ensure
    that the opinion of literary critics would be the fundamental standard by
    which *Ulysses* would be judged" (88).

15. William A. Gordon, *Four Dead in Ohio. Was there a Conspiracy at Kent
    State?* Laguna Hills, CA: Northridge Books, 1995. Gordon writes that in
    the course of his research on the campus shootings in 1970 at Kent State,
    he learned that Morris Ernst "as Davies correctly pointed out, had an
    highly unusual relationship with J. Edgar Hoover—one that baffled his
    associates in the Civil Liberties Union" (261).

16. Professor Sean Latham, e-mail to the author.

17. The bureau kept an extensive collection of letterhead stationery on file in order to identify and monitor individuals listed on the letterhead as being on the boards of organizations, associated with the organizations, or sponsors of the organizations.

18. Theoharis explains,

> Memoranda that were not to be serialized and recorded in the FBI's central records system were originally to be prepared on blue paper, bearing the caption "Information Memo Not to Be Sent to Files Section." In time, the color of these memoranda was changed to pink and the caption changed to "This Memorandum is for Administrative Purposes: To Be Destroyed After Action is Taken and Not Sent to Files." In 1942, Hoover extended this intra-headquarters special records procedure when devising the Do Not File procedure for all memoranda submitted by heads of FBI field offices (SAC's) requesting the FBI director's approval to conduct "clearly illegal" break-ins. ("Introduction," *Official and Confidential Files of FBI Assistant Director Louis Nichols,* viii)

In his 1991 book *From the Secret Files of J. Edgar Hoover,* reprinted in 1993 with additional materials, Theoharis identifies six separate secret office files kept by Hoover. There was of course (1) the Central Records System. Rounding this repository out were (2) the Official and Confidential File, (3) the Confidential File, (4) what Hoover's secretary Mrs. Gandy called the "Highly Confidential File" kept in Hoover's office under lock and key, (5) the Personal and Confidential File, and (6) the Tolson file, maintained by Clyde Tolson (3-10).

Chapter Two

1. *Sunday Express* August 19, 1928. Quoted in Edward De Grazia, *Girls Lean Back Everywhere: The Law of Obscenity and the Assault on Genius* (New York: Random House, 1992), 173 and 57. I am grateful to David Bradshaw for pointing me to these passages.

De Grazia adds "This was not the first time the editor of the *Sunday Express* had denounced a book and alerted the authorities. In May 1922, Douglas reported to his readers that he had read Joyce's *Ulysses*—this would have been a copy of Sylvia Beach's Paris edition—and found it 'the most infamously obscene book in ancient or modern literature'" (174*n*).

2. Years later, with the 1939 publication of Flann O'Brien's (pseudonym Brian O'Nolan) tour de force *At Swim-Two-Birds,* publishers would appeal quite differently to that quintessential "sister" figure when preparing book publicity. A notorious blurb by Dylan Thomas on the Plume/Penguin Books edition of O'Brien's farce advises, "This is just the book to give your sister if she's a loud, dirty, boozy girl."

3. In *Dangerous Dossiers,* Herbert Mitgang notes that two particular events seem to crop up time and again in the FBI files of American writers: the Sacco and Vanzetti case was one; the other was the Spanish Civil War ten years later. A number of the files I have seen have bureau commentary regarding both events. Any writer's involvement with or support of the Abraham Lincoln Brigade, for example, is well-documented in bureau files. To his list I would add the Scottsboro case trials.

    Richard Gid Powers notes that the Sacco and Vanzetti case interested writers and activists on all sides:

> Books, poems, and essays on Sacco and Vanzetti were appearing everywhere—something on the case seemed obligatory from any writer with progressive convictions. Walter Lippmann, Heywood Broun, John Dewey, Norman Thomas, Jane Addams, Robert La Follette, Sherwood Eddy, H. L. Mencken, John Dos Passos all enlisted in the defense. Radicals and intellectuals demonstrated on Boston Common. Katherine Anne Porter joined the Communist pickets. Upton Sinclair wrote his two-volume *Boston* about the case, although he privately became convinced of Sacco's guilt while researching the book. Maxwell Anderson's *Winterset* was based on the case. John Haynes Holmes of the ACLU compared *The Letters of Sacco and Vanzetti,* co-edited by [Felix] Frankfurter's wife, to Plato's *Apology.* Communist novelist Howard Fast said that the

case was "your passion and mine. . . . It is the passion of the Son of God who was a carpenter." Ben Shahn's Sacco-Vanzetti mosaic expressed his conviction that "this was a crucifixion itself—right in front of my own eyes." When Sacco and Vanzetti were executed at midnight on August 23, 1927, Paris's Communist newspaper *L'Humanite* headlined its story "ASSASSINES." There were riots in Paris, Geneva, Berlin, Bremen, Hamburg, and Stuttgart. (95)

4. Though he had grown up the child of poor Irish immigrants, Quinn grew to become a quite wealthy collector. He amassed a collection of literary manuscripts, including what we now call the Rosenbach *Ulysses,* housed with the collections of rare books and manuscripts at Philadelphia's Rosenbach Library. Quinn also collected Ezra Pound's and T. S. Eliot's work, and artwork by the moderns Picasso, Matisse, and Van Gogh. One website details the provenance of the "Rosenbach" manuscript, and describes how Quinn acquired the draft of the "Circe" episode of *Ulysses* from Joyce, which the National Library of Ireland purchased in 2000: http://www.worldbookdealers.com/articles/nw/nw0000000246.asp.

   In her web essay, Sophia Read notes, "John Quinn was a very important book collector and writer's benefactor. A self-confessed early starter, '(I) became a collector of books almost as soon as I had ceased to be a collector of marbles, and gave my marbles and my bicycle away'" (quoted by B. L. Reid in *The Man From New York: John Quinn and His Friends*). His friendship with Joyce began in 1916, when Quinn helped alleviate Joyce's considerable financial difficulties, and their correspondence lasted for many years. He bought the manuscripts of several of Joyce's earlier works, including *Exiles,* and provided a much needed source of income for the struggling writer" (www.worldbookdealers.com).

   Nancy Birk provides additional information about Quinn and his collections in her essay on Quinn and Joseph Conrad materials (*Rare Books and Manuscripts Librarianship*).

5. In *Hemingway: The Final Years,* biographer Michael Reynolds describes the development of *Islands in the Stream* from a "fragment of a Bimini

story that referred back to the island's heyday as a rumrunner's haven during prohibition" (128) to its development into a novel:

> [H]e knew he was writing a novel but had no idea where it would end. It was a strange enough story, mixing memory and desire on the cool sea breeze coming through the open doorway and windows of a painter's cottage. The time is 1936; the two male characters—the older painter and the younger novelist— are old friends who carry heavy personal baggage. The theme was remembrance of things past, but most particularly it would detail the condition of the artist played out against the backdrop of twentieth-century conflicts.

Reynolds adds that this was a story Hemingway had been writing "obliquely" for quite some time, "and would continue to write for the rest of his life" (136).

6. See Mary Hemingway, *How it Was* (New York: Knopf, 1976), 500-502.

Chapter Three

1. Murray Kempton provides a moving anecdote about the American playwright in *Part of Our Time. Some Ruins and Monuments of the Thirties:*

    > Clifford Odets said that when he wrote his first play he was living on ten cents a day. The truth was harsh enough to require no such dramatic license. Odets's mother had worked in a stocking factory in Philadelphia when she was eleven and had died an old woman at forty-nine. When Clifford Odets's time came before the House Committee on Un-American Activities, he told its counsel: 'I did not learn my hatred of poverty, sir, out of communism.' (234)

2. Though Powers reports that Cooper wrote four books and three movies on the FBI, he adds that "Hoover is listed as the author of record" for

Cooper's 1938 book and subsequent 1939 movie *Persons in Hiding* (197). Cooper's books on the bureau include *Ten Thousand Public Enemies* (1935), *Here's to Crime* (1937), and *Persons in Hiding* (1938). His movies on the same subject were *Persons in Hiding, Undercover Doctor, Parole Fixer* and *Queen of the Mob.* William Beverley's *On the Lam: Narratives of Flight in J. Edgar Hoover's America* also discusses Cooper's collaboration with bureau ideology and image, as well as the work of other bureau-developed writers (see Beverley, chapter 2).

3. Dale Carnegie gave up space in his newspaper column to J. Edgar Hoover once to use in his "fight against crime," Robins reports (422). Oddly enough, she adds, Hoover had a 31-page bureau file on the motivational speaker.

Chapter Four

1. The Dublin Lock-out began when employers demanded that workers sign a statement saying that they would not join Larkin's or any other union. Those who refused to sign were dismissed, and factories and workshops quickly were closed in order to force Dublin workers to terms. By the time the 22-week epic struggle ended in late January of the following year, the lock-out had affected some 25,000 workers and some 80,000 dependents. Nearly two million days of paid production had been lost. It was a crushing defeat for Larkin and his union. See Culleton, *Working-Class Culture,* 41-42.

2. Larkin's friend Jack Carney details Larkin's prison history in his short essay "Jim Larkin in America":

> Not satisfied with jailing Jim, the authorities tried to destroy him. He was sent to the worst prison in the United States, the dreaded dungeon prison of Dannemora. He was put to work in the basement operating a jute mill. Few emerged from this job without falling a victim to tuberculosis. Due to the pressure of public opinion he was transferred to Sing Sing. . . . Later he was transferred to Comstock . . . an open prison for trusted prisoners. . . . Jim did not enjoy the comforts of Comstock because there were too many convicted politicians among the

prisoners so he was transferred back to Sing Sing until, finally,
he was released. (283)

3. The 1919 assassination conspiracy came as news even to scholars who
   were familiar with Larkin's work and his life. It is not mentioned by any
   of Larkin's biographers nor is it mentioned in any of the essays in the
   exceptional 1998 centennial collection *James Larkin, Lion of the Fold*.
   Since news of the conspiracy broke in the summer of 1999, several
   journalists have followed the story, uncovering significant leads. See
   Bushe, Cullen, Foote, and O'Hanlon.

4. After the roundup in New York, detainees were called to appear before
   the Lusk Committee, an anticommunist investigative body chaired by
   New York senator Clayton Lusk. The Lusk Committee defined Larkin's
   work as "criminal" and charged him with criminal anarchy.

5. Doyle reports that "soon the migration was self-generating. The initial
   grants had functioned as supplementary seed money":

   > Under the Arrears of Rent Act (1882) and the Tramways Act
   > (1883), £133,173 made in government grants enabled 54,283
   > people to emigrate by 1891. Small numbers were also assisted
   > under the poor rates under an act of 1849. Vere Foster of
   > Belfast spent much of this inherited wealth placing 20,000 girls
   > in American homes between 1880 and 1887. The *New York
   > Herald* ran a fund to bring whole families from the west [of
   > Ireland] out, and the English Quaker J. H. Tuke acted for
   > another group of philanthropists in the same way. (207)

6. A short list would include James Connolly, William F. Dunne, Patrick
   Ford, William Z. Foster, Jay Fox, Elizabeth Gurley Flynn, Fr. Thomas
   Haggerty, Mother Jones [Mary Harris Jones], J.P. McDonnell, P.J.
   McGuire, Leonora O'Reilly, Michael Quill, and Margaret Sanger. Moreover, in the first 20 years of the new century, almost 50 percent "of the
   110 American Federation of Labor unions had stock-Irish presidents or
   senior officers," even though Irish and Irish-American workers made up
   only one thirteenth of the total male work force (Doyle, 207, 193).

   Importantly, the thousand arrests and deportations that followed
   the Palmer Raids not only affected the diverse composition of the

American work force, causing then-Harvard Law Professor Felix Frankfurter and 11 others to issue the "Twelve Lawyers' Report" denouncing Palmer for carrying out "a grossly illegal campaign of terror 'whereby working men and working women suspected of radical views have been shamefully abused and maltreated'" (O'Riordan, 72), but the culture of fear quickly affected membership in workers' clubs, long a haven for the immigrant work force. Consequently, too, card-carrying membership tapered off in the larger, more politically influential organizations such as the Communist Party of America and the Communist Labor Party, co-founded by Larkin in 1918. The bureau kept a 51-page file on Eamon De Valera, too. Under the FOIA, they released 46 pages of his file to me.

7. Here, the "Fawcett" is probably Diarmuid L. Fawsitt, a senior figure in Sinn Fein who was appointed at this time by Eamon de Valera as the Republic's trade consul in New York; see O'Hanlon, "*Inside File*: Fifth Man in the Larkin Murder Plot."

8. The committee feared that Larkin might defeat the criminal anarchy case against him (Larkin was serving as his own counsel), or that he might jump bail after his conviction and flee to Ireland in time for the January elections. They worried that his presence in Ireland would mean that he would do all possible to arouse the Irish Socialist vote against Sinn Fein (Irish for "Ourselves/Ourselves alone"), whose policies, according to the agent reporting on Larkin, were capitalistic and not in accord with good Socialist doctrine. Indeed they were not. Louise Bryant noted in a *Liberator* article "Jim Larkin Goes to Jail" (June 1920: 13-16) that while Larkin was not opposed to Sinn Fein, he was no sponsor, either. Bryant reported that during the Larkin trial the assistant district attorney was "baiting Larkin as a matador baits a bull. 'You are opposed to the Sinn Fein,' he said in his insinuating way. Larkin replied, 'I am not opposed to it but I don't sympathize with it. The very meaning of the word *Ourselves* is too small and too limited for my imagination and my enthusiasm. I am an Internationalist. I believe in freedom for the whole world'" (13). The Larkin "committee of disposal" agreed that he needed to be assassinated "for the good of the Irish Republic." The special agent in charge who reported on the meeting urged that this information be treated with "utmost secrecy" so that the agent's informant would be protected. In fact, he seemed more interested in protecting his informant than in protecting Larkin from the imminent violence.

The names of the four-man "committee of disposal" had been censored in the file with the notation "b7c" scribbled next to them, shorthand for one of the exemptions allowable under Title 5 of United States Code Section 552, Subsection (B)(7)(C): "could reasonably be expected to constitute an unwarranted invasion of personal privacy." Following my lead, Ray O'Hanlon, a journalist for the *Irish Echo,* filed a Freedom of Information request in 1999 and successfully had the censorship removed (See "The Plot to Kill James Larkin," March 15, 2000).

9. William Albertson explained in a June 1929 issue of the *New Masses* that

> They [Mooney and Billings] had been leaders of a bitter strike of the San Francisco street-car men against the bosses. In 1916 a bomb was hurled into a preparedness parade in San Francisco. Some people were killed and many wounded. The frame-up machine was oiled and put into gear. On the basis of fake evidence Mooney and Billings were convicted of hurling the bomb. They were sentenced to death. Due to mass protest of Labor, the death sentence was commuted to life imprisonment. To date all living witnesses in the case have confessed that they lied at the trial. The jurists who convicted them claim they are innocent. The presiding judge is asking for a pardon for Mooney and Billings for a crime which they did not commit. Ever since the International Labor Defense was organized it has been fighting for their unconditional release. (6)

New Masses used the term "organized murder" when discussing court-established death sentences for workers or labor organizers, as in the cases of Mooney and Billings and Sacco and Vanzetti. Albertson's discussion of the Mooney-Billings frame-up and his frustration at deaf, dumb, and blind justice reads uncannily like the Scottsboro trial shenanigans that would haunt an international audience in the coming decade.

10. The government's role in squashing union activity was for the most part successful. Some labor historians even see the decades of the 1920s and 1930s as marking the rise and fall of the American labor movement.

David Montgomery certainly argues as much in his book, *The Fall of the House of Labor, 1865-1925*.

11. Bizarrely enough, a *second* murder plot is captured and recorded in Larkin's FBI file, one planned after his pardon and release from Sing Sing in 1923. A Cleveland SAC reported that at a Chicago rally shortly after his pardon, Larkin said to his Ashland Auditorium audience that a man from Boston **[CENSORED]** warned him that a plot was on foot to have him go to Clinton, Iowa. He continued: "He warned me that if I accepted the invitation, I would be killed, for the sole purpose of preventing my going to Ireland. The invitation came to me just as he stated, and I am satisfied there is a conspiracy to put me out of the way; and the worst part of it is that this country has a part in the conspiracy, because it is linked up with the other countries." The SAC's report adds: "He declared that there are many enemies of Ireland in this country, and mentioned particularly **[CENSORED]** who prosecuted him when he was sentenced to Sing Sing. In concluding he said, 'Some may think I am going over to Ireland to pull the chestnuts out of the fire, but you may depend on it, if I pull them out, I will crack them. If I die in the struggle, there will be other leaders who will follow me as I am following those who went before me.'" Larkin's intimation of this conspiracy is amply recorded in the file reports of SACs in Chicago and Cleveland. Within ten weeks of that Chicago appearance, Larkin was deported to Ireland and sailed from New York City on April 21 aboard the S.S. *Majestic*.

Chapter Five

1. The *transatlantic review* was another literary review founded in Paris that published sections of Joyce's *Finnegans Wake*. Founded in 1924, it ran for twelve monthly issues. Fargnoli and Gillespie note "Its editor, Ford Madox Ford, guaranteed immediate acclaim for the *transatlantic review* by persuading Joyce, Ezra Pound, John Quinn, and Ernest Hemingway to serve as advisors. A selection by Joyce entitled 'From Work in Progress' was published in the journal's fourth issue (April 1924). This passage eventually became the MAMALUJO chapter of *Finnegans Wake*" (*James Joyce A-Z*, 217).

2. For more on the topic of the Black Press in the United States, see the award-winning documentary produced and directed by Stanley Nelson,

The Black Press: Soldiers Without Swords (1999). Nelson's work historiciz-
es the role of the Black Press in the twentieth century.

Chapter Six

1. Joyce's August 17, 1911 letter to the editor is printed in full in *Selected
    Letters,* 197-99. Written from Trieste, the letter opens with this acerbic
    paragraph:

    > Nearly six years ago Mr Grant Richards, publisher, of London
    > signed a contract with me for the publication of a book of
    > stories written by me, entitled *Dubliners.* Some ten months
    > later he wrote asking me to omit one of the stories and passages
    > in others which, as he said, his printer refused to set up. I
    > declined to do either and a correspondence began between Mr
    > Grant Richards and myself which lasted more than three
    > months. I went to an international jurist in Rome (where I
    > lived then) and was advised to omit. I declined to do so and the
    > MS was returned to me, the publisher refusing to publish
    > notwithstanding his pledged printed word, the contract
    > remaining in my possession. (197)

2. In his book on the culture of New York during the year of the
    International Exhibition of Modern Art, also known as the Armory
    Show, since it was held at New York's 69th Regiment Armory, Martin
    Green describes the excitement generated not only by the Armory Show
    but by a pageant put on in front of McKim, Mead & White's Madison
    Square Garden by striking textile workers and labor activists:

    > The Armory Show was a great media event, written about in
    > every newspaper and at every level of sympathy and under-
    > standing, but it was primarily meant for the leisure class. And
    > while it was going on, the political radicals of the city were
    > preoccupied with the nearby strike of the textile workers of
    > Paterson, NJ, which had begun in January and was being

organized by the most radical union of the day, the Industrial Workers of the World. . . . On June 7, 1,200 of the striking workers crossed over from New Jersey and marched up Fifth Avenue to Madison Square Garden, then one of the McKim, Mead and White's great buildings. There they put on a pageant in which they depicted their sufferings and announced their demands before a capacity audience of fifteen to sixteen thousand. (3)

Many of the same people who organized the Armory Show in 1913 also organized striking workers in the Paterson textile strike, Green notes (4). "Far apart as the Show and the Pageant stood, they spoke the same metamessage to the same people. For at that moment in history, art and politics came together and so people's hopes and fears came together also. Irony could be transcended because it seemed that everything one wanted stood together at the end of single perspective and everything one hated stood together in the opposite direction. Since then, people have looked back to that moment in envy" (4).

O'Neill notes in *Art for the Masses* that the Armory Show "not only offered many Americans their first opportunity to study such artists as Matisse, Picasso, and Edvard Munch at first hand but also brought the phenomenon of modernism to the attention of the general public. The exhibition proved an important event in American cultural history" (158). *Masses* artist John Sloan's reflection of cubism appeared in the April 1913 issue, and would be one of many cartoons to ridicule the new style in art. One cartoonist likened Marcel Duchamp's *Nude Descending a Staircase* to an explosion in a shingle factory, for example. Sloan accompanied his cartoon with this parodic verse: "There was a cubic man and he walked a cubic mile. And he found a cubic sixpence upon a cubic style. He had a cubic cat which caught a cubic mouse and they all lived together in a little cubic house" (O'Neill, 159).

3. The Catholic Church would long be a supporter of the Society's aims. As Gertzman points out, the Church could campaign "intensively against obscenity from the pulpit and through laypeople . . . [and could] act independently of [Sumner] without drawing any of the belittling press coverage to which the NYSSV had become vulnerable" (174).

4. The FBI currently sends out similar flyers when responding to FOIA requests. Their flyer outlines what the FBI doesn't do. See my discussion in chapter 2.

5. *Brancusi vs. United States* (1927-28). What the *Lady Chatterley's Lover* trials did for modern literature, *Brancusi vs. United States* did for modern art, claims a British Broadcasting Corporation promotional advertisement for a documentary on the case, filmed for the 75th anniversary of the landmark decision that defined Art for successive generations.

Chapter Seven

1. Frances Stonor Saunders gives an example from the late 1940s which, though it is beyond the scope of this project, outlines the evolution of the early maneuverings of the bureau chief:

> [A]n FBI agent paid a visit to the publishing firm of Little, Brown, and told them that J. Edgar Hoover did not want to see Howard Fast's new novel, *Spartacus,* on the bookshelves. Little, Brown returned the manuscript to its author, who was then rejected by seven other publishers. Alfred Knopf sent the manuscript back unopened, saying he wouldn't even look at the work of a traitor. (53)

2. At his death, Hoover's library contained a complete set of the Sherlock Holmes stories.

Works Cited

Abrahams, Edward. *The Lyrical Left: Randolph Bourne, Alfred Steiglitz, and the Origins of Cultural Radicalism in America.* Charlottesville: University Press of Virginia, 1986.

Abels, Cyrilly. FBI file. 1 section. Approximately 66 pages

Adickes, Sandra. *To Be Young Was Very Heaven: Women in New York Before the First World War.* New York: St. Martin's Press, 1997.

Allen, F. L. *Only Yesterday: An Informal History of the 1920s.* New York: Harper and Bros., 1931.

Anderson, Margaret. *My Thirty Years' War: An Autobiography.* New York: Covici, Friede Inc., 1930.

Anderson, Elliott, and Mary Kinzie, eds. *The Little Magazine in America: A Modern Documentary History.* New York: Pushcart Press, 1979.

Asher, Robert. "1919 Strike Wave." *Encyclopedia of the American Left.* Ed. Mary Jo Buhle, Paul Buhle and Dan Georgakas. University of Illinois Press, 1992. 523-33.

Attridge, Derek and Marjorie Howes, eds. *Semicolonial Joyce.* Cambridge, England: Cambridge University Press, 2000

Atwater, Jonas. "Rules and Art." *Masses,* Oct. 1911, no. 10: 16.

Auden, W.H. "In Memory of W.B. Yeats." *The Norton Anthology of Modern Poetry.* Second Edition. Ed. Richard Ellmann and Robert O'Clair. New York: W. W. Norton, 1988: 742-743.

Baritz, Loren. *The American Left: Radical Political Thought in the Twentieth Century.* New York: Basic Books, 1971.

Barong, Dante. "The Pittsburgh Strike." *Masses,* July 1916: 17.

Barzman, Norma. *The Red and the Blacklist: The Intimate Memoir of a Hollywood Expatriate.* New York: Thunder's Mouth Press, 2003.

Bayor, Ronald H. *Neighbors in Conflict: The Irish, Germans, Jews, and Italians of New York City, 1929-1941.* 2nd Ed. Chicago: University of Chicago Press, 1988.

Beckett, Samuel. *Murphy.* New York: Grove Press, 1938.

Benstock, Shari. *Women of the Left Bank: Paris 1900-1940.* Austin: University of Texas Press, 1986.

Berg, A. Scott. *Max Perkins: Editor of Genius.* New York: E. P. Dutton, 1978.

Beverly, William. *On the Lam: Narratives of Flight in J. Edgar Hoover's America.* Jackson: University of Mississippi Press, 2003.

Birk, Nancy. "Conrad for Sale: Some Wear at Extremities, Otherwise Fine," *Rare Books and Manuscripts Librarianship* 11:1 (Fall 1996): 25-31.

Boone, Joseph. *Libidinal Currents: Sexuality and the Shaping of Modernism.* Chicago: University Press of Chicago, 1998.

Brockman, William S. "American Librarians and Early Censorship of *Ulysses:* 'Aiding the Cause of Free Expression'?" *Joyce Studies Annual* 5 (Summer 1994): 56-74.

Brody, David. *Labor in Crisis: The Steel Strike of 1919.* Urbana: University of Illinois Press, 1987.

Brubaker, Howard. Columns. *Liberator,* May 1919: 25; February 1920: 20.

Bryant, Louise. "Jim Larkin Goes to Jail." *Liberator,* June 1920: 13-16.

Buhle, Mari Jo, Paul Buhle and Dan Georgakas, eds. *Encyclopedia of the American Left.* Urbana and Chicago: University of Illinois Press, 1992.

Buitrago, Ann Mari, and Leon Andrew Immerman. *Are You Now or Have You Ever Been in the FBI Files? How to Secure and Interpret Your FBI Files.* New York: Grove Press, Inc., 1981.

Burlingame, Roger. *Of Making Many Books: A Hundred Years of Reading Writing, and Publishing.* University Park: Pennsylvania State University Press, 1957.

Bushe, Andrew. "Secret Dossier Reveals Sinn Fein Plot to Kill Labor Leader "Big" Jim Larkin." *The Examiner* (Cork, Ireland), Aug. 3, 1999.

Butsch, Richard, ed. *For Fun and Profit. The Transformation of Leisure Into Consumption.* Philadelphia: Temple University Press, 1990.

Campbell, James. "James Baldwin and the FBI." *The Threepenny Review,* vol. 77 (Spring 1999): 10-11.

Carney, Jack. "Jim Larkin in America." *James Larkin: Lion of the Fold.* Ed. Donal Nevin. Dublin: Gill and Macmillan, 1998: 280-83.

Cerf, Bennet. *At Random: Reminiscences of Bennett Cerf.* New York: Random House, 1977.

Cerf, Bennett and Donald Klopfer. *Dear Donald, Dear Bennett: The Wartime Correspondence of Bennett Cerf and Donald Klopfer.* New York: Random House, 2002.

Cherniack, Martin. *The Hawk's Nest Incident: America's Worst Industrial Disaster.* New Haven: Yale University Press, 1986.

Cleaton, Irene, and Allen Cleaton. *Books and Battles: American Literature 1920-1930.* Boston: Houghton Mifflin, 1937.

Clecak, Peter. *Radical Paradoxes: Dilemmas of the American Left: 1945-1970.* New York: Harper and Row Publishers, 1973.

Coiner, Constance. *Better Red: The Writing and Resistance of Tillie Olsen and Meridel Le Sueur.* New York: Oxford University Press, 1995.

Crichton, Judy. *America 1900: The Sweeping Story of a Pivotal Year in the Life of the Nation.* New York: Henry Holt and Company, 1998.

Cullen, Paul. "Plot to Poison Jim Larkin Unearthed in United States." *Irish Times* (Dublin, Ireland), Aug. 3, 1999: 3.

Culleton, Claire A. *Working-Class Culture, Women, and Britain, 1914-1921.* New York: St. Martin's Press, 2000.

Dardis, Tom. *Firebrand: The Life of Horace Liveright.* New York: Random House, 1995.

De Grazia, Edward. *Girls Lean Back Everywhere: The Law of Obscenity and the Assault on Genius.* New York: Random House, 1992.

De Valera, Eamon. FBI file. 1 section. Approximately 46 pages.

DeLoach, Cartha "Deke." *Hoover's FBI: The Inside Story by Hoover's Trusted Lieutenant.* Washington, D.C.: Regnery Publishing, Inc., 1997.

Diggins, John P. *The American Left in the Twentieth Century.* New York: Harcourt Brace Jovanovich, 1973.

Dilling, Elizabeth. *The Red Network: A "Who's Who" and Handbook of Radicalism for Patriots.* Kenilworth, IL: Elizabeth Dilling, 1934, 1935.

Doan, Laura, and Jay Prosser, ed. *Palatable Poison: Critical Perspectives on "The Well of Loneliness."* New York: Columbia University Press, 2001

Donner, Frank. *Protectors of Privilege: Red Squads and Police Repression in Urban America.* Berkeley: University of California Press, 1990.

Dorril, Stephen. *MI6: Inside the Covert World of Her Majesty's Secret Intelligence Service.* New York: The Free Press, 2000.

Dos Passos, John Roderigo. FBI file. 1 section. Approximately 78 pages.

Douglas, Ann. *Terrible Honesty: Mongrel Manhattan in the 1920s.* London: Picador, 1995.

Doyle, Arthur Conan. *The Complete Sherlock Holmes.* Garden City, N.Y.: Doubleday and Company, 1930.

Doyle, David. "Unestablished Irishmen: New Immigrants and Industrial America, 1870-1910s." *American Labor and Immigration History, 1870-1920s.* Ed. Dirk Hoerder. Urbana: University of Illinois Press, 1983: 193-220.

Dreiser, Theodore. "Down Hill and Up." Typescript. Dreiser Collection, University of Pennsylvania Library.

DuBois, William E. B. FBI file. 7 sections. Approximately 935 pages.

Eastman, Max. FBI file. 1 section. Approximately 50 pages.

Ellmann, Richard. *James Joyce.* New York: Oxford University Press, 1982.

Enstad, Nan. *Ladies of Labor, Girls of Adventure: Working Women, Popular Culture, and Labor Politics at the Turn of the Twentieth Century.* New York: Columbia University Press, 1999.

Epstein, Jason. *Book Business: Publishing Past Present and Future.* New York: W. W. Norton and Company, 2002.

Ernst, Morris L. The Morris L. Ernst Archive. Harry Ransom Humanities Research Center. Austin: University of Texas.

Ernst, Morris L. FBI file. 3 sections. Approximately 600 pages.

Ernst, Morris L., and David Loth. *Report on the American Communist.* New York: Henry Holt and Co., 1952.

Eskin, Blake. "The Featherman File. Of Noteworthy Items in the Press." *The Yiddish Forward,* Apr. 30, 1999: 2.

Fargnoli, A. Nicholas, and Michael Gillespie. *James Joyce A-Z*. New York: Oxford University Press, 1995.

Felski, Rita. *Doing Time: Feminist Theory and Postmodern Culture*. New York: New York University Press, 2000.

Filler, Louis, Ed. *American Anxieties: A Collective Portrait of the 1930s*. New Brunswick: Transaction Publishers, 1993.

Finan, Christopher M. *Alfred E. Smith: The Happy Warrior*. New York: Hill and Wang, 2002.

Fishbein, Leslie. "Introduction." *Art for the Masses: A Radical Magazine and Its Graphics, 1911-1917* by Rebecca Zurier. Philadelphia: Temple University Press, 1988: 3-27.

Fitzgerald, F. Scott. *This Side of Paradise*. 1920. New York: Scribner, 2003.

Flacks, Richard. *Making History: The Radical Tradition in American Life*. New York: Columbia University Press, 1988.

Flanagan, Hallie. FBI file. 1 section. Approximately 73 pages.

Flanagan, Hallie. "Federal Theatre." *American Anxieties: A Collective Portrait of the 1930s*. Ed. Louis Filler. New Brunswick: Transaction Publishers, 1993. 140-144.

Flynn, Elizabeth Gurley. FBI file. 1 section. Approximately 100 pages.

Flynn, Elizabeth Gurley. *The Rebel Girl: An Autobiography. My First Life (1906-1926)*. New York: International Publishers, 1973.

Foley, Barbara. *Radical Representations: Politics and Form in U.S. Proletarian Fiction, 1929-1941*. Durham, N.C.: Duke University Press, 1993.

Foote, Rick. "FBI, radicals, murder, imposters part of Butte plot." *The Butte Weekly,* March 15, 2000: 2.

Fraser, Steven, and Joshua B. Freeman, eds. *Audacious Democracy: Labor, Intellectuals, and the Social Reconstruction of America*. Boston: Houghton Mifflin, 1997.

Freeman, Joshua. "Labor." *The Reader's Companion to American History*. Ed. Eric Foner and John A. Garraty. New York: Houghton Mifflin Co., 1991. 627-34.

Friedman, Andrea. *Prurient Interests: Gender, Democracy, and Obscenity in New York City, 1909-1945*. New York: Columbia University Press, 2000.

Gentry, Curt. *J. Edgar Hoover: The Man and the Secrets*. W.W. Norton and Co., 1991.

Georgakas, Dan. "Mooney-Billings Case." *Encyclopedia of the American Left*. Ed. Mari Jo Buhle, Paul Buhle, and Dan Georgakas. Chicago: University of Illinois Press, 1992. 485-86.

Gertzman, Jay A. *Bookleggers and Smuthounds: The Trade in Erotica, 1920-1940*. Philadelphia: University of Pennsylvania Press, 1999.

Gilmer, Walker. *Horace Liveright: Publisher of the 20s*. New York: David Lewis, 1970.

Gold, Michael. FBI file. 1 section. Approximately 400 pages.

Gordon, William A. *Four Dead in Ohio: Was There a Conspiracy at Kent State?* Laguna Hills, CA: Northridge Books, 1995.

Gordon, William A. E-mail message. Monday January 13, 2003.

Gorman, Herbert. *James Joyce.* New York: Rinehart and Company, 1948.

Green, Martin. *New York 1913: The Armory Show and the Paterson Strike Pageant.* New York: Charles Scribner's Sons, 1988.

Gurstein, Rochelle. *The Repeal of Reticence: A History of America's Cultural and Legal Struggles over Free Speech, Obscenity, Sexual Liberation, and Modern Art.* New York: Hill and Wang, 1996.

Hall, Donald, and Pat Corrington Wykes. *Anecdotes of Modern Art: From Rousseau to Warhol.* New York: Oxford University Press, 1990.

Hegeman, Susan. *Patterns for America: Modernism and the Concept of Culture.* Princeton, N.J.: Princeton University Press, 1999.

Hemingway, Ernest. FBI file. 1 section. Approximately 200 pages.

Hemingway, Mary. *How It Was.* New York: Knopf, 1976.

Hickey, D. J., and J. E. Doherty. *A Dictionary of Irish History Since 1800.* Dublin: Gill and Macmillan, 1980.

Hicks, Granville. FBI file. 1 section. Approximately 220 pages.

Hoerder, Dirk, ed. *"Struggle a Hard Battle": Essays on Working-Class Immigrants.* DeKalb: Northern Illinois University Press, 1986.

Holmes, Oliver Wendell, and Felix Frankfurter. *Holmes and Frankfurter: Their Correspondence, 1912-1934.* Robert M. Mennel and Christine L. Compston, eds. Hanover: University of New Hampshire Press, 1996.

Holt, Henry. FBI file. 1 section. Approximately 230 pages.

Hoover, J. Edgar. "Foreword." *The FBI Story: A Report to the People.* New York: Random House, 1956.

Howard, Michael S. *Jonathan Cape, publisher: Herbert Jonathan Cape, G. Wren Howard.* London: Jonathan Cape, 1971.

Huebsch, Benjamin W. FBI file. 1 section. Approximately 25 pages.

Hughes, Langston. FBI file. 2 sections. Approximately 500 pages.

Isenberg, Noah. "Double Enmity." *The Nation.* Jan 1, 2001: 35-37.

Jeffreys, Diarmuid. *The Bureau: Inside the Modern FBI.* Boston: Houghton Mifflin, 1995.

Jenckes, Norma. "Clifford Odets (1906-63)." *Encyclopedia of the American Left.* Mari Jo Buhle, Paul Buhle, and Dan Georgakas, eds. Urbana and Chicago: University of Illinois Press, 1992: 542.

Jerome, Fred. *The Einstein File: J. Edgar Hoover's Secret War on the World's Most Famous Scientist.* New York: St. Martin's Press, 2002.

Joannou, Maroula. *Women Writers of the 1930s: Gender, Politics and History.* Edinburgh: Edinburgh University Press, 1999.

Joyce, James. *Dubliners.* 1914. New York: Penguin Books, 1982.

————. *Letters.* Vol. 1, Ed. Stuart Gilbert; vols. 2 and 3, ed. Richard Ellmann. New York: Viking Press, 1966.

————. *Selected Letters of James Joyce.* Ed. Richard Ellmann. London: Faber and Faber, 1992.

————. *Ulysses*. 1922. Ed. Hans Walter Gabler, *et al.* New York: Random House, 1986.

Joyce, James. FBI file. 1 section. 20 pages.

Joyce, Stanislaus. *My Brother's Keeper: James Joyce's Early Years.* Ed. Richard Ellmann. New York: Viking Press, 1958.

Karolides, Nicholas J., Lee Burress, and John M. Kean, eds. *Censored Books: Critical Viewpoints.* Metuchen, New York: Scarecrow Press, 1993.

Kelly, Joseph. *Our Joyce: From Outcast to Icon.* Austin: University of Texas Press, 1998.

Kempton, Murray. *Part of Our Time: Some Ruins and Monuments of the Thirties.* New York: Random House, 1998.

Kennedy, Kathleen. *Disloyal Mothers and Scurrilous Citizens: Women and Subversion During World War I.* Bloomington: University of Indiana Press, 1999.

Kenny, Kevin. *Making Sense of the Molly Maguires.* New York: Oxford University Press, 1998.

Kimeldorf, Howard. *Battling for American Labor: Wobblies, Craft Workers, and the Making of the Union Movement.* Berkeley: University of California Press, 1999.

Kivisto, Peter. *Immigrant Socialists in the United States.* Cranbury, N.J.: Associated University Presses, Inc., 1984.

Kolocotroni, Vassiliki, Jane Goldman, and Olga Taxidou, eds. *Modernism: An Anthology of Sources and Documents.* Chicago: University Press of Chicago, 1998.

Kronenberger, Louis. *No Whippings, No Gold Watches: The Saga of a Writer and his Jobs.* Boston: Little, Brown and Co., 1965.

Larkin, James. "Affidavit of Mr. James Larkin." *James Larkin: Lion of the Fold.* Ed. Donal Nevin. Dublin: Gill and Macmillan, 1998: 298-312.

Larkin, James. FBI file. 2 sections. Approximately 500 pages.

Leab, Daniel J. *I Was a Communist for the FBI: The Unhappy Life and Times of Matt Cvetic.* University Park: Pennsylvania State University Press, 2000.

Lee, Charles. *The Hidden Public: The Story of the Book-of-the-Month Club.* Garden City, N.Y.: Doubleday and Company, 1958.

Lewis, David Levering. *When Harlem Was in Vogue.* New York: Oxford University Press, 1981.

Liberator, The. 1918-1924.

Manganaro, Marc. *Culture, 1922: The Emergence of a Concept.* Princeton, N.J.: Princeton University Press, 2002.

Mann, Thomas. FBI file. 1 section. 95 pages.

Marek, Jayne E. *Women Editing Modernism: "Little" Magazines & Literary History.* Lexington: University Press of Kentucky, 1995.

Marinaccio, Rocco. "George Oppen's 'I've Seen America' Book: *Discrete Series* and the Thirties Road Narrative." *American Literature* 74:3 (Sept 2002): 539-69.

Masses. A Radical Magazine. 1911-1917.

Maxwell, William J. *New Negro, Old Left: African-American Writing and Communism Between the Wars.* New York: Columbia University Press, 1999.

McConachie, Bruce. "Pacifying American theatrical audiences, 1820-1900" in *For Fun and Profit: The Transformation of Leisure Into Consumption,* Richard Butsch, ed. Philadelphia: Temple University Press, 1990: 47-70.

McCourt, John. *James Joyce: A Passionate Exile.* New York: St. Martin's Press, 1999.

———. *The Years of Bloom: James Joyce in Trieste 1904-1920.* Madison: University of Wisconsin Press, 2000.

Meagher, Timothy. *From Paddy to Studs: Irish American Communities in the Turn of the Century Era, 1880-1920s.* New York: Greenwood Press, 1986.

Messick, Hank. *John Edgar Hoover; An Inquiry into the Life and Times of John Edgar Hoover, and his Relationship to the Continuing Partnership of Crime, Business, and Politics.* New York: David McKay Company, Inc., 1972.

Millay, Edna St. Vincent. FBI file. 1 section. Approximately 175 pages.

Miller, Arthur. *Echoes Down the Corridor: Collected Essays, 1944-2000.* Ed. Steven R. Centola. New York: Viking Press, 2000.

———. "On Censorship" in *Censored Books: Critical Viewpoints.* Ed. Nicholas J. Karolides, Lee Burress, and John M. Kean. Metuchen, N.J.: New York: Scarecrow Press, 1993: 3-10.

Miller, Dan B. *Erskine Caldwell: The Journey From Tobacco Road.* New York: Knopf, 1995.

Mitgang, Herbert. *Dangerous Dossiers.* New York: Donald I. Fine, 1996.

———. *Once Upon a Time in New York: Jimmy Walker, Franklin Roosevelt, and the Last Great Battle of the Jazz Age.* New York: The Free Press, 2000.

Montgomery, David. *The Fall of the House of Labor: the Workplace, the State, and American Labor Activism, 1865-1925.* Cambridge, England: Cambridge University Press, 1987.

Morley, Christopher. *The Middle Kingdom.* New York: Harcourt, Brace and Company, 1944.

Morrison, Mark S. *The Public Face of Modernism: Little Magazines, Audiences, and Reception, 1905-1920.* Madison: University of Wisconsin Press, 2001.

Mullin, Katherine. *James Joyce, Sexuality and Social Purity.* Cambridge, England: Cambridge University Press, 2003.

Murphy, Richard. *Theorizing the Avant-Garde: Modernism, Expressionism, and the Problem of Postmodernity.* Cambridge, England: Cambridge University Press, 1999.

Murray, R. Emmett. *The Lexicon of Labor.* New York: The New Press, 1998.

Nevin, Donal, ed. *James Larkin: Lion of the Fold.* Dublin: Gill and Macmillan, 1998.

———. "The Larkin Defense Committee," in *James Larkin: Lion of the Fold.* 293-96.

———. "The *New York Times* and James Larkin," in *James Larkin: Lion of the Fold.* 274-79.

New Masses. 1926-1948.

North, Michael. *Reading 1922: A Return to the Scene of the Modern.* New York: Oxford University Press, 1999.

Oakley, Helen Mck. *Three Hours for Lunch: The Life and Times of Christopher Morley.* New York: Watermill Publishers, 1976.

O'Brien, Edna. *James Joyce.* New York: Viking Press, 1999.

Odets, Clifford. FBI file. 1 section. Approximately 30 pages.

O'Hanlon, Ray. "Feds Tracked Labor Leader Post Sing-Sing Stay." *The Irish Echo* (New York), March 15, 2000: 46.

———. "Feds Uncover 1919 Plot to Murder Larkin." *The Irish Echo* (New York), July 8, 1999: 6.

———. "*Inside File:* Fifth Man in Larkin Murder Plot." *The Irish Echo* (New York), Aug 4, 1999: 5.

O'Neill, William L., ed. *Echoes of Revolt: The Masses, 1911-1917.* Chicago: Ivan R. Dee, 1989.

O'Reilly, Kenneth. *Black Americans: The FBI Files.* David Gallen, ed. New York: Carroll and Graf, 1994.

O'Riordan, Manus. "Larkin in America: The Road to Sing-Sing" in *James Larkin: Lion of the Fold.* Ed. Donal Nevin. Dublin: Gill and Macmillan, 1998: 64-73.

Orwell, George. FBI file. 1 section. Approximately 35 pages.

O'Toole, James M. "Democracy—and Documents—in America." *The American Archivist* 65 (2002): 107-113.

Oziebo, Barbara. *Susan Glaspell: A Critical Biography.* Chapel Hill: University of North Carolina Press, 2000.

Parkes, Adam. *Modernism and the Theater of Censorship.* New York: Oxford University Press, 1996.

Pease, Alison. *Modernism, Mass Culture, and the Aesthetics of Obscenity.* Cambridge, England: Cambridge University Press, 2000.

Phillips, William. *A Partisan View: Five Decades of the Literary Life.* New York: Stein and Day, 1983.

Potter, Claire Bond. *War on Crime: Bandits, G-Men, and the Politics of Mass Culture.* New Brunswick: Rutgers University Press, 1998.

Powers, Richard Gid. *G-Men: Hoover's FBI in American Popular Culture.* Carbondale: Southern Illinois University Press, 1983.

———. *Secrecy and Power: The Life of J. Edgar Hoover.* New York: The Free Press, 1987.

Preston, Jr. William. *Aliens and Dissenters: Federal Suppression of Radicals, 1903-1933.* Urbana: University of Illinois Press, 1963.

Radway, Janice A. *A Feeling for Books: The Book-of-the-Month Club, Literary Taste, and Middle-Class Desire.* Chapel Hill: University of North Carolina, 1997.

Reynolds, Michael. *Hemingway: The Final Years.* New York: W. W. Norton, 1999.

Robins, Natalie. *Alien Ink: The FBI's War on Freedom of Expression.* New Brunswick: Rutgers University Press, 1992.

Roth, Samuel. FBI file. 3 sections. Approximately 320 pages.

Rowell, Margit. Preface. *Brancusi vs. United States: The Historic Trial, 1928.* Paris: Société nouvelle Adam Biro, 1999.

Salisbury, Harrison E. "The Strange Correspondence of Morris Ernst and John Edgar Hoover, 1939-1964." *Nation,* Dec. 1, 1984: 575-90.

Sandburg, Carl. *Letters of Carl Sandburg.* Herbert Mitgang, ed. New York: Harcourt Brace Jovanovich, 1988.

"San Francisco Frame Up." *Masses* Dec 1916: 15.

Saunders, Frances Stonor. *The Cultural Cold War: The CIA and the World of Arts and Letters.* New York: The New Press, 1999.

Schiffrin, Andre. *The Business of Books: How International Conglomerates Took Over Publishing and Changed the Way We Read.* London: Verso Books, 2001.

Schultz, Bud, and Ruth Schultz. *It Did Happen Here: Recollections of Political Repression in America.* Berkeley: University of California Press, 1989.

Scribner, Jr., Charles. *In the Company of Writers: A Life in Publishing.* Based on the oral history by Joel R. Gardiner. New York: Scribner's, 1990.

Segall, Jeffrey. *Joyce in America: Culture Politics and the Trials of "Ulysses."* Berkeley: University of California Press, 1993.

Shulman, Robert. *The Power of Political Art: The 1930s Literary Left Reconsidered.* Chapel Hill: University of North Carolina Press, 2000.

Smethurst, James Edward. *The New Red Negro: The Literary Left and African American Poetry, 1930-1946.* New York: Oxford University Press, 1999.

Snyder, Robert W. "Big Time, Small Time, All Around the Town: The Structure and Geography of New York Vaudeville in the early Twentieth Century," in *For Fun and Profit: The Transformation of Leisure Into Consumption,* Richard Butsch, ed. Philadelphia: Temple University Press, 1990: 118-35.

Spoo, Robert. "Copyright and the Ends of Ownership: The Case for a Public-Domain *Ulysses* in America." *Joyce Studies Annual* (Summer 1999), 10: 4-62.

Stansell, Christine. *American Moderns: Bohemian New York and the Creation of a New Century.* New York: Metropolitan Books, 2000.

Steffens, Lincoln. FBI file. 1 section. Approximately 35 pages.

Steinbeck, John. *America and Americans and Selected Nonfiction.* Ed. Susan Shillinglaw and Jackson Benson. New York: Viking Press, 2002.

Steinbeck, John Ernst. FBI file. 1 section. Approximately 95 pages.

Stepan-Norris, Judith, and Maurice Zeitlin. *Talking Union*. Urbana: University of Illinois Press, 1996.

Stephan, Alexander. *"Communazis": FBI Surveillance of German Émigré Writers*. Trans. Jan van Heurck. New Haven, C.T.: Yale University Press, 2000.

Summers, Anthony. *Official and Confidential: The Secret Life of J. Edgar Hoover.* New York: Putnam's Sons, 1993.

Szalay, Michael. *New Deal Modernism: American Literature and the Invention of the Welfare State*. Durham, N.C.: Duke University Press, 2000.

Theoharis, Athan G., ed. *From the Secret Files of J. Edgar Hoover.* Chicago: Ivan Dee, 1993.

————. "Introduction." *The Louis Nichols Official and Confidential File and the Clyde Tolson Personal File*. Microfilm.

Ungar, Sanford. *FBI*. Boston: Atlantic Monthly Press, 1975.

Vanderham, Paul. *James Joyce and Censorship: The Trials of "Ulysses."* New York: New York University Press, 1998.

Vorse, Mary Heaton. FBI file. 1 section. Approximately 150 pages.

Wallach, Mark I., and Jon Bracker. *Christopher Morley*. Boston: Twayne Publishers, 1976.

Wald, Alan M. *Exiles from a Future Time: The Forging of the Twentieth-century Literary Left*. Chapel Hill: University of North Carolina Press, 2002.

West, Don. *In a Land of Plenty: A Don West Reader.* Los Angeles: West End Press, 1982.

West, Nigel. *MI6: British Secret Service Intelligence Service Operations 1909-1945*. New York: Random House, 1983.

White, William Allen. FBI file. 1 section. Approximately 30 pages.

Whitehead, Don. *The FBI Story: A Report to the People*. Foreword by J. Edgar Hoover. New York: Random House, 1956.

Williams, Trevor L. *Reading Joyce Politically*. Gainesville: University Press of Florida, 1997.

Wilson, Sarah. "Picasso: Public Enemy." *Tate* (London), 2 (Spring 1994): 28-32.

Winslow, Horatio. "Eight Hours and a Revolution." *Masses*, Nov 1911, no. 11: 5.

Woolf, Virginia. *The Diary of Virginia Woolf*, vol. 5. Ed. Anne Olivier Bell with Andrew McNeillie. New York: Harcourt Brace Jovanovich, 1984.

Zurier, Rebecca. *Art for the Masses: A Radical Magazine and Its Graphics, 1911-1917*. Philadelphia: Temple University Press, 1988.

Acknowledgments

Throughout this project, I have been amazed and sustained by the uncompromising generosity of my friends, my family, and my students, who not only did the proverbial "bearing with me" thing but rooted for me, inspired, and encouraged me when I needed it most. Several family members, friends, and colleagues have provided the friendship, sustenance, and love necessary to see this project to completion. I am most grateful to my twin sister Carole, who, ever since we were kids, has been able to come up with the best pep talks anyone's ever heard. Her wisdom, counsel, and uncanny knack for championing people when they need it most has gotten me through some pretty nasty ordeals and has helped me finish this book. More important, she has provided a consistent model of friendship and sisterhood.

I also wish to acknowledge the unrelenting encouragement of Betty Kirshner, Nancy Birk, Pamela Grimm, Margaret Shaw, and others who have nudged me along on the way to completing this work. I also want to acknowledge Cedric Burrows for his research assistance while studying in the McNair Scholars Program at Kent State during the summer of 2002. I am grateful to Rebecca Thorndike, who helped prepare the book's index. Walter Corbella generously hunted down some of the photographs that accompany this project, and with his sense of humor, always lifts my spirits. He and Mike Modarelli have served up the milk of human kindness. I also wish to acknowledge the love and support of some wonderful friends: Lorie Bednar, Mark Bednar, Rocco Marinaccio, Tamar Rein, Christopher Jaskulski, and Melissa Jones. At important junctures I have received support and feedback from Eavan Boland, Martha Campbell, Susan Darrah, Patrick McCarthy, and Kristin Ventry. I also want to thank Susanna Fein, Yoshinobu Hakutani, David Raybin, Margaret Shaw, Larry Starzyk, and Gerry Winter for departmental and collegial support.

I can't imagine doing anything other than teaching, that's how much I love it. To my undergraduate and graduate students at Kent State University, especially those in the sections that seemed perpetually sprinkled in magical pixie dust they were so wonderful—thanks for being such remarkable people, such irresistible personalities.

The University Research Council at Kent State University supported this project with two research leaves, and covered the often-exorbitant costs of securing FBI files, photographs, and permissions fees. The University Teaching Council also supported this project by funding my travel to conferences. I am grateful to both councils for their support of my work. The English Department at Manhattan College sponsored my lecture of an early version of this project and provided me with meaningful feedback and helpful encouragement.

The Andrew W. Mellon Foundation funded my research at the Harry Ransom Humanities Research Center at the University of Texas in Austin during the summer of 2000. I wish to thank the Mellon Foundation for its support, and want to thank Nancy Birk, Kristi Long, and Patrick McCarthy for recommending me for the Mellon Fellowship.

As always, the New York Public Library has had exactly what I needed when I needed it, and then some. It is a fabulous place to work and to write and I miss being there almost all of the time. "New York is everything," John Steinbeck wrote for a radio broadcast in 1955. "It is tireless, and its air is charged with energy. I can work longer and harder without weariness in New York than in any place else" (3). I know exactly what he means.

Early drafts of this work have appeared as articles in the *James Joyce Quarterly* (32.3-4) and in *Eire-Ireland: A Journal of the Irish American Cultural Institute.* I am grateful for permission to reprint sections of those essays here. I also am grateful for permission to quote from Morris Ernst's letters housed in the Ernst Archive at the Harry Ransom Humanities Research Center at the University of Texas. Others have read drafts and/or commented on paper presentations relating to my project, have sent me articles pertaining to my topic, or have responded to questions that have come up in the course of my research. I am grateful for their comments: Nancy Birk, Kiki Culleton, Mary Culleton, Nicholas Fargnoli, Sid Feshbach, Judith Harrington, Betty Kirshner, Sean Latham, Mike O'Shea, Bob Lowery, Tammy Voelker, and James Wilson.

Finally, I am grateful to Kristi Long, who contracted this project years ago but has since left the press for another job. I wish she could have had a bigger part in the final project, and I missed having her there for it. She saw in my presentation at the Gotham Book Mart one June evening the stuff of a book, and was a veritable Griselda while I fussed around and took my time with it. I want to thank my current editor at Palgrave Macmillan, Farideh Koohi-Kamali, for her help with the project. To her dedicated assistant Melissa Nosal, to Sonia Wilson in production, and to my copy editor, Bruce Murphy, many thanks.

My family has always been a source of strength and support for me and has helped me to keep on keepin' on. Let's continue to want everything for each other.

Index